THESE LIES THAT SNARE US

RACHEL TORK

To all the strong women who wear their humor and sarcasm like armor.

Your pain is valid, even if you don't let the world see it.

CHAPTER 1
ASTER

I watched the fading sun hover at the horizon, my hands braced against the smooth stone ledge of a balcony in the Seelie Court palace.

My palace.

Ivy, peppered with wilting purple flowers, crawled up the exterior stone walls of the castle. I'd thought the flowers might fully return to life, being that my demon-possessed uncle was gone, but it seemed the dark magic had permeated itself deeply into the palace. Maybe even into the Seelie court itself.

This balcony jutted off my private rooms—once my parent's rooms—and standing there I could imagine my mother lounging on the chaise, smiling softly at my father as he talked and sipped on a glass of whiskey, perched next to her. He would say something, and she would laugh. They'd grasp hands. He'd kiss her palm. They were so, so happy.

I could almost believe it was real, but then the sun

dipped below the horizon, bathing the world in cool twilight, and the vision immediately faded away. I looked away from the darkening sky, soon to match the hair that tumbled down my back, and strode inside.

My uncle had never taken up this room, for reasons unknown to me, but I was glad, glad to have untainted memories of my parents in this place. Still, the grandeur made me a little uncomfortable, and in the last couple weeks, I'd found myself wishing for the simplicity of the shitty apartment I had until quite recently shared with Lil.

I had more furniture in this damn room than we'd had at home, period: a couch and loveseat I had never even thought to sit on faced a fireplace; the four-poster bed draped with maroon and gold curtains and covers was annoyingly enormous, and I often felt child-like as I crawled under the sheets alone most nights; there was also a low, mahogany table that was currently scattered with empty candy wrappers; and not one but two more circular tables on either side of the couch. I had no idea why one room needed so many tables or what the hell I was supposed to put on said surfaces. Lil had suggested framed photos, but the only pictures I had ever really taken were blurry selfies on my cell phone of the two of us drunk.

They were now mementos from simpler times. *Much simpler.*

I glanced at the smooth, white moonstone sitting atop one of the nightstands and sighed. Nox was somewhere in the Unseelie Court, leading a search party for Raven and the other missing members of his court. Griffin, who I'd just recently discovered to be Raven's biological father, was with him too.

Rage flared in me, as it always did when I thought of the fucked-up situation at hand. My face felt hot, and I knew my blue eyes were aglow with what I now knew was starlight. But I stuffed those feelings down quickly, taking a deep breath and heading for the bathroom.

Like the bedroom, the bathroom was ridiculously extravagant, all gleaming white surfaces and sporting a swimming pool-sized tub, an additional standing shower, and double sinks. Plus, there was an area specifically for doing makeup and hair.

Lil waited for me there, perched on a comically small chair by the vanity. Her lilac-streaked hair was pulled away from her round face, and the sleeves of her floral blouse were pushed up.

She was ready to work.

Upon seeing her, I schooled myself, relaxing my shoulders and doing all the things one does to look okay.

Obviously my attempts were for naught as she sighed loudly and said, "Deep breaths, Aster."

"I'm fine," I clipped out.

She rolled her bottle-green eyes. "Since when do we lie to each other?"

I splayed my palms on the marble-topped counter, meeting my own gaze in the mirror. My blue eyes were mercifully dull as I mumbled, "I just need to get through this meeting."

"Are you worried about him?"

I knew exactly who she meant.

Nox. My mate.

We hadn't really defined what else we were to each other beyond that. The situation was complicated at best, given that we were rulers of two entirely different rival courts. Not to mention the fact that I had yet to tell him my true feelings. Sure, I'd accepted the mating bond, but I knew deep down that there were more complex things to unravel about the nature of our relationship—things I was terrified to admit to him and even myself.

Lil was looking at me expectantly, and I cleared my throat, turning to her as I said, "Of course I'm worried."

More like terrified. Because the world seemed to have a horrible sense of humor and a knack for taking good things away from me. It wasn't exactly that I didn't trust Nox. It was that I didn't yet trust in fate letting him stay in my life.

But I had other important tasks to focus on at the moment, like getting ready—apparently. I was here, enduring the interminable blemishes of the Seelie Court palace, because tonight I had a meeting with the remainder of my small council. It was a meeting that was supposed to be held over a week ago. Before the demon prince, Abaddon, showed up at Nox's palace.

Before he took Raven.

"You're getting wound up again," she said softly, indicating her head towards the equally tiny chair just across from her. "Sit. Let me do your makeup."

I chewed on my already-raw lower lip, but obliged her, sitting lightly on the cushioned seat. My leg bounced twice before she shot me a look.

"If you fidget like that, I'll end up accidentally smearing mascara on your nose," she said.

"Sorry," I muttered, stilling my leg and shoving my hands under my thighs.

As she began to work on brushing shadow over my

eyelids, she said, "I've said this before, Aster, and I'll say it again: it's okay to let people care about you."

"I know you care about me, Lil," I replied stiffly.

She snorted. "I'm not talking about me, smartass. I'm talking about your shadow-daddy Fae king."

Who also happens to not be really much Fae at all...

I pushed that thought away. Nox had yet to really explain his true heritage to me, and truthfully, I hadn't put much effort into seeking answers. I didn't think it was because I feared what he truly was, but maybe I feared what that meant for us, or even the world.

"He cares," I said carefully as she began to powder blush on my cheeks. "I know that."

Lil paused and the brush stopped just before it hit my skin again. Then, she looked me dead in the eye and said, "He loves you. Whether he's said it or not, I *saw* his face that day. I don't think I've ever seen somebody look like that... sound like that."

I looked away, but I knew exactly what she meant. I'd heard the agonized sounds coming from him when I pushed my way back to my body, after I had died under that fated tree. The rope hadn't failed to snap my neck, and yet, due to forces still mostly a mystery to me, I'd come back. The goddess or Maiden, or whoever the hell she truly was, hadn't been entirely clear on the why nor the how.

Conveniently for me and my proclivity for avoidance, I didn't have time to dwell on it.

"We need to hurry. It won't do me any good to be late," I said to Lil, shifting the issue to the back of my mind.

"It's *your* small council," she reminded me.

"Tell that to them," I sighed.

She grimaced but finished with a few swipes of lip stain against my mouth. She knew I was right.

When I glanced in the mirror, the dark circles under my eyes were mostly gone and my cheekbones were sharper. My lips were a deep wine-red and my lashes were dark and heavy. But in my irises, something stirred as I stared at my reflection. It wasn't just starlight but something else entirely. Just a wisp of darkness, almost like Nox's shadows. But where his shadows felt harmless and mischievous at worst, this felt ominous, like dark storm clouds on the horizon.

"Time for the dress," Lil said, oblivious to the danger that lurked within me.

She got up and made for the bedroom, and I tore my eyes away from my reflection and followed her. The dress I had planned to wear had been laid out by palace maids earlier today, and it was made of black silk, green threads woven into the fabric like slithering snakes.

I stepped out of the robe I wore—not caring one bit that I was as naked as the day I was born underneath as Lil had seen every inch of me more than once—and Lil helped me step into the dress before zipping it up to my neck. The final touch was, of course, my crown—the crown of ivy, frozen in time, that my father had worn. The same crown my uncle had worn. I refused to let fear sink in at that, that I was to share in this ritual that he had once performed, instead picking it up from where it rested on the bedside table and placing it atop my head. It was lighter than I'd expected it to be, almost unnoticeable.

"You look pretty damn regal," Lil puffed out, her hands on her hips. "Go get 'em."

I raised a brow and repeated, "'Go get 'em?'"

She made an exasperated sound in the back of her throat and shoved at me as she said, "Don't be a killjoy. Go."

I dragged up a small smile, just for her, before walking out into the hallway. Four faerie guards were waiting to escort me, all wearing all-too-familiar maroon uniforms. Heavy swords were strapped to their sides for easy access, though I wasn't sure if I really trusted them to protect me. These were all fresh recruits since most of the former guards had either resigned or fled after their captain's betrayal. Truthfully, I had no idea where Ewin Wells was. He'd disappeared that day when the truth about my uncle had finally been revealed, and I didn't have the time nor support to track him down right now.

I looked at these new guards and let my smile fall, hardening my features into an unwavering, icy glare. They nervously glanced at each other before flanking me as I wordlessly began to stride down the hall.

Pale moonlight was already beginning to stream in through the tall, arched windows that lined the hall, casting an otherworldly glow upon the gleaming hardwood floor. Something in that glimmering moonlight called to me; a darkness inside that felt a lot like the voice that had begged for me to *let go* of my power just weeks ago. The same entity I'd seen in the mirror. My power was something I had yet to understand, and I was currently trying and failing to figure out where a line was drawn between it and me.

The guard's footfalls were heavy, the sound of his boots clomping against the floor and reverberating through otherwise quiet corridors. Mine were nearly silent, and I almost felt wraithlike in the palace; in that moment I thought of

Nox, about how he and his shadow magic were far from here. I was facing the lords of my council alone today.

We descended the grand staircase that led to the ground level and walked past the sweeping entrance to the throne room. Upon our approach, I held up a hand and stopped in front of the doorway that led off to the adjacent council room. The guards stopped immediately, and I took a moment—just a moment—to collect myself and quell the sudden shaking in my hands.

Then, I strode inside.

The nine lords of the Seelie Court sat around a long, oak table, Lord Jasper lounging at the head. Most of them looked at me smugly, dressed in their finery and sipping no-doubt expensive wine from gold-rimmed goblets. As I saw Lord Jasper at the head of the table, I paused. He met my stare, his expression flat and his gray eyes unfeeling.

"Move," I said, the command ringing through the near-silent room.

Lord Jasper narrowed his eyes.

"Now," I murmured, the sound like a lover's whisper—a spell.

His nostrils flared, and finally he stood, making his way to the only remaining empty chair near to the door. I walked slowly to the head of the table and then sat down lightly, surveying the men before me. All Fae. That was going to have to change if we were to properly represent the population of the court—and we really needed to get some women in here too.

Finally, I sighed and said, "War is upon us."

Lord Jasper snorted.

"Something funny, Lord Jasper?" I asked coolly.

He gave me a deprecating smile as he traced his fingers along the rim of his cup. "You know nothing of war. I've seen it before, and we are facing nothing of the sort."

I cocked my head. "Or, maybe, it's just a war like none you've ever seen before."

"I hardly—"

"Demons possess the bodies of our subjects," I cut in, and his expression darkened. "I've seen it with my own eyes. If you'd like proof, I can arrange that."

"Because your Unseelie mate holds them hostage in his dungeons?" another, Lord Ives, challenged.

I raised a brow. "They are being kept as comfortable as is possible. It's integral to keep perspective here: if they were freed from their cells, they would wreak havoc, likely kill anything in their way. Or rather, the demons inside of them would."

"I think," Lord Thestle said, "we must address the matter of the Unseelie king before we can continue on in a smooth manner."

In my lap, I clenched one of my hands into a tight fist. I had known this was coming, but I had hoped the lords of my council would take the threat of the demons seriously enough that we wouldn't have to spend much time talking about Nox. As it turned out, I was majorly wrong.

"In my so *humble* opinion, that is the most pressing issue," Lord Jasper said mockingly, pressing a jewel-laden hand to his chest.

I didn't really understand their fuss; the rivalry between our courts had never made any sense to me; but I had to tread delicately here to gain their support.

"I understand the logistical difficulty that may concern

you because of my relationship with him," I said carefully. "However, I argue that, given our current situation, a partnership between our courts can only be a good thing."

Lord Jasper's answering smile was cruel. "Because you want us to work with your Unseelie king?"

"Because we need unity now," I said sharply. "We must find a way to stop what is surely coming—an outright slaughter. We can't do that if we're fighting amongst ourselves."

"Fine," Lord Jasper said, his gaze sweeping over the other lords.

And quite suddenly, I had a distinct feeling they'd already come to a decision previously without me.

"We will ally with Nox Ether and his court of shadows, but on one condition." Lord Jasper looked me directly in the eyes, his gaze menacing, as he said in a low voice, "The Veil which separates our courts must be destroyed."

My breath caught as I tried to fully comprehend the request. I didn't know much about the Veil separating the Seelie and Unseelie Courts, other than that it limited travel and was made up of strong, ancient magic. I was also aware that it was a pretty big deal. Seelie Fae couldn't even travel through it unless given explicit permission and accompanied by an Unseelie faerie.

I was certain that dropping it, or even destroying it, would not be a simple thing. Still, I swallowed my questions and hesitation as I stood and said, "I will consider your...proposition."

Lord Jasper raised a brow. "Do."

I ignored his disrespect for now. It was all I *could* do.

Goddess, what was I going to do?

HOURS LATER, I curled around myself in bed, squeezing my eyes shut in the hope that sleep would come quickly. That, for a period of time, I could forget the mess I was in—that we were all in.

Whether I wanted to admit it or not, I had little control over my own court. The lords of my council had come to a decision all on their own, and it was one they knew I could hardly resist or dismiss. If Nox refused to do something about the Veil, it would only make them more suspicious of him and of me as well. But I had no idea what kind of magic truly existed within the barrier. I knew it had to be tied to Nox if the lords were making demands of him specifically. The magic must be something that was passed on through Unseelie rulers...but why? Our courts weren't friendly by any means but internal war between them hadn't been a common occurrence throughout history, at least that I knew of. In fact, we had banded together more than once to defeat the demons. There had to be something more to all this, some reason for the blatant separation.

In the end, it didn't really matter why it existed or how. Nox *had* to get rid of it; we needed each other right now, and our courts had to work together. All had been quiet on the demon front, but I had a bad feeling the demon prince was just waiting for the right time to strike. And then there was Raven...

No. I couldn't go there. I just couldn't. Nox and Griffin would find him. Maybe they already had. He would be safe, and then we'd figure out a way to get the demon out of him

—out of all of the possessed faeries—and everything would be fine. It simply had to be.

I rolled over, letting out a frustrated sigh. Naturally, sleep was not coming easily tonight.

When I faced the balcony, my heart skipped a beat and my breath caught in my throat. The glass doors were open, letting in a cool, citrusy breeze and a sliver of pale moonlight. Panic started to creep in, sending my body into high alert, but the alarm immediately faded away as I felt it.

The mating bond. It was an intermittent nudge at my consciousness and a small tug in my chest, making me aware of everything that was *him*.

Not so long ago, he wouldn't have been able to flit directly to this palace due to the heavy wards surrounding it, but the magic of the mating bond tended to bend some rules.

I for one was not complaining.

The bed bowed behind me, and, still facing the balcony, I muttered, "You know, it's very rude to sneak up on people."

A small, tight chuckle escaped Nox, and I turned to face him. He was perched on the edge of the bed, still wearing dark leathers. He smelled faintly of dust and sand, leading me to wonder where the hell he had just been. Strands of wavy, silver hair fell across the sharp planes of his cheekbones, caressing tanned skin. Bright amber eyes met mine and his full lips parted as he looked at me.

Goddess, I wanted to forget everything and let myself be swept into him. I could tell by the look in his eyes that he wanted to do just the same, but I forced myself to sit up slightly and ask, "Anything?"

His expression shuttered and he cleared his throat before saying, "Not yet."

I looked away, blinking away burning tears that threatened to spill out over my cheeks. I would not cry. I couldn't, not now. I needed to be strong, for Lil, for Raven, and for my court. It was not the time to falter or think of myself.

"Asteria," Nox murmured in a low voice, as if already sensing the tidal wave threatening to sweep me under.

I sucked in a breath and blinked rapidly, still not looking at him as I said tightly, "I'm fine."

"You don't need to be."

"I do."

The bed shifted as he moved closer to me, and moments later, I felt the warmth of his hand gently stroking down my back. Shutting my eyes, I added, "I'll be okay. I'm just..." I trailed off, not really sure what exactly I was feeling, only that it was too much.

Shivers broke out over my skin and my body became a livewire as his lips brushed against my shoulder and he murmured, "I know, love."

He peppered featherlight kisses up to my neck, and my back arched.

Shit. I couldn't. There were things I needed to tell him. We didn't have time for this. The world didn't have time for us to slow down and get to know each other. I wondered sometimes if there would ever really be time for that, or if our relationship would always have its impossibilities.

The events of the day shoved themselves to the forefront of my mind, and I sighed and said, "Wait."

He paused instantly, lifting his head. Our gazes clashed and a puff of air escaped my lips at the molten look in his eyes. They were slightly aglow, just like mine sometimes were.

Goddess Above, I had so many questions for him. But instead of asking any of them, the first words that fell from my lips were, "You need to drop the Veil separating our courts."

Slowly, I watched as the words washed over Nox's features. His brow rose and his mouth tightened. The glow in his eyes dimmed, and I swore I saw the hint of a shadow curling around his delicately pointed ear. Shadows that came from his wraith blood—from his mother. I still didn't know what had happened to her, or his stepfather.

Questions upon questions.

"Says who?" he asked, the question soft, though not gentle—lethal quiet, a trait I was all too accustomed to when it came to him.

I took a deep breath. I needed to stand firm on this. He had to agree with the demand. "Says me."

His brow rose further. "And which of the spineless idiots on your council told you to say that?"

Briefly, I closed my eyes, feeling that increasingly familiar burning rising in my chest. *Shut it down*, I chanted silently, the words a familiar mantra in my mind.

Nox chuckled lightly, and I opened my eyes just as he smirked and said, "You don't need to swallow it down. Not for me, love."

Clenching my jaw, I gritted out, "Nox. This is serious."

He rolled off the bed and began unbuttoning his leathers as he said, "Oh, I'm aware."

"Then...will you do it?"

He snorted. "Gods, no."

I still found it difficult to comprehend that Nox was old enough to remember a time when the goddess was just the Maiden and true Beings of Light ruled as deities. It felt huge, but having met the goddess myself, I was admittedly less impressed with her given the lackluster explanation she had provided me when I died. Not that it mattered —yet.

Squaring my shoulders, I looked him dead in the eye and said, "This isn't negotiable."

"Everything is negotiable, love," Nox said airily, pulling off the outer leathers, leaving only a black shirt underneath that showed off the corded muscles in his arms.

I dutifully ignored the way my mouth dried slightly, instead saying sharply, "Just listen, please."

He tilted his head to the side slightly, the movement almost animalistic. But he said solemnly, "I am."

"I barely have my council under control," I began, hating the way my voice was shaky and thin. "I don't have their trust or respect, but they're agreeing to work with you and to ally our courts as long as you drop the Veil that separates us."

Nox looked away, a muscle in his jaw ticking. Under his breath, I heard him mutter, "And *this* is what those idiots choose to focus on right now."

"Nox." I said quietly. "I don't know what else to do. I need to have their support."

He swept off the black shirt in a single motion and prowled over to me, bare-chested. My breath caught as he leaned over me and moved close, murmuring in a low voice, "You could just eradicate the issue."

My chest fell and rose quickly at his proximity and heat,

but I managed to steady my voice as I said, "I'm not killing anyone."

He searched my expression, and for a moment, I truly wondered what he saw when he looked at me. We had known each other for such a short period of time, at least in waking. Still, a growing part of me felt as though whatever this was between us was bigger than I even yet realized.

"So be it," he finally said. "But I'm not dropping the Veil."

"And why not?"

Our mouths were inches away now, and my pulse was pounding in my ears.

"Because," he whispered and brushed his lips against mine, "the Veil ensures balance. Light and dark are two entities and must remain so. Without that balance, without that separation, the world would come apart."

"And what does that say about you and me?" I dared, meeting his eyes.

Amber irises lit up once again, and he growled, "You will *always* be my exception."

CHAPTER 2
ASTER

I stared at Nox, wide awake and my body thrumming beneath him. "I don't think the universe takes kindly to exceptions like me," I whispered.

"Well, then, fuck the universe," Nox said, eyes flashing. His hands were braced on either side of me, caging me, just enough that I could feel the power that I knew lived beneath his skin. Power that came partially from an otherworldly Being of Light.

"Asteria," Nox said, softer now, as if somehow sensing the shift in my thoughts. "I know you have questions, and I know things are uncertain." He moved one hand, swiping his thumb across my lower lip. "But nothing is going to be solved by you worrying about it tonight. Nothing will change, not yet."

"You still haven't explained everything to me," I said as he traced the curve of my jaw. "About you, I mean. About what happened between you and your parents and how you became king."

He paused then moved so that he was sitting against the headboard. He pulled me to him so that I was practically sitting into his lap. I twisted so that I was facing him and touched his face lightly. His eyes fluttered shut as I slid my fingers over his mouth, his lips parting.

When my hand moved to his bare chest, resting atop where his heart was, he said, "I will. I want to tell you those things, I promise. But I'm..." He trailed off, then took a breath. "I'm tired, love. And I know that's not an adequate excuse, given the gravity of it all—"

"It's alright," I cut in, feeling a pang in my chest at the vulnerability in his words. Vulnerability I knew he only ever showed to me. "For tonight, for just a little while, we can put it all aside."

Nox leaned his forehead against mine and breathed, "Thank you."

"But in the morning, we need to talk," I said, nipping at his sharp jawline. "Promise me?"

His hands tightened where they rested on my hips. "In the morning," he agreed before sliding a hand under my chin, raising it so our lips aligned.

I gasped just before he kissed me softly. Quickly, though, the kiss became desperate and rough, and a soft moan escaped me. I shifted my legs so that I was straddling him, and a low groan slipped from his lips in return. One of his hands rested lightly over my neck and the other tightened at my hip. I moved rhythmically, already feeling him hard beneath me, moaning my pleasure into his ear without restraint.

Nox growled, "The fucking noises you make."

He kissed me hard on my mouth before moving to my

neck. I felt the scrape of sharp faerie canines and my back arched. Goddess, I was already so damn close. And by the sound that rumbled up from his chest, I knew he was too.

He didn't bite me like he had the night I'd accepted the mating bond, but he did suck on the delicate skin there, no doubt leaving a mark. The flimsy straps of my silky gray nightgown slid off my shoulders with a single brush of his hand, and he lowered his head, teasing my breasts with his mouth. I made a small, exasperated noise in the back of my throat, and he glanced at me, grinning.

"What is it, my star?" he asked darkly.

"Don't," I gasped.

"Don't what?" he urged, his eyes bright and wild.

"Don't tease me," I said. "Not now."

"As my queen wishes," he said, and I hardly had time to process *that* before he sucked deeply on my nipple.

I cried out, fisting my hand in the soft strands of his hair. He sucked and licked greedily, before I decided I wanted more, my hands fumbling at the clasp of his pants.

He lifted his head, helping me pull off the leather breeches. The silky nightgown was still pooled around my waist, and Nox practically ripped it away before guiding my hips over his cock. Slowly, I lowered myself until he filled me completely. And for a moment, I stayed there, completely still, my forehead pressed against his and both our chests heaving.

His calloused fingers traced over my face, as if memorizing every inch of me.

"Please understand," he breathed, "to me, nothing matters. None of it, besides you."

"We have duties," I whispered.

Just before kissing me again, he muttered, "And mine is to you."

I lost myself then, falling into the feel of him inside me and the touch of his hands on my body. The movement of my hips grew hurried, and my breaths became ragged. Without pulling our bodies apart, he moved so that I was underneath him, my legs wrapping around his narrow hips. His fingers slid between us, and at the sound of the ragged moan that dragged up my throat, his wings materialized on his back, sweeping out above us. He groaned as I slid my pointer finger across the dark membrane of one of them in wonder. They would always fascinate me.

My hand quickly slid away as he worked me with *his*. All semblance of reality fell apart as he swirled his finger in just the right spot. I soared, up and up and up, before crashing down in pieces back onto the bed.

When my eyes opened again, I found Nox watching me, his lips parted and eyes wide. I didn't have words for that moment, so instead I kissed him, trying to communicate everything I was still too afraid to say. He kissed me back, moving at a placid pace, his hand curling in mine and pinning it beside me on the bed.

I felt the moment he began to lose control. His hips snapped against mine roughly and those mighty wings curled around us, cocooning my world in darkness. The words 'I love you' nearly rose to my lips, but I pushed them away.

Not now.

Not yet.

Instead, I held him as he came, his entire body trembling, his hand still tight in mine. When he pulled out of me and the room fell into a soft silence, I found myself thinking somehow of the day I had died. Maybe it was the come down, maybe it was the unspoken words swirling in my mind, or perhaps it was the danger constantly looming.

But as I traced my fingers along his arm, I found myself saying, "I was there that day by the tree, watching."

"What?" His voice was raw, and he sounded genuinely surprised. "You mean—"

"Yeah," I puffed out. "After I had my little chit-chat with our favorite goddess, before I was back in my body, I saw everything through Lil's eyes."

Nox laid down beside me in the near-dark, his wings fading away into mere wisps of shadow. His eyes shone in the slivers of moonlight as he looked at me, brow creased. For a long, heavy moment, he was quiet. Then he said, "Then you are aware of what I was ready to do."

I shuddered slightly. I did know. He would've burnt himself out to the point of death trying to defeat Abaddon alone, and I had no doubt he would've gladly done it thinking I was gone forever.

Tracing a finger over his chest, I said quietly, "Today, Lil was here. She scolded me."

"About?" Nox murmured.

"Not letting people care," I said before I sucked in a breath and sat up.

"What is it?" he asked.

"I'll be back...bathroom."

And with that, I shot up out of the bed. Sure, I did kind of need to pee, but mostly I was chickening out of admitting anything further about my feelings.

Once inside, I flicked on the light and stared at myself in

the mirror. My cheeks were flushed and there was a bruise on my neck, but it was already fading thanks to my faerie blood. My dark hair was messy, and I sighed as I combed it back with my fingers.

When I met my own eyes again in the mirror, I swallowed hard, unnerved by my own image. In my irises, something flickered beneath the soft, blue glow. In the silence, it urged me to let go of my power and let the world crumble to ash. It craved revenge and thirsted for death—and I was deeply afraid of it.

I looked away, used the toilet, then mechanically washed my hands. Reaching into one of the drawers below the sink, I pulled out a bottle and popped a birth control pill in my mouth, rinsing it down with sink water. I only needed to take them once a week in order for them to do their job, but I had been a *tad* lax about it recently. And the last thing I needed to worry about right now was a child.

An heir.

Goddess, how would that even work? Would a child of ours rule the Seelie or Unseelie Court? Where would they call home? Perhaps both, or maybe even neither. I hated the burden I would be forced to put on any child of mine—of ours—and yet the idea of it, as much as it terrified me, felt liberating. Or maybe thinking about a future without the shackles of this reality was, regardless of the specifics, exactly what I craved.

In any case, whatever I thought about that, it wouldn't be happening anytime soon. We had a war to fight first.

By the time I left the bathroom, I was feeling a bit calmer. A part of me hoped Nox would be asleep when I went back to bed. Not because I didn't want to find comfort with him, but because I didn't want to burden him. I was still getting used to allowing him to carry some of my worries and stresses. However, I found him propped up against the headboard, staring at the blue-tinted screen of his cell phone, his brow furrowed.

"What is it?" I asked, my voice suddenly hoarse and foreign in my own ears.

He glanced my way, and it was only because of the look on his face that I realized I was still completely naked. But I refused to hide or feel self-conscious under his gaze, so I walked lightly over to the bed and slid underneath the cool sheets with him.

He shut the phone off and set it on the bedside table, sighing. "It's Griffin. He doesn't understand the term 'personal boundary' no matter how hard I try to explain it to him."

"I'm sure he just wants to keep you as updated as possible," I said. "Goddess knows I appreciate it, and so does Lil."

Nox looked away and murmured, "I know."

He shifted, lying down next to me. I rested my head on his chest as I asked quietly, "Do you think we'll actually find him?"

Nox was quiet for a long while. When he did reply, his voice was tight and laced with guilt. "I don't know, love. I really don't."

I squeezed my eyes shut, trying to calm my heartbeat. I took in Nox's scent, listening to him breathe as I curled tightly against him. We fell asleep like that, me holding onto him as his arms encircled me protectively, as if, even here, danger lurked.

I was on the dream bridge again.

Time was hardly a factor in a place like this, yet I knew hadn't come here for many nights. Not since Nox had looked past me in fear. The night Abaddon had come for Raven.

I was alone as I stared at the shimmering bridge and touched the light floating around me, like stars suspended in silky water.

I sensed Nox the moment he stepped onto the other side. Then, I saw the shadows slinking my way but fading just as they reached me.

"Nox!" I called, my voice echoing in the endless expanse of space around me.

He hesitated. I couldn't see it, but I could *feel* it. And I wondered—was he afraid of what he might see?

What *had* he seen?

Still, he did not show himself past the shadows. I took matters into my own hands and pushed my burning starlight across the bridge. Just before it reached him, he finally stepped away from his cocoon of shadows.

"What is it?" I asked, seeing the way his features sharpened as he looked at me.

Amber irises illuminated as he looked at me and said, "You need to wake up now, love."

I looked down at myself to find my skin was glowing, as if I too were a star—like I was becoming my power.

I raised my gaze back to Nox and said, "No. Not until you tell me what you're seeing."

A shadow danced around my ankles, caressing me as he said softly, "Wake up, Asteria. This is not the place."

"I don't care," I said, feeling my body start to heat and my mind begin to blur. I was losing control, even here in this place between unconsciousness and reality.

"But I do," he murmured, just before shadows rushed around me and everything went dark.

CHAPTER 3
ASTER

I awoke with a jolt. The first thing I saw was Nox, sitting up against the headboard and looking directly at me as I opened my eyes. The light was dim and the air in the bedroom cool. It had to still be early, too damn early for me to be awake already. Especially with what I knew the day would surely bring. But something was tickling the edges of my consciousness...

The dream. *Right.*

"Nox," I rasped, sitting up. "What was that?"

He sighed heavily, his bare chest rising and falling before he replied, "Another piece to an incomplete puzzle."

I stared at him, narrowing my eyes. "Explain," I ordered softly.

He glanced outside before sliding off the bed and offering his hand. I took it silently, and he led me out to the balcony. The sun was just starting to rise, tinting the horizon with pink, though some stars were still visible in the sky above. The meeting of night and day, of light and darkness. They could only exist together in this brief, hazy period of time.

Nox sat down on the chaise, and I joined him. For a moment, he didn't touch me. When he did, he only stroked a finger down my face once before dropping it to his lap and saying, "You alluded to the fact that the goddess told you who...what I am."

I pressed my lips together and whispered, "Yes."

"How much exactly did she explain?"

I shrugged, tracing my fingers over the cushion of the chaise. My nail polish was starting to chip, and I supposed that now, as a queen, I should probably try to remedy that.

"Asteria?" Nox urged, and I looked up.

"She said..." I swallowed, meeting his gaze. "She told me that your mother was the queen of the Unseelie Court but that the king was not your father. She told me about a Nephilim warrior named Sameul and how he marked her as a being of Above. She said he's the reason you have the power you do—because he's your father."

Nox's jaw was tight as he nodded, just once. I opened my mouth to speak again, but he beat me to it, saying tightly, "Then you know most of everything."

I bit my cheek then asked quietly, "Have you ever met him?"

Nox blew out a breath, staring at the horizon as he replied, "Not in waking, and I doubt I ever will."

"He's come to you in dreams?"

He looked back at me. "Just once."

Sensing there was more to it, I furrowed my brow and pushed, "When?"

He shifted, and I swore I saw the shadowy flicker of

wings at his back. "The night before I sent the demon prince back to Hell. He told me to be careful. Warned me, more like, that every decision I made would have consequences because of what I am." He shook his head and added quietly, "A cursed life."

"Welcome to the club," I said, wringing my hands.

He searched my expression and said, "Your life was only ever cursed because of me."

A small, tired smile rose to my lips. "I don't think you believe that, Nox. I think you saw something on the dream bridge, the night Abaddon came for Raven. And I think you saw something last night too."

A light breeze disturbed the loose strands of my hair, carrying with it the scent of lilacs and fresh, early morning dew. Nox's wings materialized fully, and he wrapped them around us, as if he could somehow shield me from the truth of whatever he was about to say.

"I don't know exactly what I saw," he said, meeting my eyes. "But...remember how I told you I recognized Abaddon's mark in you because it was in me too?"

"I do." My voice was hoarse and low, my pulse pounding in nervous anticipation.

"The night the demon took Raven, I saw someone behind you on the bridge. A woman."

I felt my own eyes bulge in shock. Someone else? On *our* bridge? Then again, had it ever really been just about us, or more about the connection of our power?

"She wore a mark on her forehead," Nox said, "and that mark glowed behind you again last night."

"What mark?" I asked, my voice trembling.

"I honestly have no idea. That's what I want to find out.

Some sort of symbol." Nox dragged a hand across his face. "But what frightened me was the way she looked at you."

"And what way was that?"

"A way that showed she was no friend of yours."

I scoffed. "Well, she can join the club."

"We'll find out what the mark means," Nox said, his mind somewhere else, "and we'll deal with it."

I looked him in the eye, fully knowing what he meant by 'deal with it.' "Nox," I said with a small smile. "You can't just rip out the heart of anyone who threatens me."

He did not smile back. Instead, he leaned forward and growled in an edged voice, "Watch me."

I looked away and sighed, chewing on my lip. I knew he meant it—he was willing to go very far for me. And I…I would kill for him if it came down to it. I knew that now. I suppose that should have frightened me, at least a little, but I couldn't bring myself to feel bad about the thought. He was *mine.* No one—no demon or faerie lord—would harm him.

His wing curled to hug my body, and I wondered if he sensed what I was thinking.

I took a breath, trying to calm the firestorm of emotions swirling inside. There were other problems we needed to face today.

"Weird lady aside," I said, moving to more pressing, political matters, "have you thought about what I said last night?"

Nox's features grew sharp and his eyes brightened, making him look like he truly was a terrifying creature from a strange, faraway realm. "I already gave you my answer," he said.

I straightened, my hands smoothing over the banister of the balcony. "And I told you the consequences of not conceding. My council won't support my rule if you don't do this."

"Fuck your council," he said harshly.

"I am a part of that council," I retorted. "And I agree their terms are fair."

"Because you do not understand what you ask—"

"Then tell me!" I demanded, my voice becoming shrill. "Don't keep me in the dark because it isn't the 'right' time! I'm not a child or an innocent. Not anymore."

The hard exterior of Nox's expression faltered to show the cracks beneath. He knew just as well as I did that the events of the last month had changed me, and I didn't know if it was for the better. There was no going back to the perpetually half-drunk party girl I had been, no returning to the little princess hiding her bruises and crying into her pillow each night. I was older and harder now. Every day I felt the void of hopelessness inside myself deepen, and I wasn't sure what that meant for my capacity for love. Maybe everything that had happened had finally caught up with me and made it impossible for me to open myself up, to extract as much joy and security from my relationships as I could.

Maybe I was fucked.

"I cannot do what you ask," Nox said, his voice rough. "Balance exists for a reason. Your council knows that, and they are using you to further their agenda. Believe me, love, if you bend to this you will not control them—they will own you. And trust me, you do not want to be that kind of ruler."

I stood, walking back into the bedroom as I said flatly,

"You should go. Lil will be here soon." I heard Nox stand and follow me, but I turned and stopped him at the doorway with a hand to his chest. "I need time to think about what to do," I said as he looked down at my hand. "Without you."

Slowly, he raised his gaze to mine and nodded. "I understand," he said, and I couldn't quite read whatever was in his voice. "Just be careful."

I looked away and muttered, "And when have I not been?"

Gently he gripped my chin, forcing me to look at him. "I know you are angry with me, but I do not make this refusal lightly, nor do I do it to undermine you. I would do whatever you asked, but it is not you who is truly asking."

"Fine," I said, not breaking eye contact.

He pressed his lips together and dropped his hand. He nodded once more before stepping back, his gaze still on mine. A moment later, he was gone in a flurry of shadows. When I looked back to the room, his clothes and leathers were gone too.

As if on cue, a knock sounded at the door. I pulled on a robe that I'd thoughtlessly thrown on the couch earlier, and I ran my hands down its length to smooth out the wrinkles. "Come in, Lil!"

The door cracked open, and Lil peered in. Her lilac-streaked hair was pulled back in two braids today making her look younger, and she wore light denim overalls.

"Is the storm over?" she ventured, stepping inside and carefully looking around as she shut the door behind her.

I glared at her. "Storm?"

She rolled her eyes. "I could kind of hear you, you know. Not what you were saying, but I could tell it was heated."

"Eavesdropping is rude."

She plopped down on the side of the bed and shrugged. Glancing at the disheveled, tangled sheets, she raised a brow and said, "So...hate sex?"

I shut my eyes briefly before sitting down next to her and saying, "The argument was this morning."

"Ah," Lil mused. "So, sex first, then you got mad at him. Surprising."

"Lil," I pressed. "My council gave me an ultimatum. They want him to drop the Veil between our courts. When I asked, he refused, multiple times."

Lil furrowed her brow. "Well, shit." She paused, biting her lip before she added, "Um, Aster, please don't kill me, but have you considered that maybe Nox is right?"

I sighed, picking at my nail polish as I muttered, "Of course I have, but I need my council to back me. I can't do this alone."

"You could just dissolve it and form a new council." She shrugged. "They're a bunch of assholes anyways."

"They have power, Lil," I replied softly, "and connections all around this court to high-ranking people. I don't even understand their full reach. So, I can't just tell them to fuck off."

"So," she said slowly. "What *are* you going to do?"

I rubbed my face, feeling a headache forming at my temples. There was a nervous energy buzzing around my body. I did need to do something, and now, but I didn't want to be here, trapped inside the palace walls. I was itching to do something that was actually useful, and I had a plan slowly coming together in my mind.

But it didn't involve Lil—I didn't want her to get into trouble or danger—which meant I had to get her to leave.

"I think I'm just going to take the day," I said carefully.

Lil raised a brow, obviously unconvinced. "To what? Stare at the sky?"

I shrugged but gave her my best cheeky smirk. It was the kind of expression I used to wear all the time, but now—on this new version of me who had died, come back to life, taken on a much too hefty role as queen, and was currently fighting a losing battle in persuading the lords of her own court not to let the world come to a horrible demon-infested end—the sly, easygoing smile felt foreign and, frankly, just plain wrong.

Still, I added, "It's been a while since I've had a day off. Maybe I'll reacquaint myself with Mr. Whiskey for a little while."

That seemed to make her a little less suspicious. She stood, brushing nonexistent dust off her pants before relenting, "Alright, fine. I know you're a big girl, but text me if you need anything."

"I will."

"Promise?" she pushed, holding my gaze.

I nodded. "Promise. See you later. And thanks for checking in on me."

"It's what I'm here for," she chirped with a small smile then left the room.

I waited a few minutes to ensure she was really gone before padding over to the dresser and pulling out the leathers Nox had given me a few weeks ago. I stuffed them in a bag and dressed quickly in a t-shirt, jeans, and leather boots. Then, I slipped out of the bedroom.

Just down the hallway, there was a hidden panel behind a painting that gave access to a passage. I had found it as a child while exploring and was delighted to discover that it eventually opened up into the kitchens. Back then, I had only ever used it to sneak down and steal pastries. Now, it was coming in handy as a quick escape-way.

I glanced around the empty hallway of the royal wing. It was just me here—only me left—and I shoved that thought away as I pushed aside the panel, slipping inside the passage. It was dark inside, and the walls were made up of roughly carved out stone. Condensation coated my palm as I pressed my hand to the tunnel's surface, steadying myself as I tugged the jeans off and changed into the leathers. I had forgotten how much I liked them. They fit my body like a second skin. My old self might have even contemplated wearing them to a club.

Once I was ready, I meandered down the passage for another few minutes before I reached the kitchens. The passage led into one of the large pantries, and I carefully slid aside the panel and darted behind a large pallet of flour. The kitchens were thankfully quiet, most of the staff likely serving or clearing breakfast. Still, as I slipped out of the pantry, I hid behind a large oven until I was sure it was clear—then, I ran out, grabbing a slim knife off the counter before hurrying into the courtyard beyond.

There was a large, half-wild garden on this side of the palace that eventually bled out into what I believed was a public park. The path through the garden was a rough one, so much so that it wasn't really a path at all. Still, I endured the scrape of twigs and brambles to avoid any questions as to why I was leaving the palace grounds.

Once I finally cleared the gardens and left the royal Seelie palace behind, I was left with a conundrum. The moment Nox had left, I'd decided I was going to look for Raven. I had been thinking about it for a few days but had kept talking myself out of it. I knew it was a stupid idea to go off on my own like this. I hadn't ever really asked Nox if I could come along with him and Griffin, but I had an inkling he would be hesitant. Deep down, I knew that was for good reason. I was untrained, both in weaponry and in my magic, but after our argument this morning, I just needed to be *me* for a few hours.

I needed to be a little reckless.

I skirted the edge of the park and ended up hidden in the shadows of a particularly foul-smelling alleyway. I shut my eyes and took a grounding breath, ignoring the sharp, sour scent wafting from the dumpster next to me.

I wanted to go to The Wilds; I knew that was where Nox and Griffin had been looking. It was an area of the Unseelie Court that was—from what I understood—wild. It was apparently full of dark creatures of folktale and legend. My father had once told me a story, on a rainy night when I had refused to go to bed, about a creature called the Bean Nighe. I believed every word at the time, but I wasn't sure if I really believed wild faeries like that were actually out there. Regardless, it did seem like a pretty good place for a demon prince to set up shop and hide someone.

The main issue was I had never flitted on my own before, and I couldn't exactly waltz around the Seelie Court in my fighting leathers on public transport, especially now that some people would recognize me; there were plenty of faeries who had been there that day when I had died under that tree; and with everything going on, the fewer eyes that were on me, the better.

Problem number two was I'd never been to The Wilds, so I couldn't even visualize it. And thanks to the Veil, there weren't exactly trains or buses that ran between our two courts.

Fortunately for me, I had an idea—probably a really stupid one at that, but all my best ideas were—and I let out a puff of air as I raised the knife I'd snagged from the palace kitchens to my palm. I had no idea if this would work, but I had to try.

Before I could overthink it, I pressed the blade to my skin, watching the dark-red blood well up. I didn't wipe it away or try to staunch the wound; instead, I let the blood drip down my wrist and onto the gravel beneath me.

Minutes passed, and I was just about to give up when I heard footsteps approaching. I whirled, seeing a young woman approach. She was dressed simply in a t-shirt and jeans, but there was a particular gleam in her eye that marked her as not-so-innocent.

"Asteria Fairwae," she said simply.

In the pit of my stomach, I knew what this girl was. She was a possessed faerie; a demon lived beneath her skin, controlling her mind. Who knew if the true soul was still there beneath the demon. For Raven's sake, I had to believe so.

"What do you want?" I asked, feigning innocence and balling my hands into fists at my sides.

She smiled, her gaze flicking to my bloodied palm, and flashed her teeth so menacingly I knew she'd seen right past my bullshit. "My master would like to see you," she said plainly, as though it didn't matter either way. "And he has something that you want, something you've been looking for. He's willing to bargain if you let me take you to him."

As I clenched my non-injured hand, my fingertips dug into my palm. I felt another sting as my nails pierced skin, and the demon-faerie's nostrils flared.

"What?" I taunted her. "You want a sip?"

Her lip curled. "If only you knew, promised princess."

"It's 'queen' now."

She chuckled, stepping closer to me. "What is your answer?"

I stiffened as she lifted a hand, her long nail stroking down my cheek, but I strained to keep my breath steady as I replied, "Sure, I'll go with you."

A voice in my head that sounded a lot like reason screamed, *What the hell, Aster?!* But I ignored it. This was a chance—maybe my only chance—to finally find Raven, when Nox and Griffin had so far had no success.

The faerie-demon reached out her hand, and I stared at it for a moment before taking it. When I did, the world around me slid away into a whirling vortex of darkness.

When I opened my eyes, I was standing in a wide, open cavern, lit only with a few low-burning torches mounted on the wall. And standing a few feet away, smiling, was what appeared to be a young man. But I recognized the look in his eyes. It was the same look I had seen many times when I was young and in the clutches of my uncle. This was Abaddon, the demon prince.

CHAPTER 4
NOX

My body felt heavy as I walked through the halls of my palace. I knew it was not simply the years weighing on me, or even just the events of the long-gone past. No, what plagued me now was very present and maddeningly unfixable. At least for now.

I had known being with Asteria despite our court divides wouldn't necessarily be easy, and truthfully, I didn't mind a little challenge. Her council's demand for me to lower the Veil was not even what bothered me the most; I knew these slippery people, had known many more like them in my many years of living, and I would be a fool to let their nature get to me; what I hated was the reluctant submission I could already see in her eyes.

She didn't need to bow to anyone—not even me. In fact, I'd much prefer to be on my knees before her. Still, I knew the precarious position she was in; I had been in a similar one when I first took up my crown, juggling to strike a careful balance between ruling and pleasing powerful, well-established allies. It was like a dance, this role we both held in our courts.

I turned the corner, the hallway branching off into two: one hall led further into the palace, the other to the royal Unseelie orphanage. There was really nothing royal about it, as most of the children who lived there weren't relations of anyone living in the palace, but I always made sure they knew that didn't matter. They had a home here—and that reminder was part of the reason for my visit here today. Admittedly, a part of me needed a distraction from the conundrum I was in and the ache of Asteria's absence once again. Somehow, the children always offered their own beautiful perspectives on things, and today I craved their joy.

"King Nox!" a familiar voice cried as I walked into the common area.

Almost immediately, children gathered around me, their eyes bright and cheeks flushed with excitement. The common area itself was large, spacious, and always comfortable, filled with plenty of bean bags, couches, and toy bins. This place needed to feel like a home for these children, and I ensured it was kept that way. Perhaps a part of me wanted to make sure they had the home I never had. It was a selfish thought, given I had grown up in the palace, but even I knew that stone walls did not make a home. The walls of this palace had, until recently, only ever felt like a prison, and I didn't want that for any of these children.

"It's been so long since you've been here!" one of the children cried.

Another tugged on my shirt. "Yes, nearly two weeks!"

"Is it her?" a young siren boy asked, his blue eyes shining and wide.

"Is it your mate?"

"I heard she's Seelie!"

A smile tugged at my lips at the torrent of questions bursting from their mouths. With a happy sigh, I knelt and said, "One at a time, please."

A small, round-faced faerie girl to my left named Gianna giggled, then said, "Me first!"

I glanced at her, raising a single brow. "Go on, then."

She flushed crimson, but her voice was confident and loud as she asked, "Is it true that you found your mate?"

Warmth blossomed in my chest, and I replied with a half-smile, "I did."

A stunned silence fell over the room and the warmth grew. Once, I'd had the thought that these children were likely the only I would ever have. The prospect of a child with anyone had been akin to a death sentence because of the curse Abaddon had put on me.

But now, I realized I wanted that very badly.

Not yet—not when there was so much danger afoot—but someday, if I truly ended up surviving everything that was coming. That hope was a small light in a vast darkness, yet still there all the same.

"Is that why you've not been here in *ages*?" a young boy asked, sickened by the idea of love as many young boys are.

"She has been taking up a little of my time, yes," I said carefully, "but mostly I've been doing a lot of problem solving to help a friend of ours."

"Are they in trouble?"

I offered the sheepish boy at the back a playful wink. "Not for long."

In truth, I had hope that we'd find Raven, but I had no idea what state we'd find him in. Regardless, I'd do my best to bring him back, to rid him of this demonic possession, because beyond all else I feared Asteria's pain if we failed to do so.

"King Nox?"

I realized I had gone quiet and cleared my throat before saying, "What else would you like to know?"

Several of the children glanced at Gianna, and she sighed loudly, throwing her hands in the air as she exclaimed, "Fine! I'll ask."

I waited patiently, as she gathered her courage.

"Your mate," she said, twisting her hands together, "is she really the new Seelie queen?"

I chuckled. "She really is."

"And..." Gianna paused, looking entirely unsure.

"It's alright," I said gently. "No question is wrong. You know that."

She smiled. "Okay. We just want to know if she's a goddess? Because there's lots of talk about what happened at that tree in the Seelie Court."

I paused, considering what to tell them. Technically, Asteria *was* what Gianna was claiming her to be. She was the Maiden's twin soul—and our kind saw the Maiden as a goddess. They had, for many centuries, in fact. It wasn't hard for me to see why Asteria was becoming deified now too. Her power surpassed what most living Beings could remember in this world. And perhaps it *was* like nothing ever seen before.

Finally, I settled on saying, "She is very special, to both me and the world."

The children's eyes widened just as my cell phone began to buzz in my pocket. Gianna pointed at my pocket and said, "You should take that, King Nox. It's rude to ignore a call."

I smiled. "I suppose it is. Do you all mind?"

A chorus of "no's" rang out, and I stepped out into the hall, seeing that it was Lilliana. A pit formed in my stomach. She had never contacted me on her own before, and I had a feeling this wasn't just to say hi.

"Lilliana," I said as I picked up. "What is it?"

She huffed into the phone. "You're very presumptuous, King Nox."

"Just Nox, like I've told you," I said impatiently. "Is something the matter?"

She paused, and my pulse quickened. Finally, she said, "I think Aster might be about to do something reckless."

I froze. Then, very slowly, I asked, "Where is she?"

"I don't know, in her room at the palace, I think? I'm probably just being paranoid, but the longer I think about it, the more I feel like she was trying to get me to leave this morning. She gets in these moods sometimes...I'm sure you'll figure this out soon. But anyways, it usually starts with her becoming really restless and tense. I noticed that yesterday she couldn't stop fidgeting. In the past, I would assume she'd gone out to a club or bar to blow off some steam, but given everything with Raven, I'm worried she's gone off on her own." Lilliana spoke at double speed, and even over the phone I could hear she was breathless as she finished.

"You think she went to find Raven?" I asked.

"Maybe?"

I took a quick breath, glancing back at the children who were now otherwise occupied. Then, I said to Lilliana, "Can you check her room and confirm whether she's there or not?"

"I can, but it'll take me a bit. I went home after she shooed me out so—"

I hung up the call and immediately flitted to her balcony in the Seelie palace.

I stepped inside her room to find it empty, just as my phone buzzed again. Seeing it was Griffin, I picked up immediately.

"Nox," he said shortly. "We have a new lead."

I shut my eyes, trying to calm the white-hot burn rising in my chest. My starlight magic had been growing stronger in the past few weeks, and I was still getting used to it rearing its head when my emotions ran high.

"Good," I said. "Lilliana thinks Asteria went looking for Raven."

Griffin was silent for a long moment. Then, he said gruffly, "Of course she did. We go now, then?"

His lack of hesitation told me just how well he knew me.

"I'll meet you at the usual spot in five minutes," I said, not sparing another moment before hanging up the call.

I flitted back to the Unseelie Court, ignoring the tightness in my chest; the intense worry would only cloud my mind and I needed to focus now. Once I'd tied up all loose ends for the day; telling the children I'd be back another time and notifying my advisors that our meeting would need to wait; I marched outside. When I arrived, Griffin was waiting in the private training yard where we had been rendezvousing before searching for Raven these past couple weeks. A group of my strongest and most trusted warriors, the close circle Griffin called on in times like these, were already there too. Some stood with arms behind their backs, talking to each other in hushed tones as they waited patiently. Others, less patient, took to honing their fighting techniques or sharpening their weapons. One stood behind Griffin, calm and collected as ever—Francine.

"Where does the lead point to?" I asked as soon as I marched within earshot.

Griffin was all business as he conjured a map of the Wilds with a flick of his fingers. Maps like this did not exist digitally, even in this court, mostly due to Seelie propaganda and widespread media control. Thankfully, both he and I were old enough that it didn't matter. We had other resources.

"The cave system we looked into before," Griffin said, his dark eyes intent on the map, "has cropped up again. Additionally, one of the possessed faeries in the dungeons muttered something about being underground, only an hour ago."

"And," a warrior named Evangaline said as she stepped forward, "there was a magic flare out there in that same spot around the same time."

I nodded once, my jaw ticking. We had set up digital magic detectors near all the promising areas last week. Most of the detected flares so far had turned out to be the Wild Folk messing with us, but this *had* to be it.

"We're ready," Griffin said, meeting my eyes. "Just give the word."

Without hesitation, I replied, "Let's go. Now."

He said something in a low voice to his warriors before nodding at me. My wings were a sobering weight behind me as we flitted to the Wilds—a reminder of all I had to lose.

CHAPTER 5
ASTER

"So, who are you possessing this time?"

Abaddon smiled widely, his gleaming white teeth glimmering in torchlight. He took a step towards me and said, in a voice that was unfamiliar in tone but disturbingly familiar in intent, "No one, Asteria. This is who I truly am. My true form."

I lowered my chin, taking him in. He was just as tall as Nox, but broader, with cropped, jet-black hair and a square jaw. He wore a pristinely fitted suit and shiny dress shoes—I even spotted a silver watch on his wrist—and he might have almost looked human if it weren't for the obsidian ram horns curling around his head.

"Like what you see, dearest?" Abaddon purred.

I shivered—and not in a good way. This was the creature who, along with my uncle, had abused me for years.

"Where is Raven?" I demanded as forcefully as I could muster.

Abaddon prowled over to me, running his fingers delicately over the wall of the cavern, the rock crumbling away where he touched it.

"Dearest princess...ah, *queen* now, is it?" he said mockingly, even bowing slightly. "You cannot have imagined, even in your sincerest hopes of how this would go, that I would let you off so easily?"

I swallowed, and he followed the bob of my throat, his endless, swirling gaze predatory.

"No," I said softly. "I didn't."

The demon prince stopped just short in front of me and murmured, "Good. You're learning. Shall we get on with it then?"

For a brief moment, I really thought he might actually kill me as he raised his hand to my neck, and the swell and complexity of emotions I felt had my head spinning. It conjured a flash of memory of me under that tree; I saw again the ground disappear beneath me, felt the rope around my neck, heard the snap of my bones—it made me want to vomit.

He studied my expression and chuckled. "You didn't think I would grant you such an easy death, did you? You and your bastard-blooded mate did, admittedly, outmaneuver me. But I am a demon, dearest. There's always another scheme in my pocket if the first does not work. And besides, your uses extend far beyond death, despite how satisfying that might be to witness."

I smirked humorlessly. "So, what's your backup plan then?"

I flinched as Abaddon stroked a hand down my face, his eyes empty pools of shadow as he told me, "It's not truly a backup plan. Think of it as the way things were meant to go.

Being as cunning as I am, I chose to go with an easier option. To be frank, it failed, and here we are."

I furrowed my brow as he lowered his hand and took a step back. I had no fucking clue what he was talking about. It unnerved me—the notion that the forces at play might have been working against us for even longer than we had thought—but I wasn't about to let his cryptic words distort my mindset. I would not forget my purpose for coming here.

"Where is Raven?" I said again through gritted teeth.

Abaddon sighed. "You faeries are so impatient, even with your immortality."

"What do you want in exchange?" I asked, having an inkling about how things typically worked with demons. They only gave you what you wanted through shady deals, schemes, and bargains. Perhaps, not so different from faeries, in a way.

Abaddon chuckled. "Figuring it out, are you now? Unfortunately for you, I currently have all I need. You here, and"—he glanced at his watch—"I'll give it a few hours before your Unseelie mate senses something is wrong and comes looking for you."

My stomach dipped. "So that's it? You just wanted to lure him here?" I whispered.

He laughed again and rolled his neck before lunging forward. He grabbed my arm, and I barked out a cry of shocked surprise as he began to haul me across the dusty cavern floor. Before I even realized what was happening, he was opening a barred iron door.

"A little slow to the realization, dearest. But, as I said, at least you're learning."

He threw me down onto a cold, stone floor, and the iron-barred door banged shut behind me. I lunged at it, despite the way it burned my skin, and shook the rusted bars as panicked, shrill words left my mouth. "He'll kill you!" I shrieked. "If I don't do it first!"

Abaddon only cackled as he walked away.

I tried shaking the bars again, tried dredging up my power and directing it towards the iron blistering my hands, but nothing came. I didn't know if it was from some sort of ward on the room or simply that I was too untrained to use it in such a way—it didn't matter now.

I slumped down, cursing my lack of preparedness.

"Even you won't be able to open it."

I whirled as the tired, familiar voice brushed my ears, my eyes widening as I saw a figure slumped on the floor behind me. In the dark, his green eyes were heavy-lidded and dull. His dark hair was tied back, with loose, tangled strands framing his face, and he still wore the clothes he'd been in the day he'd been taken by Abaddon.

"Raven?" I breathed.

A smile tried and failed to reach his cracked lips as he said hoarsely, "I'd hug you but I'm currently chained to the wall."

I fell to my knees, throwing my arms around him.

"Woah, careful with the chains. They're iron too—"

"I don't care," I mumbled into his chest, tears stinging at my eyes. "It's you. *Really* you."

I felt his head dip, his nose brushing against my neck as he whispered, "You shouldn't have come here, Aster. You had to have known it was a trap."

Lifting my head and searching his face for any signs of injury, I asked, "How much do you remember?"

Raven half-shrugged, wincing as he did so. "Not much. My memories of when I was possessed are all pretty blurry and fragmented."

"How is it that you're not still..." I trailed off. "The demon possessing you told us the only way to kill the demon was to kill the host."

Raven snorted. "Oh, he's not dead. I think Abaddon just moved him to a different, stronger body until he has use for me again. Waste not, want not and all, I guess. For now, I've just been the bait." His brow creased. "Why did you let it work?"

"I had to come for you, Raven."

"Come for me, Aster? What good is it if you're in here with me? This is the last thing I wanted."

I glanced around the cell then, taking in the solid, seemingly impenetrable walls, the tiny pile of hay, and the single pan of water. When I looked back at Raven, pain—and not just the physical kind—was written all over his face.

"Admittedly this was very much an Aster move, not so much the careful plotting of one Queen Asteria. Not my finest moment." I sighed deeply. "But I had to do something. Nox and Griffin have been looking for you, and they've come up empty every time. When I had a chance to find you, of course I took it."

Something dark flickered across Raven's face, and I pressed my lips together before I said carefully, "Raven, there's something you should know about Griffin."

Raven shifted, the chains groaning and rattling. "I know," he said gruffly. "I know who he is. It's been just another way for the demon to taunt me, I suppose. As if you and Lil aren't enough."

"Raven," I said softly.

He choked out an empty laugh. "It doesn't matter," he said. "It's not like he raised me. It's just a piece of information, really. I don't really see how it changes anything."

I bit my lip and told him quietly, "You should know he was frantic when you were taken. He felt guilty, I think."

"So much good that does me now," Raven muttered.

I looked away. "I'm sorry, Raven. I should have tried harder to find you sooner. We all should have."

"It's fine," he replied through a dry cough. "Is Lil okay?"

"She's fine," I said, shifting so I was sitting against the wall next to him.

"And my mother?"

"Also just fine."

"And you?"

"I honestly wouldn't know where to start answering that question." I scoffed, finding the question almost laughable. "I have a ton of responsibility and have not one responsible bone in my body."

I chuckled deliriously, and he shook his head at me in amusement.

"I'd say give yourself some credit but you're in here with me." He paused, then asked carefully, "Are you queen now, then?"

I closed my eyes briefly. "Trying to be," I muttered.

"It's complicated, isn't it? Because of him."

I looked sidelong at Raven and said, "Yes, Nox complicates things. Though, not as much as a hidden demon army hiding in both our courts."

"Right." Raven laughed hoarsely and without joy. "Sorry,

I...it'll take some getting used to. The idea of you having a mate."

I placed my already dirty hand over his and said softly, "I know, Raven. I know."

"Well, isn't this touching?" someone sneered, and Raven grasped my hand just as the door screeched. My attention snapped to the faerie standing in the door frame—the *open* door frame. She looked a little older than me with cropped, pastel-pink hair and a petite frame. From the sneer on her face and the buzz in the air around her, I surmised she was possessed.

She must have seen my attention dart to the doorway because she laughed coldly and said, "Yes, promised princess, you can come out and play for a while."

I stiffened, and Raven's grip on my hand tightened. I did not like the connotation behind her words one bit.

The faerie sighed. "Will you come out or do I have to drag you by your hair?"

Swallowing, I forced my hand from Raven's grip, meeting his imploring gaze one more time before standing and following the faerie out into the open expanse of the cavern. I had to do what Abaddon wanted—I would deal with whatever happened—I just needed to get Raven out.

Twinkling in the low light of the cavern, resting on the damp ground, was a single silver dagger. My stomach turned as I saw it, purposefully placed in the middle of the cavern, and my unease only grew as Abaddon walked back into the open space.

He tilted his head at me and said, "Your mate is close, dearest."

Fuck.

Abaddon chuckled, and I realized I had said the word out loud. I hadn't wanted this, to draw Nox and likely others into direct danger. Truthfully, I'd hoped he'd be smarter, but I wasn't exactly in the position to point fingers. This plan had been reckless from the off, and he was only doing what I had done for Raven—something stupid. And what else should I have expected? His words last night should have given me an idea of just how stupid he was willing to be for me, of how far he was willing to go.

"Jura, dear, do the honors, please," Abaddon said to the pink-haired faerie, gesturing to the dagger.

Jura abruptly grabbed my arm and shoved me to the ground before I could even think about fighting back. Not that I really knew how to defend myself—it was just another thing I had hoped Nox would teach me soon. Apparently, it hadn't happened soon enough.

As I slammed into the ground, I met Raven's wide eyes. He strained against the iron chains on his wrists and ankles, panting heavily. He mouthed something to me, and I frowned, unsure of what he'd said. He mouthed it to me again, slower this time, and instantly I knew what he wanted me to do.

'*Starlight.*'

Jura picked up the dagger, still using her unnaturally strong body to keep me down as I struggled. I glanced up at her, looking for a reason to use what I had at my disposal to remove the threat, but she was innocent in all this. She likely had a family somewhere who was hoping and praying she would one day return, and if I managed to dredge up my power now, she would likely never see that family again.

I looked to Raven again, the word 'starlight' still on his

lips, pleading me to fight, but I couldn't risk him either. Last time, Nox had helped me shield the faeries nearby. I had no idea what would happen if I let go like that again without him nearby.

My recklessness only stretched so far.

I gave Raven a small shake of my head, and a rasp left his throat. We both knew that Abaddon had involved others on purpose; the demon was well aware that I wasn't willing to sacrifice innocent lives, and he was using it against me.

"Let's begin, Jura," Abaddon said. "Let's see how loud we can make her scream before the bastard shows himself."

I stiffened as Jura lowered the cool blade to the delicate skin of my forearm. She leaned down and whispered softly in my ear, "This might hurt a little."

Then, she giggled and pressed the dagger down.

At first, I held in my screams. I breathed deeply through those few little cuts. I knew I could handle it; I had endured living nightmares much more horrifying than this. But all my bravado couldn't mask the burning when it began, and it was enough to have me forget what I was capable of enduring and why. The pain spread through my arm and into my chest until my body felt aflame. I swore I was being burned alive, but in the few moments my vision stopped blurring and tilting, I saw no fire. There was nothing there but the blood dripping down my arm.

Shrill screams echoed off the walls of the cavern, mounting in their intensity. After a while, I forgot that it was even me who was screaming. I forgot about anything but the pain. All I felt was the sensation of my skin melting, my bones cracking, and my thoughts crumbling to ash.

CHAPTER 6
NOX

The caverns were a maze. Our search party had checked here last week, but we'd never travelled this deep. Here, the only sound was the water dripping from the stalactites above into echoing puddles below, and the absence of light was dense and suffocating. Three of us held faelights, illuminating the heavy darkness, but the only thing truly guiding us now was that tug in my chest, pulling us closer. Pulling me closer to *her*.

Next to me, Griffin's footsteps were near silent even in heavy boots. He had long ago learned the grace of a warrior and was far from the scrappy boy he'd been when we had first met. His face was set—a face that was so similar to Raven's except for his dark eyes, now filled with determined fury. As loyal as he was, I knew he was here just as much for himself as he was for me.

He held both blades and firearms in his holster, but I knew the heavy sword in his hand was his preferred weapon. I had a blade at my hip too, but I found myself missing the ruby-set sword that I had used to slay demons all those centuries ago. My mind wandered to the moment I saw that sword again for the first time in decades. It was mere weeks ago, in that Seelie museum, that Asteria had listed off facts about it as if they were nothing but empty words, meaningless information about time passed. Oftentimes, I wished I could have let her stay in that world, where the wars of before and now meant little to her. But as much as I wanted to protect her, deep down I knew there was never another path for her than to face this.

There was, for a time, something meaningful in my mate working at the museum, unknowingly acting as gatekeeper to something so personal to me, but now I yearned to see it removed from that lifeless place where true meaning fell on deaf ears.

Someday soon, I would recover that sword from Seelie lands.

Griffin stopped abruptly, holding up a hand to signal to the warriors behind us. I glanced back at them, all loyal to both Raven and me—friends more than comrades, from a time before I was a king and Griffin a general.

"Do you feel that?" Griffin murmured, glancing at me.

I met his eyes in the darkness and nodded. There was a low hum in the air, signaling an energy that was quite obviously not of this world. I'd been around enough demons that I recognized their odd vibrations now. Nephilim gave off a similar energy too.

"Keep moving forw—"

I cut myself off as the first scream cut through the stale air, reverberating around the space, taunting me as it bounced from wall to wall. Everything in me iced over in panic at the sound of that scream—every thought, every muscle frozen— and for a moment, I simply stood there, my body victim to fear I so seldom felt.

Then, the ice shattered, and my vision flashed red with rage.

"Nox," Griffin said in a low, hurried voice, knowing I was seconds away from detonating. "We need to be smart."

Another scream tore through the caves around us, echoing against the stone walls and making it almost impossible to tell precisely where she was. My beautiful, strong-willed, and idiotically caring mate. She had walked right into the demon's hands to try and rescue Raven, and now she was paying a steep price for it.

"Nox. Take a breath," I heard Griffin say through the roaring in my ears. "We're going to get them out, but we have to stick to the plan."

"Fuck the plan," I gritted out as a fresh wave of screams rang out. "This changes things." I met Griffin's gaze just before I shifted into shadow. "Follow me," I ordered in a voice that belonged to nothing of this world, a deep, dark resonation of my corporeal form, "but stay out of my way when I reach them."

"There are innocents down there," Griffin reminded me.

I ignored him as the screams grew ragged. I forged ahead, flying through the cave passages, half running, half shadow-shifting, and damning all consequences.

When I reached the cavern, even in my shadow form, I stopped short, my body becoming rigid.

In the open space of the large cavern, Asteria was curled up against herself on the dusty stone floor. A faerie held her down, an unnatural smile gracing her lips. The dagger was still pressed into Asteria's skin, but I could see the faerie's work was nearly done. She'd carved something into my mate's arm—the same symbol I'd seen on the dream bridge.

As Asteria raised her gaze to mine and I saw the pain glazing over her eyes, something inside of me snapped, and the parts of me that cared about anything beyond her fractured and fell into insignificance. I hardly cared about Raven in the cell just beyond. Hardly noticed the cackle of the faerie holding Asteria down. Hardly wondered why the demon prince was markedly absent. All I saw was the blood —*her* blood—pooling on the floor and the blade of that dagger.

Her eyes were dull as she shook her head. The movement was so small, as if she couldn't manage to do any more than that. She hadn't even tried to dredge up her power and save herself. She had put this nameless faerie's life over her own.

I wouldn't.

I struck out with my wraith magic first; whispering shadows filled the room and disoriented the possessed faerie, but I could see and hear just fine in this darkness. Seconds later, my blade flashed.

"Nox, no!"

Asteria's voice was raw and weak, but I could sense her panic. Except that it was too late; the faerie's head landed on the damp floor of the cavern with a wet smack and rolled into the shadows.

Suddenly, the room flooded with faeries, likely all possessed; they spilled in from each entrance that filtered into the cavern.

I rushed to Asteria and growled, "Get behind me. Now."

She met my eyes and whispered, "I tried to save her...you killed her."

I lowered my chin. "She was dead the moment she touched that blade to your skin, possessed or not."

Something akin to conflict flashed across her expression as she attempted to haul herself up, but she faltered, her body trembling.

Gods, her arm. I was going to kill the demon, and slowly.

Before she could fall, I scooped her up in a fluid motion, cradling her against my chest.

"He's here," she rasped. "Abaddon."

"I know, love," I said in a low voice, my eyes scanning the slowly approaching faeries around us.

"And...Raven"—she was fading—"you have to get Raven out."

"I promise," I said, glancing at her as her eyelids fluttered shut. "You're going to be alright."

Then, she was limp in my arms.

I saw Griffin and the others approaching through the passage I'd emerged from, but the possessed faeries hardly seemed to notice them, too preoccupied with Asteria and me. I shook my head once at Griffin, and he nodded and began to back up, understanding my silent order.

"Bridge," a possessed faerie hissed, eyeing Asteria.

Another smiled and rasped, "Key."

I knew what was coming next.

"Breaker!"

"Keeper."

The last voice I knew in my bones, but I didn't give the demon prince a second to advance further; I let my newly stronger starlight fan out across the room, shielding only Raven behind me from the blinding blast.

When the otherworldly light faded, only ashes remained.

Griffin and the others darted into the cavern. Griffin was at the cell door immediately, breaking open the lock with ease—one of his many talents—and rushing inside. I saw him pause momentarily as he and Raven stared at each other.

From behind me, Evangeline called, "We don't have all day, Griffin. We need to move."

I saw Griffin's chest expand in a deep breath, then he nodded curtly, freeing Raven wordlessly from his restraints. He supported his son as he stumbled to his feet on shaking legs.

"Flit, now," I ordered coldly.

"Is this place not warded against that?" Evangeline asked, eyeing the burnt-out shell of the cavern around us.

My arms tightened on Asteria. "Not for a few more seconds. Now, flit."

With that, I didn't hesitate before folding myself and my mate into the cool darkness of time and space, leaving the cavern behind—hopefully forever.

When I arrived at the Unseelie palace with Asteria in my arms, Lilliana was already waiting in the infirmary. She jumped off a chair and ran towards us as I set Asteria down on one of the beds.

"Oh, goddess," she breathed, her eyes set on the blood on both Asteria and me.

The healers immediately surrounded us just as she began to wake, muttering words I couldn't make out.

"My king, is it just her arm?" one of the healers asked.

Just her arm. As if it were a simple scratch. As if she had not been awake while an intricate symbol was carved into her skin. Not only that, but I knew beyond all doubt that this weapon had been tampered with; I'd sensed the evil in the blade immediately.

"No, it's not just a cut," Lil muttered, ghosting her fingers over Asteria's arm without quite touching it. "The wound is poisoned...or something."

I glanced at her, surprised by her insight. "Has your mother been teaching you some healing?" I asked, the effort to focus on anything but Asteria causing the words to come out harsh.

She pressed her lips into a thin line, her usual bubbliness dimmed, and her features pinched with worry. "A bit."

I'd known Lil had an affinity for healing the moment I'd met her, but some things people needed to figure out for themselves.

Just behind me, I heard Raven insisting he was fine and Griffin arguing he was not, but my attention quickly zeroed in on Asteria as her eyes fluttered open and met mine.

"Nox," she slurred. "Where am I?"

"You're safe, love," I murmured, my brow furrowing as I touched her forehead. She was burning up.

"It hurts," she gasped, her back arching off the bed.

Quickly, I snatched up a cool cloth from a bowl at the bedside table, pressing it to her forehead as she began to writhe in pain. Territorial instincts kicked in as two healers surrounded her. *I* wanted to heal her, and I didn't want anyone touching her or even being near her when she was in such a vulnerable state.

"Nox."

A cool, small hand touched my arm as Lilliana said my name. I turned to her, my features set.

She raised a brow. "I know you want to go all macho, mega-protective mate right now but don't you think you can trust your own healers?"

My attention swung to one of those healers as they muttered incantations, their hand hovering above the wound on Asteria's arm. In response, a hazy, red mist rose up from the wound, and the healer sucked in a quick breath before siphoning it away into a small vial.

"I don't know who to trust anymore," I said, stepping closer to Asteria, watching as more of the strange mist was pulled from the wound. Mercifully, she'd fallen unconscious again, the pain of removing the poison too much.

"You can trust me," Lilliana said from behind me.

"Lilliana, you should go and check on your brother. Make sure he's alright," I said distractedly, clenching my hands at my sides.

Thankfully, for once, she listened and left. I heard her talking to Raven and Griffin in low tones as the healers pulled the last of the poison away.

"Do you have any idea what that was?" I asked one of them, the same young faerie who had healed Asteria after we'd come back from the Trial of the goddess.

He glanced at the vial in his hand and then back at the wound on her arm. "I'm not exactly sure, my king. My best guess is that it was simply used to make the process of doing this to her more painful. And it could, potentially, cause difficulty in healing the wound, even with her faerie blood."

"I see," I said, eyeing the vial. "Don't destroy it but keep it well hidden—under lock and key."

The healer nodded, swallowing. "I'll do that, my king."

"You may both go now," I said to the two healers. "I'll take care of her from here."

They nodded, scurrying off. I spared a single glance at the bed where Raven sat, finding him holding Lil's hand. Then, I looked back at Asteria. Even in sleep, her forehead was creased in pain, and I reached out to smooth it. She only whimpered softly, and I felt entirely helpless. Even I could do nothing about this; all I could do, at least, was be there with her until she woke again.

I laid down beside her on the narrow bed and closed my eyes.

CHAPTER 7
ASTER

My dreams were blurred and filled with images I didn't quite understand. But at the end of it all, when I turned, I was back on the bridge of light and shadows.

"Nox," I said into the darkness. "What happened?"

This time, he did not linger in the shadows for long, emerging as he said, "You're safe, love. I promise."

"Don't make promises you can't keep," I countered. "Nothing is safe anymore."

The shadows around him thickened, whispering words only for him to hear.

"I will make it so, then," he said darkly.

"Today," I began, my words slow and my voice quiet. "You did an awful thing today."

He took a step closer as he said, "Wake up, Asteria. Here is not the place to speak of it."

I shook my head, but as I reached for him, the brilliant light and shadows in the middle of the bridge collided and merged until I couldn't tell one from the other. Then, the bridge fell out from beneath me, and a gaping expanse of nothingness consumed me.

I awoke with a short gasp. I was lying against a warm, hard body, and I knew immediately that Nox had followed me into sleep.

The memories from the cavern came back to me in pieces.

Abaddon in his true form.

Raven in the cell.

The pink-haired faerie and the dagger.

Then Nox, more possessed fairies, and blinding white light—

I shot up in the cot, or tried to at least, because Nox gently pulled me back down, murmuring, "Rest, Asteria."

"No," I rasped. "You killed them. You killed them all."

He paused before letting me go. I stared at him with wide eyes. Ash stained his high cheekbones and the silvery strands of his hair.

"You," I repeated. "You killed them."

His features grew hard, and he said, "I did."

My chest felt heavy. "Don't you feel any remorse?"

"I made a choice," he said, searching my expression. "I got you and Raven out safely."

Balling my hands and trembling with a sudden, barely restrained rage, I hissed, "And you had to kill all of those faeries to do it?"

Nox closed his eyes briefly. And damn him for being so

beautiful because even in my anger, a part of me softened as I looked at him. Perhaps that was a weakness in itself.

"If you had waited, told me what you were going to do, I might not have had to do what I did. But you went alone."

I swore there was a hint of sorrow in his voice as he said that word—'alone'—and I wondered if he thought I didn't trust him fully because of my actions today. If I did, why would I have gone off on my own? The answer was a mystery even to me because I *did* trust him, so much so that it terrified me. Maybe my recklessness hadn't only been for Raven; maybe it was to fulfill some selfish desire, to show myself I could still do things alone. That I didn't need anyone.

All lingering sadness on Nox's face melted away, and he looked at me with an expression both stern and sedate. "It was my choice to kill those faeries, Asteria, and my remorse is my burden to bear," Nox continued, his voice cold. "But I made it very clear I would protect you in *any* situation, yet you took the risk anyway—you put yourself in danger, you put the cards on the table."

I was still half in my thoughts, unable to really process his words. "The demon wouldn't have showed up if we had been together," I snapped. "You know that."

He eyed me warily. "That doesn't mean it was the only way."

"Just...go," I said, gritting my teeth against the dull, pounding headache blooming at my temple.

I thought he might protest or argue with me, but as usual, he was infuriatingly amicable, slipping off the bed and standing. He stared at me for a long moment and said quietly, "You scared the hell out of me, Asteria."

My breath faltered at his vulnerability before my anger surfaced again. "Go, Nox, please. I need space to think."

He nodded and turned, leaving the infirmary with one hand clenched into a tight fist at his side.

"Aster." I heard a familiar, deep voice puff from a few beds down. "You okay?"

I looked over to see Raven sitting up in his bed, staring at me with curious eyes; he still looked bedraggled and had bandages on his wrists and ankles from the iron chains, but his focus was on me as though his situation were totally normal.

I cleared my throat. "I'm fine," I said tightly. "Besides, I should be asking you that."

Even in the dim light of the infirmary, I could see Raven raise a brow. "You know...you didn't really give him much of a choice," he said carefully.

"There is always a choice," I replied, looking down at my hands, which led my gaze to stray to my arm and the bandage there.

Raven took a deep breath. "You forget I was right there, Aster," he said as though the words pained him. "I saw what that faerie was doing to you and...Aster, it made me want to do some pretty unspeakable things. Put yourself in his position for a moment."

"Are you of all people actually defending him?" I muttered crossly, looking away.

"He's right, you know," Lil's voice quipped as she entered the room, carrying what looked like a stack of fresh clothes. She headed over to me, sitting down on the edge of the bed. "I brought you clothes so you can change before you leave," she said.

"I can leave already?" I asked.

She sighed, glancing at Raven, then back at me as she said, "Aster Fairwae, do not dodge my point."

I said nothing, not at first, and the infirmary fell into a charged silence. I realized then that it was just the three of us in here bar one healer near the back of the room, busy preparing bandages and bowls of water. The soft faelights cast a dim glow around the room, and from the single window I could see out of, it was now nighttime.

Finally, I looked back at Lil. "He killed an entire group of possessed faeries, Lil," I said, wringing my hands. "Even if they had demons in them, they were innocents. People with families and histories who might have had a chance of someday returning home."

She nodded. "I know, Aster. But from what Raven and the others said, there wasn't really another way out of that cavern."

"We flitted out," I shot back.

"Which, according to Griffin, was only briefly possible," Raven said, "because of the blast from Nox's power. There were strong wards preventing it in that cavern."

"How is Griffin?" I asked suddenly.

Lil shot me a look. "Uh-uh, Aster," she scolded. "We will deal with Raven's issues later. Right now, we're talking about you."

"No, we're not."

"Yes, we are. You lost the privilege to call the shots when you lied to me." Lil looked down at her feet, wincing as though the words hurt. She sighed and looked at me with concern etched into her features. "Where exactly did that moment end in your mind, Aster? How did you survive that encounter but not to fight your way out of it?"

Our attention snapped to the infirmary entrance to see Nox leaning against the doorframe. His arms were crossed over his chest and his wings flickered in and out of existence as he looked at me.

"Do you need something already?" I asked, a tad more coolly than I meant to.

Nox hardly reacted to my harsh words, though Lil shot me another hard look. Instead, he only said in an even, controlled voice, "I just came to see if you wanted to leave the infirmary. The healers will want to check your wound in a few days, but for now you're alright to go."

"I can walk out on my own," I muttered.

Nox pushed off the doorframe, striding over to me with long legs as he said, "Perhaps, but if you want I can take you home."

A familiar voice inside of me shied away from the idea that the Seelie palace was my home, and another growing part of me screamed that *this* was my home. Here, with him. I tried and failed to push either of those stupid, tiny voices away. Instead, my eyes began to burn, and I blinked rapidly to keep the tears from falling, averting my gaze from Nox and Lil.

"I think." I cleared my throat. "I think I'll stay here tonight. It's late anyways, isn't it?"

When I looked back at Nox, he was gazing at me intently. "It is," he said after a few seconds of silence.

Lil bit her lip, then patted my hand gently and said, "You should go get some sleep, Aster. And..." she paused, her eyes darting to Nox, then back to me. "Well, just remember what I said."

I looked away as she retreated to Raven's bedside. I swung my legs over the side of the bed and stood too quickly, causing my head to swim and my vision to blur.

Nox was at my side instantly, grabbing my uninjured arm gently and murmuring, "Easy. Take it slow."

"Right," I muttered, pausing until my head cleared.

Once it did, Nox let go of my arm, though he lingered close as I grabbed the clean clothes from atop the bed and headed for the exit. As I stepped out into the hallway, though, I paused. I had no idea where I was going, since I'd really only been in this palace a few times and most of that time had been spent in Nox's bedroom.

"I can show you to one of the guest quarters, if you'd like," Nox said from behind me, though I could tell by the tightness in his voice that he didn't want to.

Protective, insufferable faerie.

Who just saved your life, another voice whispered.

Ugh. I'd had enough of little voices in my head today. Still, the idea of sleeping alone wasn't appealing; despite my anger, the idea of being away from him right now was forming as a physical pain in my chest.

"I think," I began, "I'll come with you. But I want you to show me something first."

Nox's brow creased. "You need to sleep."

I huffed out a breath. "I'm upset with you."

He nodded and slowly said, "Yes, I know."

"So, I'm giving you a chance to maybe earn my forgiveness. Or at least tolerance."

His mouth twitched, the ghost of a smile surfacing, and he stepped closer. "We're bargaining now, are we?"

"You like that, do you?" I said lightly.

His nose brushed my cheek as he whispered in my ear, "We're faeries, love. Of course I enjoy making deals."

My breath caught, and I cleared my throat. "I want you to show me your palace," I said as steadily as I could. "I'm sure you've seen nearly all of mine, but I've only ever seen glimpses of yours."

He pulled away from me, his face suddenly more serious as he asked, "You're sure you're feeling up to it?"

My gaze slid down to my bandaged arm. Truthfully, I was exhausted, but the burning still hadn't fully subsided and I didn't think I could sleep with the pain yet, which was exactly why the idea of a distraction was appealing.

"I'm fine."

Nox paused, scanning me with his amber eyes before deciding he agreed with me on some level at the least. Then, he held out his hand to me, ring-clad fingers steady in the faelight. I took it, his callouses scraping against the soft skin of my palm as his grip tightened on mine.

"Come," he said softly, his voice a lover's caress. "Let me show you my home."

WE BEGAN IN THE LIBRARY, which I actually found entirely fascinating. After all, it hadn't been long ago that I was digging through dusty files in a museum.

The space was dizzyingly enormous, lined with large oval windows that let in beams of dim light from the crescent moon. Sturdy sliding ladders leaned against the stacks, and numerous red-oak tables were stacked with lanterns, paper, pens, and even a few laptops. I walked over to one of the study tables, skimming my fingers against the smooth surface before turning the corner to a small alcove. When I did, I gasped.

Hung in the center of the alcove was a hand-painted portrait. A tall faerie man, with short, dark hair and a cruel expression set on thin lips, wore a crown I very much recognized—Nox's crown. Next to him, a pale, dark-haired woman stood wearing a blood-red gown and a crown similar though more delicate than his.

A king and a queen.

And next to the queen was a boy, appearing to be no older than five. I recognized him right away, though his silver hair was shorter and the look in his eyes was...sad. Afraid, even.

"Ah," Nox said from behind me. "You've stumbled across one of the only portraits of my family and me. I would have gotten rid of it a long time ago, but the former king spelled it to the wall for all of *fucking* eternity."

I turned away from the painting, facing him. His arms were once again crossed over his chest and his jaw was tight.

"Why is it one of the only ones?" I asked.

Nox gave me a tight, joyless smile. "Because quite soon after this, as I began to mature and my power started to emerge, my 'father' realized I was not his son."

"Did others know?" I asked softly.

He shook his head, leaning against the table behind him. "Not exactly. It was kept a secret from most. Though there has always been gossip, and I am sure a few in the higher-ranking circles knew. People with spies and connections, like your uncle.

"But as you can imagine, the king was quite displeased when my mother failed to produce another heir. I imagine his plan was likely to kill me and place another one of his children on the throne instead. But those children never came."

"I see." My voice was a little strangled. He didn't say exactly how the Unseelie king had treated him, but he didn't need to. It was written all over his expression, both in the painting and the present. Pieces of his past were coming together, and I was quickly realizing why he hadn't been so quick to share them.

He cleared his throat and held out his hand again. "Come, there's more to see," he said.

I took his hand and let him lead me out of the library. After that, we walked through the halls to a completely empty ballroom. I stared up at the ceiling; it was made almost completely of glass so one could see the stars hanging in the sky above.

"Do you ever have parties here?" I asked, looking back at him.

He glanced around the room, his expression almost sad. "Not for a long while."

"Hmm, maybe you should."

"Someday," he replied, his smile tight. "But for now, there's one important room in the palace I'd like to show you."

I bit my lip as I took his hand again, knowing what was

coming. The most important room in his palace, in any palace, was a room of power.

The throne room.

We entered from the back, walking through a small sitting room that emerged just behind the thrones. When I stepped out onto the dais, my breath caught. The space in front of me was majestic as any throne room should be; it was long, very long, and lined with spears, shields, and armored mannequins; but it was the ceiling high above us that truly took my breath away. On it was a mural that depicted myriad unknown Beings with strange, pointed faces and animalistic features. They chased down a stag, their crude weapons held high, and if I listened closely, I swore I could almost hear their frantic, crazed cries. In all my research, I hadn't ever encountered a depiction of the Fae quite like this. I thought they might be a spin on wild faeries of the hunt. Then again, ancient art had never been my true focal point during my studies.

Tearing my eyes from the mural, I saw that banners with the sigil of the Unseelie Court hung across the walls. The thrones themselves were made of what looked like shining obsidian. I approached one, sliding my fingers over the cool, smooth glass. In another life, where I wasn't queen of another court, I would likely sit on these thrones with Nox.

As I turned away from the thrones, his gaze slid to mine and he said, "Not what you imagined?"

I swallowed. "No, pretty much what I imagined. It's just odd, thinking of you here, holding court and all."

Nox's lips twitched. "You'd prefer the version of me who orders takeout from a penthouse?"

"'Prefer' isn't the right word," I said, glancing down at

my feet. "It's just that this part of you is still unfamiliar to me."

"Someday soon," Nox said, stroking a finger down the back of my hand, "you should sit in as I hold court. Then, you can see."

I nodded, and quite suddenly, out of nowhere, exhaustion was a heavy weight dragging me down. I took a step back and stumbled. Nox immediately caught me and, in a swift motion, pulled me up into his arms, carrying me.

"Nox," I grumbled. "I can walk. You don't need to carry me everywhere like I'm some damsel in distress."

He looked down at me, and I was surprised to find his irises glowing.

"You are not a damsel in distress," he said roughly. "But what you are is my mate who was tortured horribly today. You need to rest, as much as you say you're fine. I know, love. I can feel it, how tired you are. So, please, let me take care of you."

I relented and let myself relax in his hold, and he seemed content to walk with me for a while in silence.

"You shouldn't have done what you did today," I said, breaking the peace with what was very much on my mind. "Some of those faeries were probably members of your own court."

"But you understand why I did it?" he asked.

Now the anger had faded, I understood it as much as I hated it. I understood my own role in it too. I was still acting like the Aster with no responsibilities beyond managing my own alcohol intake to get myself to work on time. The stakes were way too high now, and my actions didn't just impact myself anymore. I had to be better than to run off on my own like that.

I may not have killed those faeries, but I played an undeniable part in their deaths.

I nodded against his chest, and he sighed.

"Good," he said, relief coating his words. "Let's get you to bed."

CHAPTER 8
ASTER

When I woke up, I was alone in Nox's bed. I sat up, watching as early morning light filtered in through the windows. The door to the balcony was half-open, and I rose, padding over to it. When I emerged outside, I saw Nox leaning against the railing, staring out at the sunrise.

His court lay all around us. The palace grounds extended far, filled with sprawling gardens that I somehow imagined looked best at midnight. Beyond all that, I could hear the sounds of the city, already bustling, and I was once again reminded of a simpler time where I'd be rushing to a bus, late for work, mingling with the public and pretending I was normal. In the Unseelie Court, the night was just as busy if not more than the daytime, and, not for the first time, I considered how much more suited I was to this way of life.

Unseelie. Seelie. It was all so stupid.

Nox didn't turn as I approached and stood next to him, splaying my hands against the cool, white stone that made up the balcony pillars and banister. It reminded me a bit of moonstone, like the one he had given me when we had just met.

"Nox?" I said quietly, my voice raspy from sleep.

He finally looked at me, something tired and worn in his expression. This was the man he so rarely showed to the world, the one who had centuries of burden on his shoulders and decades of guilt haunting him.

He let out a heavy breath, then said, "I am trying to think of a way to make things right, because I cannot do what you ask me to do even if I know why you ask it. It will disrupt the balance of the world at a time when we desperately need to maintain some semblance of stability. I am entirely sure your council knows this, and they're using an ultimatum to attempt weakening me."

I looked him directly in the eye and said, "They don't believe another Long Night is coming."

"No, love, they don't." Nox's jaw shifted. "Right now, they are likely plotting to use you to manipulate me."

I looked away from him and to the rising sun. "Is it working?" I asked.

From the corner of my eye, I saw his grip on the banister tighten as he said, "Nearly. I find myself actually considering doing what you ask, even though all of my advisors and generals would beg me not to."

"Have you told Griffin?" I asked. "He's your general, right?"

"He is. And yes, he's aware."

"He must *not* like me," I said, chewing on my lip. "First, I try to persuade you to drop the Veil, then I put you and an entire group of your warriors at risk."

The sun finally spilled over the horizon, flooding the world with light. I squinted as my eyes adjusted.

"He likes you," Nox said. "He thinks you're a bit headstrong, yes. But you saved Raven yesterday, Asteria. You gave Griffin a chance to try and make things right with his son. He'll thank you at some point, I'm sure, in his own way."

I swallowed hard at the words forming in my mind. "I'm sorry. For going off on my own like that. It was stupid."

Nox looked at me, raising a brow. "It was. Stupid...and incredibly brave."

"Thanks, I guess?" I said with a half-smile.

He smiled slightly too, though it fell as he looked at me. I furrowed my brow and was just about to ask what was wrong when he spoke.

"Next time, let me come with you," he said, his voice quiet. "I just lost you, and I-I don't want to ever feel that again."

I looked down, feeling my heart wrench at his stuttered words. He was normally so put-together and confident, but even I knew that everything that had happened during the Trial had terrified him. It hadn't been fun for me either—broken neck and all—but then again, I hadn't cradled the dead body of my mate, thinking it was all over before it had barely begun.

I shuddered at the thought.

"I so badly wish I could tell you everything will be alright," Nox said, his long fingers sliding under my chin and lifting it so I met his gaze.

"I know," I replied simply. There was nothing else to say.

He searched my face for a moment before asking, "How do you feel about a little field trip today?"

I paused. I knew I needed to get back to my council with an answer soon. But maybe it could wait just *one* more day.

"Where?" I asked after a moment, raising a brow.

Nox grinned. "A nod to your museum days, I suppose."

"That's where we're going, then? A museum?" I scrunched my nose. "Why?"

"Because I've had enough of guessing...waiting." His fingers slid from my chin to my cheek, his thumb swiping against my lower lip. "We're going to figure out what that mark I saw on the dream bridge is."

BEFORE WE LEFT for what Nox kept referring to as "the Archives," I stopped at the infirmary to visit Raven. He was sitting up in bed when I entered, drinking what looked like a mug of steaming coffee and talking to Lil, who was perched on the cot across from his.

They both stopped talking as I entered, and I snorted and said, "Secrets aren't fun."

Lil huffed out a laugh. "We're not being secretive. We're just in awe of our gorgeous queen."

"Uh-huh," I deadpanned. "What were you talking about, then?"

Lil pressed her lips together, glancing at Raven. He opened his mouth, closed it, then finally said, "We were talking about Griffin."

"I see," I said carefully. "And...how do you feel about it all?"

Raven huffed out a mix between a grunt and a laugh. "I searched for my father for years, and to know he was here, where I grew up—all this time—and I didn't even know it. It's strange."

"Did he know?" I asked, sitting down next to Lil.

Raven cleared his throat. "According to him, no, not for most of it. My mother kept me a secret until I was older."

"So...they've talked?" I ventured.

"Apparently," Lil said with a shrug. "No wonder my parents have been fighting. My dad must know about the whole thing."

"Wow," I puffed.

Raven sighed. "Yeah. But before you go all doe-eyed and soft feeling bad for Griffin, you should know my mom offered to finally have us meet when I was living in the Seelie Court, and he refused."

"Oh," I said softly. "Raven, I'm sorry."

He shook his head. "It's fine. It isn't like this guy has to mean anything to me. I mean, it's just blood, after all."

I looked away, feeling a pang of loss in my chest as I thought of my parents, and it must have been written all over my face as Lil said, "Blood can mean as much or as little as you want it to."

Goddess, I knew that. My uncle was a prime example. I met her eyes, expressing my gratitude wordlessly for fear I'd start bawling.

Raven nodded too just as I sensed Nox at the entrance.

"Ready, love?" he said sweetly.

"Where are you two going?" Lil asked lightly.

"Research," I said airily, waving my hand flippantly in the air.

She snorted. "Are you going to expand on that?"

"Nope," I popped out before walking over to Nox. He

wore tight, dark pants and a leather jacket, and *damn it* he looked good. Like really, really good.

Maybe we could forgo this afternoon and just...

A glint in his eye told me he somehow knew just where my mind was wandering to.

"Tempting, isn't it?" he murmured, confirming my suspicion.

"What is?" Raven said, and I felt heat rush to my cheeks.

Lil let out a laugh, grinning as she looked at me and said, "Raven, I don't think you want to know. Or maybe you do—"

"Okay, we are leaving," I cut in quickly, avoiding everyone's stares on me. "Right now."

I headed into the hall, and Nox followed. I'd only travelled a few paces when he stopped in front of me and held out a hand.

"We're flitting?" I asked.

"Yes," he replied, his voice husky and edged with something dangerous. He was very much still thinking of what he'd felt down the bond a moment ago—in all honesty, so was I.

I took a breath before taking his hand. Abruptly, he pulled me close and whispered in my ear, "Just now, in that room, do you realize what happened?"

"I projected the fact that I'm horny to everyone?" I guessed in a low voice.

Nox's laugh was full of dark intent. "No. For just a moment, everyone in that room desired you."

"That's...awkward," I muttered.

Nox pulled away, only slightly so he could look at me. "You are entrancing," he murmured, one hand grazing my neck. "So, it's not surprising that even your friends are drawn to you."

"Lil and I have history." I breathed deeply, hoping for the best. "If you didn't know."

He grinned. "Oh, I know. It doesn't concern me."

I tilted my head in question, dubious. "And you don't want to rip her head off for it?"

A gleam entered his gaze, and he brushed his lips against my ear as he said, "No. And you know why?"

"Why?" I dared.

"Because I am yours." He tugged on my earlobe with his teeth. "And you are *mine*."

I gasped as his breath brushed my ear and he flitted us into whirling darkness; the world disappeared around us, and seconds later we were landing in a lobby of what could only have been the Archives.

CHAPTER 9
ASTER

The Archives put the museum I'd worked at to shame.

The ceiling was high and painted with a mural—a common feature of Unseelie Court, I'd found—that looked like a depiction of the heavens. My eyes couldn't quite believe what I was seeing, but hanging from it was the skeleton of something I hadn't truly believed existed.

"Is that—"

"Yes."

Yup, that was definitely the remains of a long-extinct dragon. It stirred a curiosity in me that feared I was losing to my new role as queen.

"You'll catch up," Nox said with a cheeky smile. "Eventually."

I nudged his shoulder playfully and forced my gaze away from the dragon to the space below. Numerous cubbies lined the wall, each with their own desk, chair, and lamp.

And behind the huge, maple reception desk were a few special, likely monthly, exhibits.

A sliver of satisfaction wormed its way in as I imagined Miriam—my previous and very bitchy boss—standing here. She would be jealous, no doubt. Hell, I was a little jealous.

"Nox, darling," a woman said sultrily. "It's been far too long."

Warning bells went off in my head at the insinuation behind her tone, and they only rang louder when I turned to see a long-legged faerie with silky red hair approaching. Nox was still practically embracing me, my ear still tingling from his bite, and he released his grip as the woman approached.

The woman smiled warmly at me, and the bells quieted, just a little. "And this must be her."

Her?

Nox's hand warmed my back as he glanced at me and said, "*Asteria*, this is Hemma, an old friend. Hemma, this is Asteria, my mate."

Hemma gave me another smile and bowed her head slightly as she said, "It's an honor, Queen Asteria."

Surprise bubbled up in me at her use of my title. I hadn't realized it would be respected in the Unseelie Court or that so many people would already know. Then again, I supposed I was their king's mate. Disrespecting me would pretty much be shitting on Nox too.

After the shock ebbed, I returned her smile and said, "It's nice to meet you."

Hemma put her manicured hands on her hips, and I took a moment to admire the pantsuit she was rocking. She glanced at Nox before saying, "So, I presume you've come here for a reason?"

"Yes," he replied, his voice pitched low and serious.

He reached into the pocket of his jacket and pulled out a folded piece of paper. I furrowed my brow as he unfolded it, not quite sure what it was. But as soon as I saw what had been drawn on the paper, my stomach dropped. It was a depiction of a symbol I had seen before, one that I recognized from the very scar on my arm. It looked like a crescent moon with a pin through it, and surrounding it was a four-pointed star.

"We're trying to find the meaning and origin behind this symbol," Nox explained.

Hemma cocked her head as she studied it. "Hmm." Hemma's eyes narrowed. "I'm not sure I've seen it before. Or at least not quite like this."

"What do you mean?" I asked uneasily.

She glanced at me and said, "Well, at first glance, it seems to be a few well-known symbols smashed into one."

I looked at the symbol again and a lightbulb went off in my head. "The crescent moon is the goddess' mark, isn't it?" I asked.

Hemma nodded then eyed Nox. "And I believe the pin represents the sword that both she and your mate used to defeat great evil. I've seen it illustrated this way before. Do you know the origin of the sword?"

The question was just for me because, obviously, Nox had to know, since he was the one who'd actually used it to slay demons. That was just another story I needed him to tell me.

I cleared my throat. "I don't," I said.

She raised a brow at Nox. "Really? You didn't think to tell her?"

He remained silent, sliding his hands and the paper into his pockets. Hemma sighed loudly, and I would have laughed if I weren't so on edge.

"It's rumored to be a gift, granted to the goddess from the Beings Above," Hemma said. "I understand that your court currently has possession of it?"

I cleared my throat and said, "We do. Though it wasn't my decision."

She nodded. "I don't doubt it."

I creased my brow, tilting my head at her. But then, behind us, I heard doors opening and Hemma glanced over my shoulder, her lips pressed together.

"Nox, the Archives are all yours," she said, a little disgruntled. "I trust you can explain anything I've missed."

Nox nodded, beginning to guide me away.

I stopped and turned on my feet. "Hemma," I said. "You didn't say what the four-pointed star meant."

Her brow pinched. "It's a debate amongst scholars. Some say it's simply a symbol from the Beings of Light."

"And others?" I pushed.

She eyed me for a moment with an expression I couldn't decipher. "Others say it was a stolen mark. And that, originally, the mark came from a powerful, unnamed demon. A ruler of Hell. Excuse me, I have patrons to attend to."

And with that, she turned and greeted the group of faeries and humans that had just entered. When I looked at Nox, he had a contemplative expression on his face.

"Let's go," he said. "We've got some digging to do."

I worried my lip between my teeth but nodded and followed him into a slightly smaller room. It was filled to the brim with piles of books and rolls of parchment, and I wandered over to one of the many desks as Nox disappeared into the stacks.

A dusty, almost ancient smell clung to everything, and visible particles drifted in the air where streams of sunlight filtered in. It was beautiful, and on any other day the room would have taken me, but a pall of anxiety loomed as I considered the collective weight of everything I should have known about the world but didn't. In these moments, I felt unprepared and downright stupid.

With a sigh, I plopped down on a cushioned chair just as he returned, a stack of books and papers floating behind him. They drifted over to the table before landing with a gentle plop.

"Nice trick," I said.

He chuckled. "Only the best for you."

I snorted then reached out, running my hands over the books and scrolls before plucking one out. The spine of the book I opened cracked, and I smiled slightly. It had been too long since I'd done this: researched and learned. I used to love all of that—I had been top of my graduating university class for a reason— and now, I began to lose myself in the rush of it again.

Nox was quiet, looking at his own book as I turned the pages, scouring them for anything about the strange mark. Most of what I saw was mythology and lore about old runes and symbols, as well as theories about some rare, nearly forgotten words in the Old Language. I shut the book and moved on.

And so went the afternoon, drifting away as the sun dipped lower and faelights and electric lamps began to illu-minate the space around me. I hardly noticed the time passing. There was ink on my hand from the notes I had been scrawling on a spare piece of paper, but nothing was making sense and I had found little beyond what Hemma had told me.

In most texts, the four-pointed star was thought to represent hope and light. I only found one passage referencing its potential link to demons, but it was vague and lacking any solid information. The crescent moon, in this case, tilted on its side, was the goddess' mark. Paired with the sword, I was pretty sure it meant something along the lines of 'triumph over evil,' but I could find nothing that made sense of the combination of the three.

I shut the book I had been reading and sat back, rubbing my eyes. "I give up," I muttered. "There's nothing here. Not about the symbols paired together like that, at least."

"Yet," Nox said, his gaze scanning me. "This library is extensive."

"Joy," I muttered.

He didn't smile or respond at all, but he looked at me intently.

"What is it?" I asked bashfully. "Ink on my nose?"

"You're very beautiful when you're concentrating."

I met his gaze, refusing to shy away from the compliment. "We should probably go. If we're done here."

He stood, walking over to me. When he was just behind me, he brushed the hair back from my shoulder and said softly, "When you read, you get a little line of concentration between your nose and your brow. And you talk to yourself, though I can never hear what you're saying. It's too quiet. When you discover something, your eyes widen and glow a bit." He leaned down, brushing his lips against my neck. "It's all very fascinating to me."

My back arched in the chair, my body immediately responding to him before my brain could put a thought to it. But still, I found the wherewithal to say, "Nox, we're in a public space."

"Anyone could come in," he murmured. "So, we better be discreet."

With a flash of breathless darkness, he flitted us to what had to be somewhere within the stacks. My eyes narrowed, and he grinned savagely.

"Play with me, love," he breathed, lowering his lips to mine.

He kissed me softly at first, and I nipped his bottom lip, my hands running down his chest. When I reached lower, he let out a pleasured groan, and I grinned against his mouth as I palmed him through his pants.

When he eventually pulled away to look at me, his expression was wicked, and before I really knew what he was doing, he lowered to his knees before me, kissing my inner thigh. I shuddered as he moved higher, his hand cupping me.

"You'll have to be quiet," he lilted, amber eyes slightly aglow as he glanced up at me. "Can you do that?"

"Yes," I breathed, threading my fingers through his hair.

He let out a low noise, tilting his head back slightly as I ran my fingers through the silky strands. But seconds later, he refocused, unclasping my pants and tugging them down. His mouth was immediately on me, parting me with his tongue. With one hand, I gripped the bookshelf behind me, biting my lip to keep from crying out. He gripped my ass as I writhed, and with the other hand he began to slowly pump his fingers in and out. A small whimper escaped me, but I swallowed the moan that followed.

He glanced up at me and murmured, "Good girl."

I nearly came just at the words and the euphoric look on his face. But he paused before slowly circling my clit with his tongue. I tightened my grip on his hair in protest, and he chuckled, the sound vibrating against me.

"No teasing?" he said.

Goddess, I was so close, but I heard someone enter the room from a few stacks away. I froze, but Nox didn't move away from me. Instead, his lip curled before he continued, content to do exactly what he had been doing a moment before. I sent him an imploring look as I desperately tried to keep quiet, something that was becoming more and more difficult.

"Nox? Asteria?" she called, just as I felt myself start to fall.

Before the moan unwittingly escaped my lips and echoed through the library, Nox rose up, smoothly covering my mouth with one hand while finishing me off with the other.

"One moment, Hemma!" Nox called back as I panted against his palm.

There was the sound of shuffling as Hemma left the room. Slowly, Nox lowered his hand.

"You…" I rasped, shaking my head.

He grinned. "Don't lie, love. You liked it—the danger. The notion that she could have turned the corner and seen us at any moment."

"Maybe I did," I said airily, though both he and I knew it

was true; the whole thing had been completely erotic, and I had *loved* it.

"You might just have a little Unseelie in you after all," he said, planting a quick, hard kiss on my mouth. "But you're right, we should get going."

I snorted. "Oh, now you want to leave."

He glanced at me as I tugged my pants back into their proper place and smoothed my hair down.

"If you want more, you need only ask," he said darkly, mischief shining in his eyes. "Though, the chances of Hemma coming in again only grow by the minute."

I huffed out a breath, ignoring the heat that was already starting to reignite in me and said, "We can go."

"Hmm. I'm disappointed."

I rolled my eyes at him, and he chuckled. But as we walked out, passing the table where we had essentially wasted the afternoon finding nothing, my amusement faded.

Nox looked at me, his expression set into one of determination. "We'll figure this out."

"Yeah," I muttered. "And the answer will probably only add to this mess."

He didn't say anything. He didn't need to. I was probably right; whatever this symbol meant, it couldn't mean anything good. The mysterious woman behind me on the dream bridge was just another player in this game at a time when we desperately needed to level the field.

"Would you like to go back to the Seelie Court?" Nox asked just before we left the library.

I shut my eyes briefly. "I should."

He waited, and when I opened my eyes, I couldn't decipher his expression at first. It seemed almost to express anger, but soon, it became quite apparent to me that he looked on edge and territorial. He *wanted* me to come back with him. He probably wanted me to always choose that answer.

It was precisely why, in the end, I felt sure of my decision. We couldn't let our relationship, whatever it was, get too tangled up in the politics of our courts and the duties to our people. Even I, the newbie queen, knew that.

"Yeah, I think I will go back."

"Alright," he said. "But take Lilliana back with you."

I snorted. "Lil is not a dog I can just call on to do my bidding."

"I dunno about that," a familiar voice chirped.

Turning, I saw Lil herself in the doorway. She looked absolutely content, sipping on a to-go cup of coffee and wearing a ratty t-shirt and jeans.

I looked between her and Nox before demanding, "Did you...when did you call her?"

Nox shrugged. "You were very engrossed in your research, but I figured we might eventually need some help."

"Sorry," Lil said, sounding wholly unapologetic. "I know I was supposed to be here earlier, but Raven and I were talking."

"It's fine," I said, eyeing her. "We're going home."

I ignored the way I choked on the word 'home.' Everyone else did too.

"Fine, fine," Lil said with a wave of her hand, her glittering pink nails catching the faelights. "Let me text Raven and then we can go."

She typed rapidly on her phone screen, and I turned to Nox. "I'll see you later," I said.

He pressed his lips together tightly, that territorial look still sharpening his features.

"Soon," he said.

Lil looked up just as I added, "And Nox?"

"Yes, love?"

I tilted my chin so I was looking him directly in the eye as I said, "I haven't forgotten about my request regarding the Veil. I hope you haven't either."

Nox opened his mouth to reply but I was already walking away, my arm looped in Lils'. She shot me a look as we strode out of the library and into the lobby of the museum. I only shook my head slightly, not speaking until we were outside.

"Two things," she blurted out as we stepped onto the path.

I raised a brow. "Yeah?"

She sighed, obviously perturbed at my lack of concern as she said, "One, you just handed his own ass to him on a platter. Which kind of scares me, given that's the all-powerful Unseelie Night King in there."

"He's not going to do anything to me—"

"Oh, I know," Lil cut in. "I'm more worried about myself. And two," she continued, taking a breath, "how the *hell* are we gonna get back to the Seelie Court, since I assume you didn't cold-bitch walk away from him only to run back in there and catch a ride."

I smirked. "I didn't."

"So..."

With a flourish, I snatched my cell phone from my

pocket and pressed call on one of the contacts Nox had so graciously added.

"Asteria?"

Griffin's voice was gruff, but I could hear a hint of alarm in his tone. I'd never once contacted him personally, and I was sure he was worried it was an emergency.

"Yep, it's me," I said, dragging Lil along as I crossed the street.

Around us, the Unseelie Court was beginning to rev up as night set in, the streets crawling with people. Daytime had definitely not been the party hour for the citizens, but now that darkness was falling, the city was waking up. I needed to go clubbing out here someday—though maybe when Beings possessed with demons weren't potentially roaming the streets and doing goddess knows what.

"What do you need?" Griffin asked as my gaze followed a group of human girls, wearing flashy dresses and chunky heels, approaching the already-long line snaking out of a dance club.

"Oh, just a favor," I said coyly.

Griffin huffed into the phone. "So, you're not in danger?"

"Hardly."

"What does that mean?"

"No more danger than normal," I clarified. "But can you meet Lil and me outside the Unseelie Archives? We need a ride."

"And where is Nox?"

"He's getting some much-needed space to think."

There was a long moment of silence, and I almost thought he was going to bring up the Veil and perhaps scold me, but he only grunted and said, "I'll be there in a few."

The call cut out, and Lil snorted. "Damn," she said. "I think you made him pissy."

I kicked at a few loose stones on the cobbled sidewalk. "You shouldn't listen in just because you can."

Lil made a fake pouty face before curtsying and saying, "Have I upset my queen?"

I bit my lip to hide my smile. Goddess, I was so grateful for Lil at times like this. She made me feel normal. Like I was still just Aster, not a queen or some sort of twisted savior.

"Do you think Nox will come looking for us?" Lil asked. "Since he has no idea how we're getting home?"

"Maybe," I said. "But I think he might've gotten the message. Besides, I'm a big girl. He knows that."

Lil shifted on her sneaker-clad feet, pressing her lips together.

I leveled a look at her and said flatly, "What?"

"Aster," she said carefully, "I know you're a big, strong, independent woman. We all do. And no one is questioning your ability to make decisions. But be careful. There are people who will want to manipulate you, and you're going to need to be able to trust someone to help you."

"Are you insinuating that it should be Nox?"

Lil let out an exasperated sigh. "He's your *mate*, Aster. Who else—besides me and Raven, of course—are you supposed to put your trust in?"

"My thoughts precisely," a deep, gruff voice responded.

I turned to see Griffin standing there stiffly, still wearing battle leathers. Did the man wear anything else?

Straightening, I said, "Can you just take us home?"

Griffin raised a dark brow. "No 'please'?"

An unexpected laugh bubbled out of me. "You want me to grovel, *general?*"

He flicked a piece of nonexistent dust off his sleeve and said, "No, of course not. But simple manners would be appreciated."

I had no idea Griffin could be, well, sassy. There wasn't really a better word for his current behavior.

"Have you talked to him yet?" Lil asked, changing the subject.

All humor fell from his face, his features tightening as he replied in a low, quiet voice, "I think it's best I let Raven come to me when he's ready."

"And is that what you told yourself years ago, when you decided not to meet him?"

I watched, a pit in my stomach, as Griffin's tan face visibly paled.

Clearing my throat, I said, "We should be getting back. I'm sure my council is eager to speak to me. And Lil, baby-girl, you need a bath."

Lil narrowed her eyes at me, but I saw her try to discreetly sniff herself. Griffin gave me a grimace that I think was supposed to be a smile before holding out his hands. Lil glanced at me, and I nodded my assurance. Then, we each grasped a hand.

Griffin's palm was unsurprisingly rough and calloused from what I assumed was years—probably even decades or centuries—of wielding weapons. His grip tightened on mine as the world fell away into the cool, dark wind of nothingness. This was the in between; the lack of being anywhere, and I was growing to love it.

When we reappeared into existence and I could breathe

again, we were outside the gleaming gold Seelie Court palace gates. An all-too-familiar spike of fear surfaced in me as we stood there. Years of abuse from my uncle here would take a long time to forget. Maybe I would never truly forget it. Maybe that was just the nature of what had happened to me. Whether I liked it or not, it had shaped me in many ways. I supposed I just had to learn how to make peace with the memories that would never fully fade away.

As if he could sense my sudden distress, Griffin's hand remained in mine for a moment longer than necessary. He gave it a subtle squeeze before letting go and bowing slightly.

"Your Majesty," he murmured. "Lilliana."

"Thanks, Griffin," I said, my voice rasping with sudden emotion.

He rose up and met my eyes, nodding once. "Let me know if you need anything, Asteria."

I was suddenly struck by Griffin's actions. He had come to my rescue more than once, while still hardly knowing me. Sure, Raven had been involved and he was endlessly loyal to Nox, but today he didn't have to answer my call.

My lips parted with the realization as he began to walk away. "Griffin! Wait."

He turned. "Yes?"

I tilted my head. "Why do you even care?"

"About?"

"About"—I made a vague, waving motion around myself—"me. I mean, I'm pretty much your enemy by most standards. Or at least your rival. And I know you don't agree with what I'm asking Nox to do."

There was something flickering around Griffin's dark

brown irises—a deep contemplation, hardly noticeable if you weren't really looking.

His brow creased and he said, "Those things may be true. But at the end of the day, you are my king's mate. That means I protect you above almost all others. And…" He hesitated, as if considering whether to say the rest. "You are the most important thing in the entire world to my closest friend. In the Unseelie Court, we protect our own." He bowed his head one last time and said, "Goodnight, Asteria," before disappearing in a whirl of wind and shadow.

"I ASSUME we're meeting about the Veil."

Outside, night had fully set in, and the room was lit with colored lamps and glowing faelights. Each of the lords around the table had a crystal glass of whiskey. I'd been offered no such courtesy of a refreshment of my own, but I let the slight go for now.

"You assume correctly," Lord Ives said.

In his tone I was surprised to detect a curious hint of gentleness, and for a moment I held his gaze. A memory snagged, but it became lost to me as immediately as it had surfaced, and I was left only with a feeling that it wasn't a bad memory. He had been a friend of my father's, once, and one of the few lords on this council that had served under both my parents and my uncle. Nevertheless, in more recent years he'd become no more blameless than any of the lords here for displaying bigotry and ignorance, and I wondered then what his reasons for betraying me so horribly were—and if it mattered whether they were good enough or not.

I took a breath, dismissing the lost memory, putting it behind me with the rest of my past. It didn't matter, not now.

I placed my palms on the cool wood of the long table in front of me. "I have questions," I said shortly.

"And we are running out of time," Lord Jasper sneered.

I narrowed my eyes. "Time for what?"

"Your questions," Lord Ives cut in. "What are they?"

Briefly ignoring Lord Jasper's comment, I decided to address the individual treating me with at least a modicum of respect, even if I did not know the real reason for it. "What exactly is the Veil?" I asked earnestly, turning my gaze to Ives. "None of you have attempted to explain that to me, nor the true consequences of dropping it."

"Ah," Lord Ives said, almost to himself. "You've been speaking to your Unseelie mate."

I bit back the retort of '*obviously, you old twat,*' and instead said, "I'd like to weigh the options here. Decide whether this is really what we need right now."

"Whispering secrets, spinning dreams," Lord Ives muttered.

My gaze heated, totally up to my eyeballs with this shit. "Why, Lord Ives, would I agree to something I do not understand? And why exactly would one such as yourself degrade me for seeking that understanding, if your ends were honest?"

Lord Jasper sighed *again* before he said, "Who are you to trust, if not your own council?"

"And how am I to trust my own council if they are not forthright with me?" I countered.

Lord Jasper and Lord Ives exchanged a look; one of the

other lords coughed on a sip of his whiskey, sputtering his apologies; and I swept my eyes around the table, challenging them all to speak up.

"The Veil," Lord Ives began, "is a powerful magical barrier. It was created after the first Long Night by an Unseelie king named Ivan Wight. His reasons for creating it are hazy and misunderstood, especially amongst Seelie Fae. But some claim it was to protect the citizens of his court."

"Because some Unseelie Fae have magic that appears too similar to that of demons?" I half-asked, half-stated as I attempted to fit the puzzle pieces together. "And people were afraid of that after the Long Night."

Lord Ives grimaced. "That is one claim. There has always been disparity between our courts, but some records state their power increased after that initial Long Night. Since then, the responsibility of upholding that Veil falls upon each Unseelie ruler."

"Doesn't that drain them?" I asked, my brow creasing. If keeping the Veil in place weakened Nox, I couldn't fathom why the lords of my council would want to destroy it.

Lord Jasper tapped his fingers against the table as he said coolly, "Quite the contrary. The magic of the ruler and the magic of the Veil feed upon one another, strengthening both. The Unseelie are cunning creatures, are they not?"

I swallowed. "So, that's why you all want to destroy it? Because you think he's too powerful?"

And then, it dawned on me.

My magic was directly linked to Nox's through the mating bond. No one had ever told me that, but I had felt it on several occasions since I'd accepted the bond. I knew for sure after he obliterated all those faeries in the caverns with his starlight. My strength had a connection to his and his to mine.

I stood abruptly, and Lord Ives said softly, as if trying to calm a startled animal, "Asteria, please sit."

"You don't simply want to weaken Nox," I said, my voice low and aggressive. "You want to weaken me as well. You knew I wasn't fully aware of the intricacies of the mating bond. You knew I wouldn't know until it was too late."

I could feel it building in my chest—could feel the white-hot burn of starlight surfacing. I knew that it was only a matter of seconds before my eyes illuminated with that otherworldly glow, and that if I didn't take a breath, it would take a few more seconds after that before my council was burnt to a crisp.

"The power you and your mate possess," Lord Jasper said icily, "once served our world. But now it unbalances it."

"It is *needed*," I hissed. "If you idiots listened for a second you would know we are on the brink of absolute destruction. And we should be preparing for that, not questioning power or balance between our puny courts."

"Ah," Lord Ives puffed out, "but we should always question power and balance. Even Nox Ether's father did that, and it's precisely why his life ended with his son burying a blade in his back."

I blinked heavily.

Once, when I was very small, a playmate hit me square in the face with a ball. The impact was unexpected, and my nose cracked with the force of it. I remember brushing it off, continuing to run and play as though it had never happened, before reality caught up with me and I noticed the pain in my skull and the taste of blood in my mouth. It was only then that I started bawling and my father rushed to console me.

My reaction in these moments had always been delayed by my own desire to ignore the shitty truth in front of me. I always wanted to pretend, a defense mechanism to protect my feelings, but in the end, it always caught up with me—the pain always followed—and now was no different.

After moments of stillness, of quiet contemplation, I felt the air knocked from my lungs.

I knew my uncle had taunted Nox about his father before—or who everyone thought was his father—but I hadn't thought he meant Nox had *killed* him personally.

Lord Ives said the words with a purpose—hell, everything said in this room was carefully calculated. Words were his blades and he had used his to unsteady me.

I swallowed and leaned my suddenly shaking hands against the table. "If I had known your insistence to drop the Veil was only an attempt to sabotage my mate and me, then I would have never even considered it. You've wasted time—precious time we have little of."

"You will not have our support without this action," Lord Jasper cut in sternly.

"You are making a mistake—"

"Asteria Fairwae, choose wisely." Lord Jasper stood, and the court began to stir, ready to leave. "We will give you one more day."

One day.

There was no more time to argue. The council departed, and I watched as Ives idled, his expression one of deep frustration, sipping what was left of his whiskey as Lords bustled around him. It was in this moment I caught the memory I'd lost earlier; in my mind's eye, I saw a hazy image of Lord Ives sneaking me a ginger cookie under the table, placing it into my tiny hand as he sipped amber liquid in my father's study.

Lord Ives looked up from his empty glass and met my gaze. We stayed like that for some time—as though we had all the time in the world—until his resolve wavered, and he left.

CHAPTER 10

NOX

"She's very headstrong. Almost detrimentally so."

I looked up from the absolutely *riveting* finance report I had been studying to see Griffin standing in the doorway to my office, his arms crossed over his chest and a smug look on his face.

I set aside the report for now and stood. "I figured she had found a way home without me."

Griffin snorted. "Yes, she called me like a dog and then insisted I take her and her little friend back to the Seelie Court. And you know how much I hate going there."

"Have you spoken with her at all since Raven and Lilliana came here?" I asked, eyeing him. "Evelyn, I mean."

Griffin made a low grunting noise that very much let me know he didn't want to discuss that particular subject—not now and probably not ever. Good thing he had friends like me.

"This conversation isn't about me," Griffin finally said, shifting awkwardly.

"Then what is it about?"

Griffin raised a single brow. "Asteria. She's reckless."

"And?" There was an edge to my voice as the word slipped between my teeth. Nonetheless, Griffin didn't back down. He knew me too well.

"And it's going to end up biting her in the ass. The moment she reclaimed her title, a target that had already been on her for her entire life only grew more tempting for those who have and will want to hurt her. Her council has already begun to take advantage of that. Not to mention the fact that she's your mate, which makes things even more precarious."

I ran a hand over my face and muttered, "I'm quite aware."

"Have you told her precisely why you can't drop the Veil?" Griffin held my gaze, his dark eyes adamant.

I strolled past him, out of the office and into the kitchen of the penthouse. I came here when I needed to not be a king, to find respite from the stressors or royal responsibility; it was a role I'd never really expected to have and one I'd still not fully fallen into. Griffin and my closest advisors would think that ridiculous, but in my heart I'd always felt out of place in this position—I'd never left behind completely the desire to run away from it.

And today was most definitely one of those days.

Before I responded to Griffin, I flicked my fingers, opening a cabinet. A bottle of bourbon floated out, poured itself into a glass, and then lifted again, settling back into the cabinet.

"Hmm." Griffin walked over and poured himself a glass as well. "That bad? Because it is for me."

I knocked back the liquid, savoring the burn as it slid down my throat. "She doesn't know everything," I said heavily.

"And why don't you just tell her?"

"Because." I began to pace, my shoes clicking on the hardwood floor. "I've waited too long. Telling her now would make my reasons look selfish, and I don't want to give her a reason to not believe me."

"Are your reasons selfish?" Griffin asked.

I poured another glass of amber liquor and took a slower sip this time, then replied, "No. But you already knew that. Why even ask?"

Griffin grimaced. "Just checking in, my friend. We all can use a little self-reflection sometimes." He set his already-empty glass on the granite countertop before sauntering over to the couch. For a moment, he just stared at the soft cushions, the television, and my collection of films. Then he shook his head and muttered, "The world moves too damn fast."

"Careful," I said, striding over to join him. "You'll make yourself sound old."

He shoved my arm lightly. "Funny, oh ancient one."

"Don't remind me," I muttered.

Griffin finally sat down on the couch and asked, point blank, "So, when are you going to tell Asteria the real reason for your refusal to drop it?"

"There's more than one reason and you know that," I replied, sitting next to him, poised uneasily on the edge of the cushion.

"Yeah, sure." He chuckled darkly. "And I'm sure it has

nothing to do with the fact that her magic *and* yours would weaken without the Veil."

I curled my fingers, clenching my hand into a fist. It was true, every word that he said. Sure, what I had told Asteria about the balance between light and dark wasn't a lie—the balance would be disrupted, causing every magical being's power to become off-kilter, and the world would descend into chaos, at least for a while—but it would also weaken both of us at a time when we desperately needed to be as strong as possible. She needed to be able to protect herself, and I needed to be able to protect her. At all costs. Even if that cost was her amiability or even trust towards me.

"I've hit a nerve, haven't I?" Griffin said, though his tone was far from teasing.

I uncurled my fingers, flexing them as I said, "She died, Griffin. I felt her leave and felt the bond between us snap and fall away."

He was silent for a long moment, then I felt a hand on my shoulder. "I know, brother. But fear can be a poison to love. You know that."

"All too well," I muttered. Taking a short breath, I added, "I'm not him."

Him.

Wesley Ether: the former king of the Unseelie Court and ever-willing participant of my foulest memories. I could still hear him screaming at me and my mother the night he finally realized I was not his son. A slap, then knuckles smashing into her delicate face. Blood on the fine carpet of their bedroom. Her arm shielding me. And she had healed me that night, when *I* should have been taking care of her...

"Nox," Griffin said, startling me out of the memories.

I glanced at him. "I'm good."

He held my gaze for a moment, long enough that I knew he didn't believe me, but he made no comment on the horrors we both knew were playing out in my mind. Instead, he glanced down at his phone and said, "Raven just texted me."

"And?" My voice was suddenly thin. I could feel exhaustion creeping in.

"Lil contacted him. Asteria just met with her council and...I don't think it went well."

Within seconds, I was standing, all fatigue and self-centered thoughts of sleep fading away into nothing. Wordlessly, I grabbed a leather jacket that had been slung over one of the chairs by the counter, moving so fast I slipped into my wraith-form momentarily. Griffin met me by the door, grabbing my upper arm and gruffly saying, "*Do not* kill any of the Seelie lords. We can't afford that kind of political headache right now."

"No promises," I said darkly, slipping out of his grip and flitting.

When I landed at the Seelie palace gates, the guards waiting there eyed me warily. Their expressions ranged from a mix of terrified to rageful as I slipped through the solid bars of the gates, nothing but a shadow.

"Nox Ether," one of them spat. "You are not welcome here."

I let my gaze slide over the guard. Average build, dull brown hair and eyes—Fae, by his scent. He barely fit into the maroon guard uniform, likely a hand-me-down from a previous recruit—maybe one from that bastard Ewin's old gang he called his guards.

I could kill him, easily.

"Is that any way to talk to a king?" I asked, my words slow and laced with seductive darkness.

To his credit, the guard hardly flinched as my shadows began to snake up his arm, though it earned him a couple of idiot points too.

I sighed heavily, making a decision. "Move. All of you."

"Or what?" The bold guard dared, even as I could see his hands begin to tremble.

"Or I *make* you," I hissed, lowering my chin just as the shadows reached for his throat.

His hand drifted up, and he gasped. "Can't...breathe."

"Hmm, what is that I hear? An apology?" I chuckled humorlessly. "Well, I have much more important things to do, so..."

His eyes bugged out in fear just before I released him with a flick of my fingers. I strode towards the entrance as he crumpled to the ground in a heap. The rest of the guards stepped well out of my way as I stormed into the palace.

Admittedly, I could have just flitted right onto Asteria's balcony, but that feral, covetous side had pushed me to put on a display. Just a small one.

Maids and more guards jumped out of my way as I stormed through the halls, none bothering to stop me. When I reached the royal wing, the sound of shouting pricked my ears. *Her* voice. My wings flicked into existence behind me, and when I saw none other than Lord Jasper Orla lingering in the hall, they flared out wide behind me.

"Move," I barked. He didn't deserve any pleasantries or even silky deception.

Lord Jasper narrowed his eyes. "I wondered if they

might call on you. Which is precisely why I thought to linger here."

"Move."

"I don't think so," he said in a low voice. "You could pose a threat to our queen. In fact, I think you already have."

My patience was wearing thin, even as Griffin's order echoed in my ears. Fuck his order, I was king for a reason. Even if I knew I was an ass for even thinking that.

"She is my *mate*," I growled. "I would never harm her."

"Hmm," Lord Jasper rumbled. "Perhaps. But the fact that you are Unseelie could very well harm her. Not to mention the target on your back. I wouldn't be so quick to think curses are solved easily or that the Beings beyond are quick to forgive. They have so much time on their hands, don't they?"

Narrowing my eyes, I took a step closer to him. "What the fuck are you saying?"

His eyes flickered. The bastard knew something I didn't and was quite obviously taunting me.

"I'm saying," he began, "demons are tricky creatures. Even the mysterious creatures of Light have their own forms of treachery. And believe me, I am quite aware of *exactly* what you are. Wesley Ether told very few, yes, but even Unseelie spies talk when they're given enough...motive."

"Give me one reason not to kill you where you stand," I snarled, already feeling the familiar warmth of starlight at my fingertips.

Even that didn't seem to perturb Lord Jasper though. Instead, he took a step closer to me and said airily, "There are many reasons. The simplest amongst them being that Theodore and Dianna Fairwae had many secrets that would have died with them if it hadn't been for a select few, including me. Secrets directly related to their daughter. Secrets I'm sure you will want to know."

"*Fuck!*"

Both our eyes flicked towards the door at the end of the hall as Asteria shouted and glass shattered.

Lord Jasper's mouth quirked. "How very regal of her."

He finally stepped aside and added, "I suppose I'll let you pass today. But just know, if you truly cared for her, you would make sure to never set eyes upon her again."

And with that ominous warning he swept away, his heeled boots clicking against the marble floors.

Fucking bastard.

But as much as I wanted to rip his innards out and force-feed them to him, he had somehow become an important player in these games. This was no bluff—I'd seen deceit for self-preservation a thousand times—no, he knew something. Besides, Asteria needed me, and I wouldn't waste more time on him when my path to her was clear.

As I pushed open the door to her chambers, the scene before me was one of rage unleashed. Everything that could break was broken, tapestries and soft furnishings ripped and discarded, and pacing amongst it all was my mate, completely incensed.

"You called him?" she said, her nostrils flaring.

Narrowing my eyes, I stepped carefully around the shattered glass on the floor and looked up to see Asteria staring at me with burning blue eyes, the neck of a broken bottle grasped in her hand.

"Do not do what you're thinking about doing, love," I said in a low voice, holding her glowing gaze.

Her face was flushed with a vexation I'd never seen in her before, and it was both beautiful and terrifying—I couldn't look away.

"Asteria," I said, a warning. "Don't."

Her lip curled into a snarl. "I don't like secrets."

And that was all she said before hurtling the broken bottle directly at my head.

CHAPTER II
ASTER

Infuriatingly, Nox caught the bottle head right in his slender fingers. My chest heaved with what I knew was mostly irrational anger, but it slipped away—at least partially—the moment I saw dark red blood running down his wrist.

"That was very rude," he murmured.

I swallowed, my eyes still on the blood staining his skin. He hardly seemed to notice it though, tossing the bottle to the side. For just a moment, he glanced at Lil, who was sitting on the edge of the bed, wringing her hands. Her lilac hair had come loose from his braid, framing her flushed face and making her look truly frazzled.

I'd exploded like this a few times before, the previous time when my ex-boyfriend Jude had broken up with me a few years ago. All the anger and hurt had just built and I snapped, wrecking mine and Lil's apartment. Not even the burn of tequila had been enough to dampen the red-hot emotions that day.

Now, with my asshole council, sucky ability to lead anything or anyone, and my mate who had *a lot* to explain...

Well, the world was just kind of asking for it.

"I'm sorry, Aster," Lil said hurriedly. "But someone needs to calm you down. And I'm obviously failing so—"

"Calm me down?" I hissed. "What am I, some obstinate child?"

Nox's attention slid back to me and his wings were suddenly very much visible. He must have seen me staring at them because he said, "One of your council members was lurking in the hall."

"Why?" I snapped.

"Making threats and taunts," Nox said in a low voice. "Half of which could've been empty."

"But?" Lil said softly, her eyes shining and wide.

"We are running out of outlets for information," Nox said, sounding strangely solemn.

Lil cleared her throat and stood from her perch on the bed. "I'm going to go steal some muffins or something from the kitchen. Just, um, text or whatever if you need me, Aster."

With a final look in my direction, she tiptoed her way around the broken glass and left the room, shutting the door quietly behind her.

I clenched my jaw hard enough to hurt as I surveyed the damage: two broken vases, four shattered tequila bottles, and a destroyed pillow were amongst the fallen victims. Then, my eyes drifted to the far side of the room, and as if the wreckage from my outburst wasn't embarrassing enough, I espied the vibrator I'd hurled at the window. Naturally, Nox's attention drifted in that general direction too, because—as usual—I would get away with nothing.

"At least it didn't break the glass," he said, a gleam in his eye.

I looked away, quite suddenly feeling very, very exhausted. Nox titled his head and ordered, "Sit on the bed."

"What—"

"I'm just cleaning up," he explained, his voice forcefully light; I could still pick up on threads of barely concealed tension in his tone—not that I blamed him.

I huffed out a breath and did as he said. Moments later, shards of glass flew around the room, landing in a neat pile before popping out of existence. The vibrator lifted and landed next to me, on the bedside table, with a graceless thud.

"Thoughtful," I muttered.

Nox raised a brow. "If I'm leaving you unsatisfied, please tell me."

Stupid heat rose to my cheeks but I forced it away. "We need to talk. And not about *that*."

He cracked his fingers before striding over to the bed. "What do you want to know?" he asked, leveling my gaze.

"Don't play coy," I snapped. "I know you've been keeping things from me."

"I have."

I expected him to at least bluff a little, and his stark honesty somehow made it more difficult to be angry at him. Still, I kept my tone cool. "Tell me the truth about the Veil's magic. The entire truth."

"I presume you already know or have guessed," Nox

said, twirling a stray shadow around his finger before flicking it over to me.

I swore I heard whispers as it drifted past my ear, but it faded away into nothing before I could decipher what it said.

"I know," I began, "that it affects your magic. And I think it affects mine too. Because of the mating bond."

Nox nodded. "Destroying the Veil would very likely weaken me considerably, for a time, until my magic leveled out again and found a new equilibrium. And yes, our magic is connected because we are mated, just as our dreams are. Though, it would affect you and me uniquely, every magical being in both courts would also feel the effects on their power."

"It would cause chaos," I whispered. "At least for a time."

"Precisely," Nox replied.

I stared outside for a moment before I said hollowly, "What do I do? My council is giving me an ultimatum. I can't deny them, but at the same time, I can't make you do what they're asking."

"Make them bow under your power," Nox said, and I looked back at him, startled by the seriousness of his suggestion. "Lesser men will think they have the right to control people like us. Don't let them."

"Like you didn't let your father control you?" I said quietly.

Nox's body became unnaturally still, even for a faerie. "I presume your council also taunted you with something else." He searched my gaze before he continued, "Perhaps, something about me and my past."

I picked at a loose thread on one of the pillows and replied, "I don't judge you for your past, Nox. I just want to hear it from you, not from them. Not from anyone else."

He took a deep breath and his wings faded away into wisps. For a moment, I thought he might push the question off. But instead, he carefully began. "Wesley Ether desperately wanted an heir, as all kings do. He had been in power for a time and needed to secure his throne. But my parents were married merely in title, as far as I observed or anyone told me. For two faeries to conceive a child...it is difficult without love involved."

My gaze slid to his. "I didn't know that," I said.

He nodded. "One of the greater mysteries of our kind, and one of the burdens and difficulties of an arranged marriage," he said, almost too dryly, "Still, they tried. And then I came along."

I swore he shuddered then, as though his own beginnings disturbed him.

"He figured it out by the time I turned five. That I did not look like him nor carry his scent nor the imprint of his magic. My mother did what she could to protect me." He paused, and I reached for his hand, half-expecting him to push me away. He didn't, letting me gently thread my fingers through his as he continued. "The story after that, for a time, is similar to yours, love. He despised me and didn't fail to show it in every creative way he could. For a long time, no one but my mother tand a select few knew, so I was still technically heir to his throne, but I knew he never intended for that to actually happen."

"Wait," I said. "But what about the second Long Night?

You saved the entire realm with what you did. He had to have thought that counted for something."

Nox's finger stroked once down mine. "To him, the display of my power was only a sobering confirmation that I was anything but a full-blooded faerie or his son at all," he said flatly. "Once the demons were gone, I was mostly sequestered. In his eyes, I'm sure I had garnered enough attention. But I liked to sneak out and train with the new palace guard recruits. There was a young faerie who I became close with. And we eventually decided to make a run for it together."

"Griffin?" I guessed.

Nox's lip twitched, the ghost of a smile at his mouth. "Indeed. Wesley didn't even come looking for me."

"And your mother?"

Any lingering amusement on Nox's face fell away. "Her heart had been long broken, but I still feel immense guilt that I fractured it even more because of my actions."

"So, you think she actually loved your father?" I asked quietly. "I mean, your true father?"

Nox looked away as he replied, "She never gave up hope that he would come back for her, like some hero in shining armor. But they were from two different worlds and what she wished for was simply impossible."

"And do you think he loved her?"

He looked at me again, his features sharp and anything but human. "I don't even know if a Being like that is capable of love. At least not in the way our world views it."

'Remember that your mate is not merely a creature of your world.' The goddess' words of warning about Nox echoed in my mind. She had told me his actions might not always

make sense, and she was already shaping up to be right. Only days ago, he had killed without any remorse I could pick up on, all to save Raven and me. A part of me wondered if he'd enjoyed that power, even if only a little, just once.

Maybe Nox had more of his father in him than he was aware of or wanted to admit to, and maybe the Beings Above were not as benevolent as everyone thought they were.

I shoved the thoughts away for now. We had bigger problems to worry about.

"But you did go back eventually," I said carefully.

Nox swallowed. "Yeah, I did."

I waited—waited to hear the bare truth of what he did.

"I never wanted to be king," Nox said, "but Wesley had sat on the throne for too long and the power was beginning to go to his head. I returned initially on the request of a few of his council members, to try and reel him back to reason. He was speaking of war with the Seelie Court when there was no cause for it, no sane motive for conflict."

"What were his reasons?" I asked, furrowing my brow.

Nox shrugged. "The ramblings of a madman, or so we all thought at the time, I suppose. He claimed the Seelie royals were liars and that the very thing they'd accused us of was what they meddled in."

"Demons," I said, my voice ringing out in the heavy air.

"Yes," Nox replied simply. "But that is not why I did what I did." He looked me directly in the eye as he went on. "My mother sided with my father's council and me, and she tried to reason with my father as well. The day after I returned, late in the night, Wesley called me to the throne room. When I arrived, he was holding my mother with a blade to her throat. She wasn't even struggling. And she could have stopped him; I've told you she was part-wraith and could whisper and control the shadows like I can. She was powerful, but she had given up.

"My father, half-mad, told me he was saving her—from the coming demons, from the war, from...me. And I watched—"

Nox faltered, and it took everything I had to let him regain his composure on his own, to not embrace him in a hug that showed how much I was there for him through moments like these.

Finally, he lifted his chin and breathed deeply through his nose. "I watched as he slit her throat," he said so quietly it was almost inaudible. "I didn't think he would actually do it. I would have gone to her immediately if I had. And then he just let her slump to the floor as she bled out. He even taunted me, asking me what good my power would be now. I held her as she died, as he watched, and when she was gone he simply stood and walked out of the room. Just like I never expected he'd do what he did, he didn't expect me to do what I did next."

"You killed him," I said quietly.

"I stabbed him in the back with my mother's blade." Nox nodded. "And I have never regretted it. Not once."

Curling my arms around my knees as I pulled them to me, I only said, "I understand."

He eyed me. "Does it frighten you, what I did?"

A tight laugh escaped my throat. "No, of course not. I was just thinking..."

My thoughts drifted, though I couldn't have picked one

out if I'd tried. I was somewhere else, processing, not processing—it was difficult to tell.

Finally, after who knows how long, Nox pulled me back in with a simple question. "What are you thinking, love?"

"Neither of us could save the people we loved. All the power we hold, and it was good for nothing when it came to death. It only propelled it forwards." My fingers dug into my skin as I said the words. Because no matter how young I'd been or how good my intentions were the night my parents died, I had been the one who killed them.

My power.

Nox's power hadn't done the same, but it had driven his father to do what he did. Maybe it was a poison, this power, never meant to be in this world in the first place.

"There are things we still don't know," Nox said, gazing out the window as the sky darkened. "Just in the hall now, Lord Jasper taunted me with secrets."

"Like what?" I asked.

We *really* didn't need any more damn secrets.

Nox's expression grew clouded, and I had the sudden sense he was about to say something very important.

"Secrets about you," he said finally, his voice heavy.

I shut my eyes. There were so many pieces to this puzzle, and it felt like we were still missing nearly all of them. The world was on a tilt, held in my barely capable hands. I was the third coming of the Evening Star, and I couldn't control my own court or even my own emotions.

Opening my eyes, I looked around the room, where the broken glass had been scattered mere minutes ago. When I turned my attention to Nox again, there was a touch of feral sharpness to his features as he looked at me. And quite suddenly, I craved that. I craved the possessive, baser side of our natures. The piece that screamed: *mine.*

No matter what came, I wouldn't let anyone take him from me.

His amber irises pulsed with light, and I felt heat pool low in response. I wanted *all* of him, complications aside, and the residual anger from earlier only fueled the red-hot desire in my core. Every emotion was riding high in me, and I knew he could sense all of them, the rage and the want alike.

Between one breath and another, he was on his feet, tugging at my hand.

"What—"

"Trust me, love," he said, each word coated with dark promise.

"Can I?" I challenged him, standing too and tilting my chin so our heated gazes collided.

"Always," he replied.

Then, the only warning I had was his arm looping around my waist before we folded into nothingness.

When I could see again, we were in a familiar, modern kitchen: his penthouse.

My brow creased. "Why are we here?"

"Because I don't want an audience," he whispered as he leaned in, nipping at my ear. "And I don't want anyone else hearing the noises I'm going to inspire from you."

"And what makes you so confident I'll be making any noises?" I said breathily, just as I slid my hand between our bodies. He hissed as I stroked his already-hard length through his pants.

"Play nice," he muttered against the sensitive skin of my

neck. "Or don't," he added. "But know I won't let you leave this penthouse without you knowing exactly what I wanted to do to you in this kitchen the moment you touched my wings."

And with that, he hiked me up onto the granite countertop and lowered to his knees before me. I gasped, the desperation for what was to come overwhelming my senses, and then his hands were deftly unclasping my pants.

"Hips up," he ordered, his gaze burning into mine.

I obeyed, and he slid my pants and underwear off in one fell swoop. I had to give it to him—he was efficient when he wanted something.

He trailed his mouth up my inner thigh and whispered, "Do you like me on my knees before you? I hope so." He sucked against my skin, and I groaned in pleasure. "Because I will bow down before you again and again until you realize you own me. My secrets are yours"—his hands tightened on my legs—"as are my body and my heart. If it takes centuries of this for you to realize it," he uttered, his mouth curved into a delicious grin, "then so be it."

He parted me with his tongue, wasting no time as he circled my clit. My hips jerked, but with one hand he kept me down on the counter. I grasped his hair with my hand as he dipped a finger into me with his other.

"Nox," I gasped.

He paused, glancing up at me, his gaze raking over me. "Touch yourself," he ordered gruffly as his finger curled inside of me.

For just a moment, I felt a seed of self-consciousness blossom, but he held my eyes, challenging me, refusing to continue until I did as he said. The moment ended, and I dragged my shirt and flimsy lace bralette off, tossing them to the side. Nox watched, his gaze sliding over every inch of me. He was still completely clothed, yet I held all the power here.

I trailed a finger up my stomach, skirting the bottoms of my breasts, and he rewarded me by pumping his finger in and out. When I began to tease my nipple, he added another finger.

I lost all semblance of time as he began to lick and suck again. But as I felt the pressure begin to increase, I realized I craved more than this. I craved *him*.

"Fuck me," I whispered. "Now."

He didn't even pause before pulling away, and I whimpered at the momentary loss of contact.

"Bend over against the counter, love," he growled.

Yes. This was what I needed—to feel everything completely. I needed to know just what it felt like to be alive and free of restraint—to know I was living again, that I was serving myself and not some bigger purpose I didn't fully understand, even after everything that had happened.

I bent over and felt his cock brush against my backside as he leaned in and said in my ear, "Tap the counter if you need me to stop."

"Understood," I rasped.

He fisted a hand in my hair and, with hardly any hesitation, filled me completely. My back arched as I felt myself stretch; it was almost too much, almost, before the bolts of pleasure hit me and I was sent into bliss. It was devastating, the way it felt as he pounded into me without abandon. His hand slid from my hair to the curve of my neck, squeezing lightly. A loud moan escaped my lips, and his hand tightened, just enough to make my back arch more.

"*Fuck,*" he hissed as his hips snapped against my backside roughly.

"I'm...close," I gasped.

He let out a deep sound of pure arousal, and I gasped as he pulled out and said, "Turn."

I didn't need to be told twice, facing him just before he flitted us directly to the bedroom.

He wasted no time at all, sliding back into me, and my legs wrapped around his hips as he angled them deep. His hand pinned my wrists above my head as he kissed me roughly, nipping at my bottom lip just as his wings flared out behind him.

"Nox," I pleaded, wanting to touch them.

His eyes flashed. "If I let you do that, my star, this will be over."

I felt sharp canines prick my lips, suddenly realizing his teeth were out too. I curved my neck upwards, baring it to him. It felt primal, an animalistic way of telling him I trusted him absolutely, even with my life. Nox's breath hitched and his grip on my wrists loosened. He lowered his mouth to my neck, lightly nipping against the skin just as I reached up and dragged a finger against the sinewy surface of his wing.

His reaction was immediate. He groaned loudly and lost any last semblance of control, slamming his cock into me. I scraped my nails down his back as the pressure in me built and built. He slammed to the hilt, and we both came at the same time, stars blasting through my vision as a strained moan of gratification dragged up his throat.

For what felt like a while after, we remained entangled as our bodies floated back down to earth. Eventually, he laid down next to me, pulling me close against his hard chest. I breathed him in, trying to forget, for just a moment, the mess we were all in.

When Nox spoke next, his voice was rough and soft all around the edges at the same time. "When your council reconvenes," he said. "Let me come with you."

I lifted my head to look at him, raising a brow. "Do you really think that's a good idea?"

He ran a hand through my hair, and I resisted the urge to lean into the touch or outright purr.

"I think…" His voice trailed off, then he amended his uncertainty, stating firmly, "I have an idea. Something to propose to them."

I narrowed my eyes but said, "I'm listening."

CHAPTER 12
ASTER

When I returned to the Seelie palace a day later, courtesy of Nox, I walked straight to the council chambers. I'd changed into something more 'presentable' at the penthouse, since Nox had clothes there for me now. I tried to ignore the small pang in my heart at the thoughtfulness of that—now was not the time to go all ooey-gooey and doe-eyed.

Now, I needed to be a cold-hearted queen.

My heeled boots clicked against the marble floor as I approached the heavy door that separated me and the lords of my court. Not bothering to knock, I pushed it open with a flick of my hand and strode inside.

As I had thought, the lords were already gathered, an hour before we were set to meet. Conniving bastards, all of them. Still, I pasted a cool smile on my face as they all looked up at me, surprise coating many of their expressions. Lord Jasper looked as he usually did—thoroughly unimpressed by me. I ignored that, though I did not ignore the way he sat in *my* seat at the head of the table. Again.

"Move," I said, "and don't make me have to ask you again."

Slowly, he looked up at me from his spot in the high-backed chair. "As you wish," he said in a low voice. "For now."

A fire flared in my belly, but I quieted it, shushing the power that so quickly tried to come to my aid. It was starting to seem like an overly exuberant child to me, always tugging on my sleeve and offering help I didn't need. Still, it was a child that could kill—but killing was absolutely not the answer I needed.

All the lords at the table looked at me as I took my seat, Lord Jasper sliding into a chair directly to my left.

I swept my gaze around before I said with a sly half-smile, "We have a guest today."

Immediately, I felt a tug of gratification through the mating bond, an approval that gave me confidence ten-fold, and seconds later, the door flew open. Several council members stood from their seats as Nox strode in. I had to give it to him—the man knew how to make an entrance. His wings tucked in and fluttered for just a moment as he walked through the door before spreading wide behind him, enormous and menacing. He wore one of those pristinely fitted black suits I'd seen him in so often when we first met, and the Unseelie crown sat atop his silver waves, making him look like some sort of dark, devastating businessman.

Kohl-lined eyes met, and before any of the lords could protest, Nox said in a booming voice, "I have a proposal for you idiots. It is your choice whether you take it or leave it.

But know this: you will not have my court's amiability or future cooperation if you choose to overthrow Queen Asteria Fairwae, the rightful heir to the Seelie throne, because of *my* actions or decisions."

The expressions around the room ranged from terrified to rageful. Lord Jasper narrowed his eyes at me, and I dutifully ignored him.

"What's the proposal?" Lord Jasper spat, still looking at me.

"I will not destroy the Veil separating our courts," Nox said, laying his hands flat on the long table before him.

Someone opened their mouth, presumably to protest, but the sound was abruptly cut off, a puff of air escaping the lord's mouth.

"Ah, ah, ah," Nox scolded as if talking to an insolent child. "I'm not done speaking."

The lord's hand went to his throat; shadows lurked there, dancing around his neck, pushing their tendrils into his skin. It was bewitching, watching the shadows move, and in that moment I felt the urge to know them more, to know *what* exactly those shadows were made of and where they came from.

"So," Nox said with a sigh as the shadows drew away and the faerie lord took a gasping breath, "my proposal. Where was I? Ah, yes"—he tapped long fingers against the table—"I will not destroy or drop the Veil, but I'll offer you a bargain. I will allow for freer travel between our courts. We may work out the particular logistics of that as your queen wishes." He paused again, then added, "This is my only and final offer."

Silence fell in the council room, and my pulse thrummed

as my heart beat nervously against my ribs.

"Agreed."

I didn't at all expect most of the lords to agree and neither did Nox, and I jumped as none other than Lord Jasper barked his acceptance.

Nox's eyes narrowed. "Just like that," he murmured, the words less of a question and more of an accusation.

Lord Jasper's mouth curled. "Just like that, Nox Ether. Don't you want me to take your offer?"

Nox's chin lowered and he said softly, "Of course."

"And," Lord Jasper added enthusiastically, "I think it's high time our court knows it actually has a queen."

Even Lord Ives' bushy brow rose. "You're suggesting a coronation?"

"Of course," Lord Jasper said, each word dripping in false innocence. "It's only customary, is it not?"

"It...is," Lord Ives confirmed tentatively, obviously confused by Lord Jasper's sudden change in attitude. "So, we shall begin preparations?"

He looked at me for confirmation, and I found myself saying, "Yes, begin preparations."

I'd pretty much completely forgotten about a coronation. It hadn't seemed important in the midst of everything else, but I supposed it was something I *probably* should have demanded earlier.

Oh well.

"Then we are all agreed," Lord Ives said, his brow still comically high. "An official royal coronation would be best?"

Nox was glaring daggers at Lord Jasper as he said, "We are agreed."

Goddess, that man was so presumptuous, but all the

council members seemed to eat from his hand, all murmuring words of agreement and wobbling their chins assuredly—like their assurance meant anything at all to Jasper, which it absolutely did not.

I was about done with his arrogance.

After a beat of silence, I said, "Meeting adjourned." Then, after a second thought, I added, "Except for Lord Jasper."

From across the table, Nox gave me a slight nod. I knew I had done the right thing, asking Lord Jasper to stay behind. I had questions for him, and I knew Nox sure as hell did too.

The lords shuffled out of the room, quite obviously avoiding Nox and his restless shadows. When the door closed and it was just the three of us, Nox moved so swiftly I hardly realized what was happening. The next thing I knew, he had hauled Lord Jasper out of his seat and slammed him against the wall.

I stood abruptly as Nox demanded, "What the hell are you playing at?"

Lord Jasper's features twisted; I expected anger, but he looked...smug. There was no other word for it.

"It is not me you should fear," he told Nox.

"And what is it I should fear?" Nox pushed, shadows pressing up against Lord Jasper's neck.

A shiver danced its way up my spine as Lord Jasper replied, "The truth."

Nox paced back and forth in my room, his crown long discarded atop the bedside table and his silver waves mussed from the number of times he had run his hands through it.

"The fuck is he playing at?" he muttered under his breath for the tenth time.

And again, I replied tiredly, "I don't know."

Nox muttered something completely incomprehensible. At first, I thought my exhaustion had sent me truly off my rocker, but I questioned if, maybe, I'd heard something I wasn't meant to understand.

I raised a brow. "Did you just talk in the Old Language?"

He waved a hand dismissively and said, "I slip into it sometimes when I'm thinking."

"Really?" I deadpanned. "You just 'slip' into the ancient, lost language of the Fae sometimes?"

Nox leveled a look at me. "It's not lost, just fallen out of fashion like many things do over time. And remember, love, I'm quite old."

"Oh, I never forget," I said, snorting.

A small smirk threatened to surface but ultimately refused, his expression quickly returning to one of agitation.

I sighed and said, "Nox. Chill out for two seconds."

He stopped pacing, turning to stare at me from where I was sitting on the edge of the bed. "He knows something."

"Obviously."

"He's withholding information."

"Yep."

Nox took a step towards me, his arms crossing over his chest. "Are you not worried at all?"

I shrugged, anxiety churning my stomach. The truth was that I was very worried. So much so that even thinking about what Lord Jasper might be withholding and why made me want to vomit, cry, and run away at the same time. So, I was leaning on a trusty old habit—avoidance.

Nox leaned against the bedpost and said, his voice a fraction softer, "We can't just pretend this isn't an issue."

He knows me much *too well.*

I squeezed my eyes shut. "Not even for one night?"

I heard him sigh, and the bed bowed next to me. When I warily cracked open my eyes, he was sitting next to me.

"What would you do with one night?" he asked, his expression open.

I pressed my lips together. I honestly had no idea. It had been so long since anything felt normal. But maybe that was my answer—I just wanted to feel that way, even if only for a few hours.

"I'd ask you to take me on a date," I finally said.

One surprised brow rose. "Really?"

I snorted. "Is it so hard to believe that I just want one normal night with you? We've never really gotten that. It's always been demons and family issues and 'oh, wait we're mates.'"

This time, a true smile surfaced on Nox's face, like sunlight breaking through a storm. "Is that how it went?"

I squared my shoulders. "Give me one normal night. Then, we can deal with all of this. I'll be the queen I'm supposed to be, and you can go back to being the scary Night King."

A fraction of humor left his expression, softening the harsh lines of his mouth and jaw. "It's a deal, love," he said. "On one condition."

"And what is that?"

"We're going to my court."

My lips twitched. "Oh, I expected that."

With that, I stood, sauntering towards the giant closet where I'd shoved most of my stuff from the apartment Lil now lived in alone. I still helped her with the rent, because I pretty much left her in the lurch with no notice whatsoever and what kind of friend would I be if I didn't? But despite having thrown all my clothes into boxes and moving them here pretty efficiently, I'd dragged my feet unboxing everything. So, it all remained there, on the floor, getting more creased by the day.

Whatever.

I opened one and found precisely what I was looking for, conveniently at the top.

As I left the closet and dragged off my shirt and pants, Nox watched, eyes flickering. I gave him a smirk as I stepped into the silky silver dress. Once the dress was on, I turned and quipped, "Zip me up, please."

He strode over in seconds, his hands warm against my back as he slowly pulled the zipper up. His touch lingered for a moment, his hands drifting down my back.

"Ready, then?" he asked in a low voice.

"Shoes, then we go," I replied as steadily as I could. With a flick of my fingers, the black boots I wanted shot towards me from the closet. Nox caught them before they could slam into my face, and he knelt in front of me.

"Lift," he murmured, his fingers grazing my calf.

I did so and then he laced up the boot, repeating with the other. When he was done, he rose slightly and kissed my hip before straightening fully. I took a deep breath as my body shivered with need.

That was for later. For now, were going to have fun.

Nox took my hand, and without a word, we flitted.

The air was slightly chilled as we stood outside a packed club. The street seemed to be party-central of the Unseelie Court; the entire road was lined with clubs, bars, and scantily clad bodies. Against the wall outside several of the clubs, Beings of all varieties got to know each other *very* well. I swear I even saw someone flash a pierced nipple.

"Dreams, darkness, and desire," Nox murmured in my ear. "Remember, love—my court thrives on the night."

"Mm, I see that," I said, my voice breathier than I intended.

"Shall we?" Nox said, gesturing at the club ahead. A neon sign boasting the name 'The Midnight Rose' hung above the entrance. From inside, bassy music thrummed and purple and red lights flashed.

"You're sure?" I half-shouted. "I mean, you're not freaking out about all the people and the fact that some of them could be...you know," I lowered my voice, "possessed?"

His hand skimmed my back. "Of course, I am. But you asked for one night. I'm giving it to you, and I don't do things half-assed."

My lips lifted, my worry floating away. "Good, then. Do we get to cut the line because you're king?"

Nox chuckled. "Unfortunately for you, love, I'm glamoured."

"Wait." I furrowed my brow. "I don't see anything different."

He grinned. "I know. You're the only one I've let see past it."

"Did you at least make yourself hot?"

Nox laughed, and I smiled just hearing the sound of it. "Making sure you can still be seen with me?" he mused.

I snorted. "Maybe."

He let out another short laugh before taking my hand and pulling me forward into the line. In front of us, a group of two faerie's and three shifters sipped out of embellished flasks. Behind us, giggling human girls traded turns with an entire bottle of pink, lemonade-flavored vodka.

Nox chuckled and said in my ear, "Thirsty?"

I flicked a silky curtain of hair over my shoulder and mused, "Perhaps."

Within seconds, he waved his fingers and produced a glass filled with a very appealing looking cocktail. I fought to keep my smile under control as he waited for me to try it. When I took a sip, my smile grew.

He'd just made the best damn cocktail I had ever tasted —and that was saying a lot, since I'd consumed *many* cocktails in the past.

"Like it?" he asked as the line shuffled forward.

Taking another sip, I smirked and said, "You already know I do."

He reached out, swiping away a bead of liquid on my lower lip as he said, "It's always polite to ask."

I nipped at his finger and his expression darkened. From behind, an obviously inebriated girl asked, "Can your faerie boyfriend get us fun drinks too?"

Another one of the girls exploded into giggles and then slurred, "Yeah, and can we steal him too?"

Even though the girls were very drunk and very harmless, territorial instincts rose up quickly in me. Canines pricked my mouth as I smiled at the girls.

One of them took a step back, stumbling on her heels as she said, "Woah, sorry girl. We get it."

Satisfied, I turned back to Nox and found him looking at me with an amused expression.

"Something funny?" I asked boldly.

He shook his head. "Oh, nothing at all."

The line moved again, and finally we were inside, the pulsing beat of the music already finding its way into my bones. The flashing lights of the dancefloor drew me in, and I grabbed Nox's hand, tugging him towards it.

The black, marble-topped bar was crowded with patrons, but I didn't mind. I wanted to move more than I wanted another drink. Not that the dancefloor was any less crammed with bodies. The smell of hundreds of different perfumes drifted through the air, mingling with the scent of alcohol and sweat. Humanity at its very finest.

I dragged Nox to the center of the dancefloor just as the beat of the song dropped. I twined my hands around his neck, and a giddy laugh escaped me as I began to sway my hips. He rested his hands low on my back, pulling our bodies close together as we picked up the beat.

"I remember," he murmured in my ear, "this is how I first saw you. Free and uninhibited."

"And very drunk," I added.

His lips curved and he agreed, "Yes, and very drunk."

For a while after that, we didn't talk, at least not aloud. There was something to the way bodies moved in certain spaces. Here, each movement spoke volumes; every touch meant something; whether just for a night or forever. And as I fell into the haze of it all, I felt something rising within me; I was uninhibited, burning with wild expression, responding in every way to the sensual nature of everything around me.

"Easy, love," Nox murmured in my ear.

I glanced up at him. "Am I..."

"Your eyes are glowing, just a tad," he said with an unconcerned, lazy grin.

I felt heat rush to my cheeks as panic crested. "I'm not trying to dredge it up. The power, I mean."

He nodded. "I know. It's probably just responding to your heightened emotions and all the stimuli around us. It used to happen to me when I was younger."

Cool relief swept through me. It comforted me that my starlight wasn't intentionally trying to fry the entire room. It was just...excited.

"Would you like to go?" Nox asked, tucking a strand of hair behind my ear.

I sucked in a breath. "Yeah," I puffed out. "I think I'm hungry."

"Good," Nox said, taking my hand. "I know just the place."

NOT TWENTY MINUTES LATER, we were tucked into a booth in the back of a diner about two blocks from the club. On the way here, Nox had taken one look at my boots and asked to carry me. I had stubbornly refused, and now my feet hurt, but I was a big girl and I didn't need him to coddle me everywhere we went. Even if I knew he probably—definitely —wanted to.

Territorial, protective faerie.

"So," I said, "what do you even order here?"

The menu was enormous, ranging from pancakes to stir-fry and everything in between. I was currently debating between sweet or savory.

"Whatever you want," he said, lounging back. "That's kind of the point. They have everything you could ever think of here. Which makes it a great place for when you're drunk and anything and everything sounds good."

I snorted. "You, drunk?"

"Sometimes," he said, then amending, "at least I used to be, sometimes. This place has been around for a long time."

"With Griffin?" I guessed, and he nodded. I paused, then asked, "What exactly did you two do when you were off on your own?"

Nox opened his mouth to reply, but the waitress took that exact moment to appear and say, "Well, I didn't expect to be hosting royalty today."

My brows rose. "She can see you?"

The waitress, a very tall faerie woman with steel-gray eyes and dark-brown skin, said, "Yes, darling, *she* can see both of you."

I felt my cheeks warm. "Sorry. I didn't mean..." I trailed off, and the waitress laughed.

"Wow, I don't think a Seelie queen has ever apologized to me before. I'll add that one to the list."

A surprised laugh escaped me, and I grew even more surprised as I saw a wisp of shadow curl around the woman's pointed ear.

She was a wraith. Or at least part-wraith, like Nox.

"Nox, dearest," the woman said, eyeing me. "They say very interesting things about your mate."

They?

Nox traced what looked like a star with the tip of his finger on the tabletop as he replied, "I'm quite aware, Luci."

"Um," I began, "what exactly are you two talking about?"

Luci put her hands on her hips. "The shadows whisper about everything, darling. But they especially have an awful lot to say about you. Same thing happened when I first met Nox...oh, a century ago?"

"About," Nox said, wincing slightly. "But Luci, we're here for food, not to talk of shadows. Asteria was wondering what to order."

I was definitely not done asking about what the shadows were saying. But admittedly, I *was* hungry.

Luci glanced at me, as if she could decide what I wanted to eat by simply looking at my clothes or the color of my hair.

"Hmm. I'm thinking...spicy stir-fry noodles with a side of chocolate cream pie."

For a moment, I was sure Luci was completely crazy. But then I realized that her suggestion actually sounded good—like strangely, oddly good.

"How did you know?" I asked, staring at her in amused bewilderment.

She held out a hand, and I handed her my menu as she explained, "I've worked this job for a long time, darling. And the shadows help sometimes too." She gave me a wink, then asked Nox, "The usual?"

He nodded and she took his menu before striding away. I shook my head, slightly in disbelief.

"Well, wow," I said, laughing.

Nox smiled softly as he looked at me.

"What?" I asked.

"I'm just very glad to be here with you," he said simply.

My breath caught in my throat; there were words I could say in that moment, just three little words I felt and knew were true. After all, we weren't really fighting any more, were we? We had finally come to a solution together. But I knew withholding my true feelings had never really been about our argument involving the Veil. It was fear, which had only grown with Lord Jasper's ominous warning. I wondered if Nox felt that fear too; he hadn't said he loved me since the days before Abaddon's return. Or maybe he was just waiting for me to return them.

In the end, I settled on saying, "I am too. And thank you for tonight."

He frowned slightly. "It pains me that I can only give you one night of peace."

I nudged his foot from under the booth. "Let's not waste it worrying."

His expression instantly softened, and he took a deep breath. "You're right. As usual, of course."

I laughed. "Most people would not say I'm 'usually' right about things."

"Well, I'm not most people," he said with a glint in his eye, just as Luci came back with the food.

I stared at her for a moment as she set the plates down and said, "That was...really quick."

Luci chuckled. "It's something we're known for here. Enjoy, and let me know if you need anything else."

She left and I hardly waited before digging into my noodles, which were just the right amount of spicy. I was nearly halfway done scarfing down my plate when I realized just what Nox had ordered.

I looked him over, and I couldn't help but laugh. "Chocolate chip pancakes? That's your 'usual'?"

"With whipped cream," Nox added just as he licked some of it off his lower lip.

Oh, dear goddess. That mouth.

I cleared my throat, trying to ignore the fact that I was already pretty turned on. Except that we were faeries and Nox definitely knew that already. I felt heat rise to my cheeks, and Nox shook his head slightly.

"Keep looking at me like that, love," he said, "and you're going to end up spread out on this table in front of me."

"That's a lot of people seeing some very personal areas of me," I challenged, glancing around at the other patrons in the restaurant.

"Then it's a lot of people I'm going to have to kill," Nox said darkly.

A thrill ran through me at his words. It was pretty messed up, but I think I knew by this point we were both a little fucked.

I swallowed and Nox tracked the bob of my throat with predatory intent. I desperately needed something else to focus on or, he was right, we were never going to make it out of this restaurant without getting our hands on each other.

"The shadows," I said, my words shaky. "Explain them."

Nox tapped his fingers against the table and said, "They are all the same and yet very different."

"What do you mean?" I asked, my voice catching as I felt his foot drag up my leg.

"I mean," he said, and I felt a cool caress on my inner

thigh, "whether given to one by a demon, such as in the case of shadow walkers, or born to them, in the case of wraiths, the shadows all essentially function the same. And they all come from the same place."

"You said they aren't sentient," I said, swallowing a gasp as I felt another caress, higher this time.

Nox's face betrayed none of what I knew he was doing as he said, "Mm, no, they aren't. Though, from individual to individual, they do differ. And they are loyal to that Being only. For example, my shadows would not speak directly to Luci's."

"But could they tell you things about her or her shadows?" I asked, fighting to keep my voice even.

He was not touching me and yet he was. Cool, phantom caresses teased at my underwear and tickled my thigh.

"They could," Nox replied just as the phantom hands *really* touched me.

I fisted my hand in the silky material of my dress as my legs spread apart on instinct. I quickly pressed them together again, but the shadow caresses only teased them wider. The only sign that Nox was affected at all was that one of his hands was gripping the edge of the table.

"They tell you secrets then?" I managed.

Nox's lips parted as one of my hands darted to the table too, gripping it until my knuckles were white to keep from crying out.

"Yeah," he purred, finally visibly affected by everything going on beneath the table.

I sucked in a breath. "I need to...bathroom," I choked out.

He nodded once, and I darted to the single-person

restroom in the back. Before I could shut the door, I felt resistance as Nox swept in, his mouth immediately on mine. I ran my hands through his hair and a rumbling groan vibrated in his chest.

He hiked me up the sink and I demanded, "Keep using the shadows."

His eyes flared. "You like it?"

"I do," I moaned.

He stared at me in awe for a moment before muttering, "Fucking gods."

He kissed me again before I could form another word, and a phantom hand pressed my throat. He helped me hike up my dress, and I scrambled to undo the clasp of his pants. Our movements were both clumsy and hurried, everything about this red-hot and full of need.

He pushed into me roughly and I gasped, my back arching and my hands gripping his shoulders to stay steady on the sink. He braced his arms on either side of me, caging me in as his mouth captured mine with searing kisses.

"Harder," I breathed between one kiss and another.

I needed to feel all of him, everywhere and all at once.

His gaze caught on mine. "Hold onto me, love."

"Always," I said, and his eyes widened.

After that, the world broke apart and floated away. His thrusts were deep and hard; my nails dug bloody crescents into his shoulders; his shadows curled around my neck and teased my peaked breasts. Everything was us and nothing else mattered.

I shattered, and he covered my mouth with his hand to smother the moan that would have echoed loudly in the small space. He angled my leg up with one arm before I even came down from the high, and I nearly screamed. He panted out my name as he came too, his body tense and seizing up with release.

"Fucking hell," I gasped, leaning my forehead against his shoulder.

He let out an endearingly boyish laugh and agreed, "Fucking hell."

He let me down, and I did my best to make it look like I hadn't just been thoroughly fucked in the bathroom—a feat I was actually fairly decent at, given my history. Nox, naturally, hardly looked frazzled, aside from the slight flush to his cheeks.

"Ready?" he asked slyly as I smoothed down my bangs.

I turned and laughed, "Yeah. Do you think Luci will know?"

Nox snorted. "I'm sure. She doesn't miss anything, and I'm sure her shadows will think it's hilarious."

Strangely, I didn't feel embarrassed as we emerged from the bathroom and slid back into our booth. Nighttime here was something else entirely, beckoning with the sensual nature of the darkness. I was fairly sure what had just gone down in that bathroom was probably happening all over the court right now. Which was kind of a weird thought to be having as I took a bite of chocolate pie, but whatever.

We finished eating, and Nox paid a very amused looking Luci before we left. Once we were back out on the street, I realized it had to be getting close to dawn, as the smallest hint of light peeked out on the horizon.

"Come with me," Nox said, holding out his hand again. "I have something I want to show you."

Wordlessly, I nodded and took his hand.

He pulled me close, and we flitted, landing directly on a hillside overlooking what had to be the edges of the city.

"There it is," I said as I gazed over the sprawling landscape beyond, half dense forest, half rocky, almost desert-like expanse. "The Wilds."

A bird called out shrilly, drawing my attention to that seemingly unending stretch of trees beyond. In our mostly civilized courts, I had never seen such uninhibited wildness. Even from a distance I could see the enormous, gnarled branches of the trees sweeping into the sky. They reminded me of guardians, and perhaps they were, keeping vigil in one of the last untamed places in our world. The desert beyond the woods stretched out into the horizon, and I wondered how anything could survive in such a place.

Nox nodded. "This is the edge of established civilization. Out there, there are no laws or rules. Chaos that even my court cannot claim reigns free."

"I see," I whispered just as the sun met the horizon and a golden hue filled the space around us.

"I used to come here as a boy," Nox said quietly. "I'd often think about running into the woods out there and just leaving it all behind. Maybe some wild creature would end me, but at least I'd be free."

"Why didn't you ever?" I asked, looking at him.

"I think I was waiting for something to stop me from running." His answering smile was slightly melancholy. "Hope."

My lips parted before I dared, "And do you think you ever found that?"

His arms encircled me, and he leaned his forehead against mine as he murmured, "I think I did."

CHAPTER 13
ASTER

We returned to the Seelie palace just as the sun fully crested over the horizon. All I wanted to do was fall into bed and sleep the day away. But, unfortunately for me, there were things to do. More importantly, there were guests to greet and entertain. Well, *a* guest. Because as soon as I'd stepped into the little dining and sitting room where I typically ate my meals, Lil appeared and breathlessly told me the news.

My cousin was coming for the coronation, and she was showing up sometime within the next three days.

Technically, Bells Waverly was my second cousin, the daughter of my father's cousin Marianne, and one of my few remaining blood relatives. I impulsively had no idea why she would decide to show up now; she could have visited or helped at any time after my parents died, could have cared way before now to show up, though I supposed her mother had probably made those decisions back then, as she had only been fifteen at the time; but then I remembered that it's not just my birthday or a celebration of some trivial milestone in my life, I'm being *coronated*, and if that isn't the time to show up for a second cousin, when is?

"Maybe," Lil said around a mouthful of jam-laden biscuit, "this is her finally trying to reconnect."

"Maybe," I sighed, rubbing my eyes.

Lil snorted. "Rough night?"

I felt a smile tug at my lips. "No, good night. Just no sleep."

When I looked over at Lil, she had set her biscuit down and was shaking her head.

"What?" I demanded.

"Your face," she said incredulously.

"My face?"

Lil rolled her eyes. "Aster, you are so obviously in love with him. I mean, you're in deep, girl. And let me guess, you haven't said a word about it to him?"

I chose that moment to take a strategic sip of the steaming coffee in front of me. Lil groaned.

"Asteria Fairwae," she said, using her strict, no-nonsense voice. "You can't keep running away from your emotions like this. I can't let you. Just call me the avoidance police."

"What's the trouble this time?" a familiar voice said from the doorway.

I looked to see Lil's mom standing there, her hip leaned against the frame and a basket of sewing supplies in her arms.

"Evie," I said, smiling genuinely. "What are you doing here?"

"Yeah, what *are* you doing here?" Lil scoffed. "And how did you get in?"

Evelyn feigned a laugh. "Good to see you too, my darling daughters."

I swallowed hard at those words. I knew Lil's mom had always seen me as one of her own. Still, hearing her say it always tugged at a sensitive place in my heart, even with her recent betrayal. Goddess knew my uncle had given her little choice in the matter of bending to his will.

"I'm here to help you get ready, Aster, dear," she said fondly. "For your coronation."

"Mom, it's not for another week," Lil groaned. "Her hair and makeup can wait."

Evelyn reached out and fussed with a stray strand of Lil's lavender hair as she said, "I'm not an idiot, Lilliana. But I thought I could help tailor one of your mother's dresses to fit you, Aster. You know, it might be special to wear something of hers on a day like this."

A lump lodged itself in my throat, but I managed to say, "Yeah, that would be nice."

Evelyn smiled softly. "Good. Shall we go pick one out then?"

I nodded, and after a brief silence, Lil asked, "Mom, do you want me to see if Raven wants to come here so you guys can say hi?"

Evelyn's lips pressed together. "Yes, please do. I'm sorry I haven't invited him home, it's just..."

"Yeah, yeah, Dad's an ass, we all know it," Lil muttered, typing rapidly on her phone.

Evelyn's lips thinned further and, trying to diffuse the tension, I said, "I think I'll probably wear the dark blue one, with the gems and the silver embroidery. It was always her favorite."

"That sounds lovely," Evelyn said.

I smiled and we headed out of the dining room, ending up in my room.

Evelyn measured me but paused as her hands hovered over my arm. The scar there from the poisoned knife hadn't faded and still remained a little red.

"You had this looked at, right, Aster?" Evelyn asked, her brow furrowed.

I cleared my throat. "I did."

"The healer said it might take longer to fully go away," Lil added. "Since the knife was poisoned."

"Do you know what the poison was?" Evelyn asked.

Both Lil and I shook our heads.

"Well, if it's ever possible for me to get a look at it, let me know. I'm concerned some of it might be remaining in the wound, but I won't know how to get rid of it if I don't know what it's made up of."

"Demon's brew," Lil muttered, and I choked out a laugh.

"What do you mean?" Evelyn asked, her gaze falling back to my arm.

I avoided the sudden urge to scratch it as I explained, "I don't think a faerie created the poison. It was in a blade used by a possessed faerie, probably given to them by the demon prince."

"It was you," Evelyn whispered. "Lil told me King Nox's forces rescued Raven. But it was you, wasn't it?"

I grimaced. "I'm fine, Evie. Really."

She pulled me into a sudden embrace and murmured, "You are far too young to have gone through so much, dear."

"Mom?"

Evelyn let go of me and froze as she turned. Standing in the doorway was Raven, and behind him Griffin was already taking a step back, his eyes wide.

"I'm sorry," he rasped. "I didn't realize..."

Lil's mom seemed to be at a loss for words too. She opened her mouth, shut it, then finally said carefully, "It's alright. And thank you. For helping to bring him home safely."

I saw Griffin's jaw work overtime, but he only replied, "It's all I could do. I wish I could have done more."

Evelyn flinched, and Lil opened her mouth to speak but no words surfaced.

Without another word, Griffin was gone.

Raven cleared his throat. "Um, he's been helping me train," he said as if he didn't know what else to say.

Well, that was news to me. To Lil too, apparently, because her brows rose.

"That's nice," Evelyn said, the steadiness in her voice wavering.

"Yeah," Raven said awkwardly. "I mean, he's not actually a bad guy."

"I know that," Evelyn said, a little too softly.

I took a breath, then asked, "Do you three want some time alone? We can finish the measurements later."

"You don't have to," Lil said quickly, giving me a pleading look. I shot her a look right back. After all, she was the one who'd just lectured me about not running from my emotions.

"If you don't mind, dear," Evelyn said after a beat.

"It's okay," I assured her gently. "I need to start training too one of these days. Maybe now is a good time."

Raven gave me one of his smiles he reserved just for me and said, "Better now than never. But beware: they take it seriously over there."

I laughed tightly and playfully shoved at his shoulder as I made to leave the room, saying, "Okay, big guy."

Raven stopped me just before I stepped out and said in my ear, "Thank you, Aster."

I wasn't quite sure exactly what he was thanking me for, but I accepted it, saying, "Of course."

He let me go, and I walked back to the dining room. I debated just texting Nox, but I was feeling impatient, so I pulled from my pocket the moonstone I still carried around for emergencies. This wasn't really an emergency, and for a moment I considered leaving it, but I—maybe a little self-ishly—wanted him to get here quickly. So, I pressed my lips to the cool, milky-white surface, visualizing his amber eyes and starlight hair. Seconds later, the shadows in the corner of the room stirred, and my heartbeat quickened.

When Nox became fully corporeal, he immediately asked, "Is everything alright?"

Concern instantly sharpened his features as he took a step towards me, wings flickering in and out of existence. He was barely keeping a damper on his baser instincts.

"I'm fine," I assured quickly. "Griffin was just here with Raven."

Nox seemed to relax, just a bit. "Is it problematic? Griffin being here?"

"Oh, no, not at all," I said. "Not usually. It's just that Lil and Raven's mom is here. She came this morning to help me start getting stuff ready for the coronation."

Understanding flooded Nox's features. "Ah," he said.

"I wanted to give them all some space," I explained. "I mean, sans Griffin. He bolted pretty quickly."

"Of course he did," Nox muttered, his jaw shifting.

I bit my lip. "They have some pretty intense history, huh? Evelyn and Griffin, I mean."

Nox's brow rose. "That's one way to put it. But I assume you didn't call me here to chat about them?"

I snorted. "Okay, well now I'm intrigued. But, no, I wanted to see if you could teach me how to...you know...how to defend myself." The words came out awkward. Physical training was something I was really damn unfamiliar with, and it made me feel uncomfortably vulnerable to admit that.

Nox's lips twitched and he stepped even closer to me as he said, "I'll teach you that. And with time, I'll teach you to not only defend yourself, but to be something others fear. More so than now, even."

I scoffed. "People aren't afraid of me."

Nox shook his head. "That is simply not true, love. Don't think word of what you did and exactly what you became after the Trial hasn't spread, despite the efforts of your council to keep it quiet."

"What I became?" I echoed.

He held out a hand. Eyeing him, I took it, expecting him to flit us out immediately. Instead, we walked down the hall and out to the gardens in the front courtyard. Nothing bloomed, and I could almost believe it was simply because it was too early in the season, but I knew that, truly, it was due to the demonic magic that had infiltrated the palace for so many years.

"Touch one of the flowers," Nox told me, his eyes flicking to a patch of long-gone night-blooming roses.

"Why?" I asked, my stomach suddenly churning.

"Just try this, love. Then, we'll go train, I promise."

I bit the inside of my cheek but let go of his hand, padding over the half-frozen earth to the flowerbed. As I crouched down, Nox knelt beside me.

"I have a theory," he murmured.

I stared at the wilted petals. "And what is that?"

"When the Maiden, a young girl named Amely, became the goddess and the first coming of the Evening Star, people said odd things began to occur," Nox said, his voice nearly whisper on the howling wind around us.

"I didn't know that was her name," I said softly, my eyes still on the flowers.

"Yes," Nox said, and I could hear the slight smile in his voice. "Even gods and saviors have names. Histories and personal lives. We make mistakes, like anyone else."

We?

Someday, if the world survived all of this, I supposed I would be reduced to a section in some dusty history book. That was weird to think about and definitely not comforting at all.

"But Amely was rumored to have an ability reminiscent of many of the Beings of Light," Nox continued. "The very gift of life itself."

'You are much more than a fragile life force. You are life. You are light.' The goddess had told me as much, I just hadn't known what it had meant at the time. Had she literally meant I could give life itself?

Surely not.

"I never had such a power," Nox said, taking my hand and guiding it toward the rose bed. "But I was never meant to have the power of Light. You always were."

Finally, I understood what he wanted me to do. I took a deep breath as my fingers brushed against a dried, crumbling petal. At first, nothing happened, which was honestly fine with me, but then I began to sense something—an awareness, a pulse.

Life.

I could feel it, straining and barely holding on, like frayed threads hanging down from a vast night sky. And all around those fraying threads were others, pulled tight. Some were half-frayed and damaged, others were completely whole, but they were all very much alive. And I could not only sense that but *see* it. Which was an insane mix of both mind-blowing and terrifying.

"Asteria?"

Nox's voice felt far away, even though I knew he was sitting right beside me.

"I see it...all of them," I whispered, feeling the petals beneath my fingertips. They were soft and delicate; fragile, like a first breath.

"Open your eyes, love," Nox said in wonder, an unmistakable reverence in his voice.

I hadn't even realized I'd closed them, but I did as he said. And when I looked at what was in front of me, I gasped.

The entire bed of roses was alive and blooming before me. It should have been impossible, with the cool temperature outside and the rancid magic of the palace grounds, yet I had somehow made it happen.

Nox laughed, a surprised, light sound, and said, "Maybe I can teach you to heal after all."

I swallowed. "I don't know if this is the same."

He caught my eye. "No," he said slowly. "This is like nothing I've ever seen before."

"But I've never done this before," I said, shaking my head. "Why now, all of the sudden?"

Shrugging, he replied simply, "I think that sometimes, all it takes is for someone to open our eyes in order to see our true potential. Now"—he stood—"shall we?"

I blinked heavily, still shocked at what had just occurred. But I got to my feet, dusting dirt off the knees of my jeans, and placed my hand in Nox's. "You need to teach me how to flit too. It's annoying that I always have to have someone drag me from place to place."

Nox chuckled, the sound deep and resounding. "One thing at a time. For now."

We flitted and landed in a courtyard I had never seen before. Before I could take it all in, Nox turned to me with a playful grin and snapped his fingers. Momentarily, a leather bodysuit appeared.

"For you, my dear."

I scoffed and snatched up the leathers, and I was just about to find a more *private* corner or alcove to change in when Nox snapped his fingers again. For about three entire seconds, I was completely naked. Then, just as instantly, the bodysuit molded to my body, and I was clothed again.

"Nox!" I hissed.

He only smirked.

Bastard.

"Ready for training?"

I whirled and a burning rose in my cheeks as I saw Griffin striding towards us in similar attire to me.

"You look...startled," Griffin said, a brow raised. "I don't know what you did, but I didn't see a thing, I swear. And if I had, I'd probably be lacking eyes right about now, courtesy of Nox."

I huffed out a breath. "You both are *ridiculous.*"

Griffin looked to Nox, frowning incredulously, and mouthed the words *'what did you do?'*

Nox merely shrugged like he were nothing more than a schoolboy feigning innocence.

Griffin shook his head and turned his attention back to me. "So, I won't lie to you, you are going to be wishing you were never born in about half an hour," Griffin said, his feet planted on the dusty ground of the courtyard.

I rolled my eyes, taking in the area around me. Stone walls rose up on all sides, peppered with narrow windows, though strangely I didn't feel too caged in. This was not a prison but a place of becoming. Of molding—training. On the wall behind Griffin, there were racks of wooden training swords, shining daggers, and bows; and along the opposite wall were quivers overflowing with arrows, targets for shooting, and fighting dummies.

"He's right," Nox said, pulling me out of my perusal.

I balled my fists at my sides. "I'm ready."

"Alright," Griffin grunted. "Let's test your stamina and strength. You won't make it far without either. Ten laps around the courtyard and then we'll start with core exercises."

Well, this was going to be fun.

"One more minute, Asteria!"

I was on the ground, covered in dust and sweat, holding a plank. It took me back to the days when Lil and I had a brief friend at the Seelie Court University who'd been obsessed with exercise. She'd once suggested a movie night plus workouts. Where a sane person would *drink* every time the villain appeared on-screen and proceed to get blind drunk, we did a thirty-second plank.

It truly was one of the worst nights of my adult life.

"Can't I just...stop?" I gritted out, adding, "Fuck!"

Griffin snorted. "Colorful language won't stop the training, but feel free to use it if it helps you. I'm going to push you, and you are going to thank me for it later."

My core felt like it was on fire. "I will not be thanking you," I hissed.

"When we're seconds away from losing a battle and your speed, strength, and ability to persevere are the only things keeping you from being cut down, you will be glad you chose to train," Griffin said, adding, "Minute's up."

I collapsed to the ground in a heap, lifting my head just as he crouched down and held out a hand. I shook my head and rasped, "Give me just a second before we go again."

Griffin smiled, though—as usual—it kind of just looked like a grimace. "We're done for today, Asteria. Though, I'm happy to know you would continue if I advised you to."

I warily took his hand, half-expecting him to try some fancy hand-to-hand combat move on me, which would have really sucked because we hadn't even gotten to that yet.

Thankfully, he simply helped me up, just as Nox reentered the courtyard.

"And where did you go?" I said sullenly, wiping at my forehead.

He smirked, striding over as he said, "To do some very boring, very important things."

"That's not vague at all," I muttered.

Nox's smirk only grew wider as I frowned.

Griffin sighed and said, "Well, you two have fun. I'm off."

"Tomorrow, Griffin?" Nox said, glancing his friend's way.

"Tomorrow," Griffin agreed before disappearing through one of the many shadowed entrances to the courtyard.

"What's happening tomorrow?" I asked, crossing my arms as I looked at Nox.

He swiped his thumb across my bottom lip, the movement so comfortably casual, and replied, "Training. We try to do it together as often as we can."

I resisted the urge to nip at his finger before he dropped it to his side. "I see," I said. "Bromance time."

"Ha-ha," Nox deadpanned. "Do you want a bath?"

"Are you suggesting I smell?" I countered. I definitely did, but he was not allowed to insinuate that.

Loyally, he said, "No, but I figured it might feel nice on your muscles."

Warm water did sound pretty freaking awesome right about now, so I relented, "Yes, fine. But I am also requesting a massage."

"Ah." His lip curled. "So, you want me in the bath as well?"

"I mean, *duh*," I said casually. "You can stay clothed if you want, but that would be kind of silly."

His eyes glinted. "Coy little thing, aren't you?"

I gave him a sly look, and I felt the whisper of something cool around my ear. I couldn't quite catch what the shadow was murmuring as Nox was already heading for one of the entrances, not bothering to make sure I was following. That was something I loved about him. Sure, he definitely coddled me sometimes, but he also understood the simple fact that I was independent. I always had been, partially out of necessity, and it wasn't a trait that had disappeared simply because I'd found my mate.

I followed after him, my limbs already aching. We soon emerged into a smaller hallway and followed the path of glimmering faelights that lined the dark marble floor. Up ahead, the hallway opened up into a lighter space, courtesy of a large, circular window.

"How did the Unseelie Court ever get such a horrible reputation?" I asked Nox as we walked. "I mean, it's not that bad here."

Nox played with a wisp of shadow, the tail of it curling around his pointer finger. "Modernization has made the whole of our kind tamer," he explained. "Just a few decades ago, things were quite different. Wilder."

I felt the weight of the words as he said them. And as much as I loved having a cell phone and the ability to microwave my lukewarm coffee in the morning, there was a part of me that intrinsically knew this was not how it was supposed to be. We were creatures of the wild. Of the hunt. Of dance and song and desire—even in the Seelie Court.

"This court was once home to many creatures that most

would call nightmarish," Nox went on as we stepped into the larger, lighter room. "But through laws passed when I was only a child, they became sequestered to the Wilds. I'm told that it was once territory of the Unseelie lands. Now, it is a place of exile."

"Couldn't they have fought the laws?"

"Maybe," Nox replied simply. "I assume they would rather be free to be who they are, even if it is a caged freedom."

The words resonated within me, and for some reason I thought back to my date with Nox, losing myself on the dancefloor amidst the bodies. That, I realized, was why I craved it so often, why I had drank and fucked and pretended—it was a beautiful illusion of sweat and alcohol soaked freedom.

I would have to examine that particular realization later.

"Beasts, the lot of them," an irritatingly familiar voice said.

I resisted the urge to do some inappropriately aggressive things as none other than Wista practically floated into what I now realized was a sitting room. Today, she wore a tight pink turtleneck and jeans that admittedly did great things for her ass. That alone nearly had me snarling at her; I knew *exactly* why she had worn them.

"That's very rude, Wista," Nox said easily, "and I doubt you would dare say that in their presence."

Wista lifted her chin. "I'm not afraid of your kind."

"Maybe you should be," I said smoothly.

Wista glanced at me, and a delicate blush rose to her cheeks. "Are you threatening me?" she said in a high, girly voice.

"Nope," I replied with a smile that showed each and every one of my teeth.

Nox cleared his throat. "Asteria, love, shall we?"

"Mhmm," I hummed, my eyes still on Wista as she glared at me. I could feel her gaze burning into me, even as Nox and I left the room and made our way up a *very* pretty winding stairwell; stained glass let in streams of sunlight, casting a colorful glow around us as we climbed.

"Sorry," I said flatly when we reached the top. The apology was pretty lame, but hey—at least I tried.

Nox pushed open the door to his chambers, and I relaxed as we entered, a true sign that this place was becoming more and more familiar to me.

"Do you know," he began, "why Wista stays in this palace?"

"Because you wanted a fuckbuddy?" I grumbled.

Nox grimaced. "No."

"Then why?"

He brushed a strand of hair away from my face as he explained, "Because she's an oracle."

My eyes widened slightly as I remembered that sweet little girl. "Like Lena?"

Sadness flickered across his features. "Yes."

I looked away. "And why does she dislike me so much?"

Nox hesitated. "She foretold something she doesn't wish to happen."

"And it has to do with me?"

"Not necessarily," he replied, but I could hear in his voice that there was more.

Water began to flow into the enormous tub, and the sweet, heady scent of rose filled the air as Nox flicked his fingers and a bottle of bath oil poured itself into the water. I watched him carefully as he tugged his shirt off and shucked off his leather boots.

"Nox," I said. "What did she see?"

His muscled shoulder rose up in a deep breath. "Can you trust me? Just this one time?"

"I don't like secrets," I said, echoing my words from a few days ago.

"I know, love. But this is information that I don't even..." He trailed off, running a hand over his face. "Just trust me, for a little while."

"And if I say no?" I asked, stripping the leathers off my body and stepping into the tub.

He didn't reply, instead stepping into the water and sitting behind me. I didn't stop him as he swept the hair off my shoulder and began to rub the sore muscles there.

"Tell me in three weeks," I said, staring at the shelves on the wall, full of more colorful bath oils and salts.

He paused. "Your birthday."

"How did you know?" I twisted to find his expression pained.

His mouth thinned and he merely said, "This information is not a gift to know."

I sighed, turning and reaching for a bar of soap. "What's another curse, then?" I whispered.

He laughed but it lacked any real humor. "Here, let me," Nox said gently, taking the bar from my hands.

I let him, relaxing as he rubbed soapy hands down my back. I wasn't done pushing about what Wista had seen, but it was quite obvious he wasn't going to budge, at least not yet. Which was fine. I could wait.

Instead, I said, "So...tell me the deal with Griffin and Evelyn Hephaste."

Nox's hands paused before I felt him shift in the water. "Griffin met her when she was a year or two younger than you are."

"Wait," I said. "But she met Lil's dad when she was older than I am now."

"Precisely," Nox said.

"Well, shit," I muttered.

He cleared his throat. "Yeah, and court divides back then were an even more serious issue than they are today. Relationships between Beings of the two courts, especially Fae, were completely taboo."

"How did they even meet then?"

Nox's hands slipped away from my bare back, and he set the soap down. "Let's dry off and I'll tell you the rest."

"Alright," I said quietly.

I stood, water streaming down my body in rivulets. I folded myself into one of the fluffy, white towels from the shelves under the sink. Then, I padded into the bedroom, helped myself to a pair of his boxers and a band t-shirt, and sat on the bed, waiting as my hair dripped onto the covers. Nox smiled as he saw me, softening the harshness of his features.

"What?"

"Nothing, love. I just think you should wear my clothes more often."

I swatted at him as he sat down. "Not the time. Finish the story." He looked a little conflicted for a moment, and I added, "And don't feel bad for telling me. I doubt that

Griffin or Lil's mom would mind, and I think it's kind of important for me to know."

Nox nodded, just once, before settling back against the headboard. I joined him, lying across his lap as he spoke.

"Evelyn was a little like you when she was younger. She didn't care much for the court divide and was flippant about following rules."

"That does *not* sound like her," I said, my voice muffled.

"Hmm, well people change," Nox said, sounding a little sad. "But as I understand, she liked to party. The night they met, Griffin had dragged me out to some bar that had pretty loose rules about who they let in. To be frank, a lot of criminal activity happened in that bar."

"Fun," I said, and I kind of meant it.

Nox snorted. "Well, somehow, Evelyn had snuck across the borders. A half-Unseelie friend, I believe, was the story, since the Veil only allows Unseelie Fae to flit across its borders."

"So, even if I could flit here, I...couldn't?" I asked.

"No, you could, because we're mated. It's rare enough that faeries from different courts form a mating bond that my forefathers didn't even think about that when they created the Veil. Our magic just allows for it."

"Good to know."

"Mhmm. Shall I continue?"

I traced little stars on his leg with my finger and replied, "Yeah, sorry."

His hand threaded through my hair and he went on. "So, they met that night in the bar. Cell phones weren't widely used then, so Griffin gave her a moonstone. Which, if you didn't catch, is a fairly big deal. Admittedly, I tried to tell him not to do it because a moonstone in the wrong hands could mean bad things for our court. But he trusted her, after just one night. He knew, I suppose.

"After that, they kept in contact and saw each other when they could. But it was only a matter of time before Evelyn's family discovered the relationship. And they punished her and Griffin both for it."

"Goddess, how?" I whispered. I'd never met Lil's grandparents and I'd always assumed it was for good reason. Now, I figured I was about to find out why.

"They forced Evelyn into a betrothal. Which, again, at the time, wasn't uncommon."

"And if she refused?"

"I believe the insinuation was they would make sure she never saw Griffin alive again. I think he tried to convince her not to do it, but she was too afraid for him. She married Lil's father, and for a while, that was that."

I swallowed hard. I had a very bad feeling about where this was going next.

"About a year later, she contacted Griffin through the moonstone; I don't think he even thought that she still had it; but the short of it was, she was unhappy in the marriage and her husband was growing impatient. He'd hit her."

Nox paused and my throat felt tight. I'd never thought Lil's dad was a great person, but I had always hoped he wasn't actually evil.

"There was nothing I could do to stop Griffin from going to her. He didn't come back for three days, and I nearly went into the Seelie Court myself to find out what had happened before he showed his face again. Evelyn had told him she loved him and to never come back. I've never seen Griffin like that, not before and not since. Devastated is a mild way to put it."

"Were they...I mean, are they mates?" I asked.

Nox sighed heavily. "Honestly, I don't know. After what happened, I never asked Griffin and he's never been inclined to tell me one way or another."

"And Raven..." I trailed off.

"I think Raven is a result of those three days Griffin disappeared," Nox finished. "Griffin didn't even know he existed until years later, when Evelyn contacted him completely out of the blue and told him."

"But wasn't Raven at your court when he was a kid? How did Griffin not realize it then?"

"The orphanage is separate from the palace and few but the caretakers and I ever visit the children there."

"Damn," I whispered. "Poor Griffin."

"Indeed."

I sat up then and asked softly, "Do you visit them often? The kids in the orphanage?"

Nox looked a little bashful as he replied, "As often as I can. I suppose they remind me a bit of myself as a child, which is probably selfish because at least I had living parents, but—"

"No, it's valid," I said, touching his cheek gently with my hand. "I want to come with you sometime."

He swallowed. "If you truly want to, I'll take you." His features softened into a smile. "They'll be excited."

"They talk about me there?"

Nox's eyes were sparkling like stars as he said, "They talk about you everywhere, love."

CHAPTER 14
NOX

In the morning, I flitted Asteria back to the Seelie Court palace—reluctantly. I hated taking her there, knowing that being there pained her. But in the same way I had to learn to walk the walls of my palace without fear, she needed to as well. It was a bitter truth of our reality as rulers in the places we had once been abused.

By the time I got back to my palace and into the training courtyard, Griffin was already hacking at a wooden dummy. I approached him silently, blade ready, but he sensed me nonetheless, whirling and meeting my blow.

He was my war general for a reason.

As I went on the offense for once, I said between strikes, "I heard Evelyn Hephaste was there at the palace yesterday."

"Did you now?" he grunted, slamming his blade into mine.

I feigned a movement to the left, but he saw right through it and I ended up with his blade pointed at my chest.

"Dead," he said in a low voice.

"What a waste," I shot back. "I'm so much prettier than you." I looked to him and smirked, but his mouth remained set. I huffed. "Are we not going to talk about this at all?"

Griffin mumbled something about it being none of my business, and I shoved at him—brotherly love at its best—and said, "It absolutely is my business, given that her daughter is Asteria's best friend. We're both likely going to be seeing more of her."

"Joy," Griffin grunted, his back to me.

"Griffin."

He whirled, and only then did I see his eyes shining with angry tears.

"She had a *daughter* with that bastard, Nox. And I do not fault Lilliana at all for it, but you know what it takes for our kind to have a child."

"It might not have been love. It could have been a fluke," I said with a lighthearted shrug. "It happens."

He ran a hand over his face. "I doubt it. She stayed with him."

I raised a brow. "To protect you."

"Even still? From what?"

Looking up at the cloud-covered sky, I replied, "As far as I know, her parents are still living. Maybe she thinks their threats still stand. And they very possibly could. Or maybe she's afraid of her husband, especially now that there are children involved."

"I would kill him before he touched them. Either of them," Griffin growled.

I looked back at Griffin. "You care for her, don't you?" I

said, the protectiveness in him swelling the already booming pride I had for the man. "Lilliana, I mean?"

He shrugged. "She's still a part of Evelyn. How could I not?"

"You still love her," I said, holding his gaze.

"I wish I didn't," he said, his voice cracking. "It would make this all so much easier."

"Nothing about this, any of this, was ever going to be easy," I replied, no longer just talking about him. Nothing about our lives was simple.

We stared at each other for a moment, and I wondered if we were both thinking the same thing. That we couldn't fix this—couldn't protect those we loved the most.

We both jolted as a mildly familiar voice said, "Your Majesty, General."

I turned to see one of the newer recruits standing a few paces behind me. Griffin picked the royal guard members personally and with careful consideration, so I trusted all of them. But during those few seconds in his presence, I sensed there was something off about this boy. I just didn't quite know what.

"I have information, my king," the guard said stiffly.

I looked to Griffin, who expressed what I felt, a dubiousness about the guard and confusion over what was causing it. He stood with his hand poised, ready but discreetly so.

I turned back to the guard, a quizzical brow raised. "About?" I pushed, circling him and feeling my wings prick at my back, readying to fight.

His mouth curved into a cruel smile and warning bells sounded in my head.

"Lilith's Mark," he whispered before shoving his heavy sword towards me.

I sidestepped on instinct, my wings flaring. Seconds later, Griffin leapt in front of me, his blade meeting that of the guard's. The guard let out a low snarl, kicking out and unbalancing Griffin with surprising strength for his size. Griffin grunted, and I raised my own weapon as the guard barreled towards me. I met his first blow, the force of it reverberating up my arm. That was the moment I knew for sure this was no mere guard; he was hardly full-grown, likely barely trained, yet was just as strong as Griffin or me.

"You want to know," the guard taunted. "I know you do."

I lowered my chin, sure of what he was now. "Enough, demon. Tell me what you're here for."

He laughed, the sound unhinged. "You think you will get the information you want so easily?" A slow smile spread across his face. "She is in more danger than you can even imagine."

At that, my vision flashed red, an instinctual rage at the threat of my mate burgeoning inside me, and it clouded my focus enough that I didn't see the second blade in his hand, aimed straight for my heart.

"He *what*?"

Asteria's voice was tinged with notes of anger, her all-too usual defense mechanism.

"It's fine, love," I assured her over the phone. "I don't even have a scratch on me."

"And the guard?" Her voice shook slightly.

"Dead," I said flatly. "We disarmed and cornered him, but he had a dagger hidden. Before we could question him, he turned it on himself."

"He was possessed."

"Yes," I said, my tone sour over the loss of more of our own. "I'm nearly certain."

I didn't tell her the rest of it over the phone; the information felt too sensitive to utter on a call that could be traced. I had no idea what it meant—Lilith's Mark—but I did have a very bad feeling it was related to the woman I'd seen behind Asteria on the dream bridge.

"Are you coming here now?" she asked.

"I'm about to leave. Is Lil and Raven's mother still there?"

"No, she left about an hour ago. But she said she might be back either later on today or tomorrow."

"Understood. I'll be there shortly."

"Right. I..." She hesitated before dismissing whatever was on her tongue entirely. "Well, see you soon."

I wondered what she'd been about to say, and for a moment I hoped for those three little words. I'd never gotten them from her and had resolved not to pressure her by saying them again; I would stay with her forever even if I never got them as she had my heart completely, yet I had to wonder because of those unspoken words if I did or ever would have hers. Selfishly, I wanted all of her. She could never know just *how* selfish that was, and I couldn't help but think that maybe it would be better if she never gave herself completely to me.

Putting those thoughts aside for now, I flitted to the

Seelie palace grounds. When I arrived, the guards didn't even look my way. In fact, they averted their eyes as I passed by.

Odd.

I walked directly to Asteria's rooms and found her and Lil sitting on the bed and talking quietly. Raven sat on the small armchair near the window, tapping his fingers impatiently. They all looked my way as I entered the room, Raven standing up from the chair.

"What happened?" he demanded.

"Did you tell them?" I looked at Asteria. She nodded, though by the look in her eyes, I could tell she knew there was more to it all.

"Griffin," Raven said. "Is he—"

"He's fine," I replied. "More annoyed that our training session was interrupted than anything."

Raven made a low, indiscernible sound of acknowledgment, but I could see the poorly hidden relief on his face.

Lil cleared her throat and pushed, "There's more, isn't there?"

I glanced at Asteria, and she simply said, "It was obvious you didn't tell me everything."

"I know."

She kept her eyes on mine, her gaze serious and beautiful. "What is it?"

"Have you told Raven and Lilliana? About the dream bridge?" I asked carefully.

"The what?" Raven said, his tone a little disgruntled.

Lil snorted. "You mean your wet dream connection?"

I felt a smile fight its way to my lips as I turned to Raven, his expression even moodier now, and explained, "It's a mind connection, exclusive to Unseelie mates. I can see Asteria in my dreams, and she can see me in mine."

"And it's *not* a sex thing," Asteria muttered, shoving at Lil.

Yet, I thought slyly. I swore Asteria somehow heard me because her gaze flicked to mine for a moment.

I didn't think I would ever get used to that. Around her, not even my thoughts were safe.

I cleared my throat, setting *that* aside for later, and said, "The night Abaddon came for you, Raven, I saw a woman standing behind Asteria on the dream bridge. She wore a mark on her forehead, one I'd never seen before. We tried to figure out what it was to no avail. But today..." I looked back at my mate. "The guard claimed to have information about Lilith's Mark."

Starlight stirred in Asteria's icy blue eyes, reacting immediately to the perceived threat, and I watched as her lips parted. "I don't know why or how," she whispered. "But somehow that sounds familiar to me."

CHAPTER 15

ASTER

Both Nox and Raven were pacing around my room in the Seelie palace, Lil and I still sat on the bed, eyeing each other as they strode back and forth.

"Do you think they realize they're doing it?" she whispered in my ear, grinning.

I snorted. "I really don't think they do."

She caught my gaze, her large green eyes earnest as she asked quietly, "Are you okay? I mean, this is all a lot."

"This has all been a lot for a while," I said, grimacing.

Lil touched my cheek with her hand. "I know, Aster. I know."

A place in my heart, only for her, warmed, and I felt better instantly—at least momentarily.

"Thanks for being here," I said as she pulled her hand away from my face. "I know it's been weird with Griffin and your mom, and now this."

"Yeah, it is all pretty dramatic. But where else would I be?" she said, smiling. "You're my person, silly."

I blinked rapidly and muttered, "Ugh, Lil, you cannot make me cry now. My eyeliner is the best it's been in weeks today."

She laughed. "As if you care. You always wore the smeared makeup look great anyways."

"Are you insinuating I cried a lot?"

"Hmm, maybe. But mostly that you had a lot of sweaty bathroom stall sex. Don't worry, though, I won't tell Nox."

"Maybe he won't mind since we…" I trailed off, and Lil's brows rose. "Well, let's just say if bathrooms could talk there'd be one in the Unseelie Court with a *lot* to say."

"You dirty, dirty girl," Lil said, smacking the back of my hand. "This is why I am so wary of public restrooms."

"Are you two done?"

We both looked up to see Raven standing a few feet away, glaring.

"Um, is there a problem, dear brother?" Lil said.

Raven and Nox exchanged a look.

I rolled my eyes and said, "Will you two stop acting like caged animals? None of this will be solved because you're pacing around my bedroom."

"I promise you're still both very big, bad, faerie men," Lil added. "You can sit, it won't convince me otherwise."

Nox opened his mouth, likely to protest, just as there was a knock on the door.

"My queen!" a voice called.

Gingerly, I stood from the bed and walked over to the door. Nox's wings flickered in and out of sight, and he tensed as I opened the door. Thankfully, it turned out only to be a guard, one I still didn't know the name of, and one I'd wager remained unpossessed; his energy was that of a doe, all buggy eyed and nervous, and every demon we'd met was their own special shade of arrogant at best.

"Is something the matter?" I asked.

The guard shook his head stiffly. "No, my queen. But there is a relation of yours in the entrance hall, claiming to be here for your coronation."

Right...Bells. I'd completely forgotten my cousin was coming.

"Alright," I said wearily. "Let her know I'll be there in a few minutes and offer her something to eat and drink while she waits."

"It will be done, my queen," the guard said, before turning and marching away.

"That is something I'll need to get used to," Lil said as he left. "He was so formal."

"Do," Raven snapped. "Aster is a queen now, not just our friend."

"Okay, cool it, Raven," I said, rolling my eyes. "I better get going." Nox, Raven, and Lil all made for the door, and I put a hand up. "Woah, guys, I appreciate it, but I haven't seen Bells in years. Maybe I should just do this on my own."

"That, love," Nox said, "is precisely why we are coming with you. None of us know this girl, and one of my guards just tried to kill me."

"Right," I muttered. "Can't trust anyone."

"He's not wrong," Raven pointed out.

"Damn, Raven, you're agreeing with Nox?" Lil said playfully as we all spilled out into the hallway.

Raven grunted, and I held back a smile. This was just what I missed. The everyday banter that had somehow grown to include Nox. My family, I realized, this was them.

Sure, the girl waiting in the entrance hall had my blood, but these were the people who truly mattered in the end.

I took a deep breath as we descended the wide, marble stairway that led down to the entrance hall. Flowers had once hung everywhere in the spacious, airy palace, but now they were few and far between. The arched windows still let in streams of sunlight, and the distant sound of trickling water, flowing from one of the fountains in the numerous gardens outside, filled me with a surprising sense of tranquility. For the first time in a while, I believed I could make this my home again, at least with time.

We left the stairway behind and turned the corner. I took a deep breath as a head of long, golden hair turned. Blue eyes, matching my own, crinkled, and a sweet voice exclaimed, "Oh my goddess, you've grown to be so beautiful!"

I forced a smile to my lips. "Hey, Bells."

She pouted, her full lips tinted a blush rose. She wore a sweater dress of the same color, along with white fur-lined boots and a delicate collection of gold necklaces sitting at her collar. She looked just as I remembered. A good girl in the most traditional of senses.

"It's been almost fifteen years, and all I get is 'hey'?" Bells said, her eyes wide with surprise, but her mouth was still tilted in a sly smile.

At first, I thought I might brush past it, keep everything locked away, every grievance and pain regarding our past and her visit, but I couldn't. There were lies and secrets and bullshit everywhere I looked, and I couldn't stomach more.

If she wanted this, whatever *this* was, she would do it my way—with the truth in front of us.

I kept my cool demeanor but said quietly, "You never came, Bells. All those years, I didn't hear from anyone. Not even you."

Her expression faltered as she took a step closer. Nox was instantly at my side, and Bells froze at the sight of him.

"I'd heard the rumors," she said softly, almost as if to herself. "But it's true." She took a breath, then bowed her head slightly. "It's a pleasure to meet you, Nox Ether."

I glanced at Nox, whose amber eyes were narrowed, assessing my cousin. Finally, he said, "Do you have no explanation to offer her?"

Bells' delicate complexion paled slightly, and she looked at me again. "Asteria, I'm sorry," she said in a hushed whisper. "My mother forbade it. And I know I should have tried harder, but I just..." she trailed off. "That's all I can give you. It's your choice whether to forgive me or not."

I looked at her for a long, long moment. She was definitely holding her breath, and I let her for just a few seconds longer before I said, "I forgive you—but only if you help me get through this awful coronation."

A smile broke apart her face. "Can I...can I hug you?"

Nox glanced at me, as if saying, *Tell me if this is okay.*

I gave him a slight nod, and he stepped back as I let Bells embrace me. She was slightly shorter and softer than me, and the material of her dress was warm against my cheek as I let her hold me.

"I'm so sorry for your loss, Asteria," she whispered. "I never got to say that to you, so I'll say it now."

I pulled back, fighting the sudden, churning nausea in my stomach at her words. I didn't deserve her sympathy, not really. My parents would still be standing here today if not for my power. Still, I was grateful for the gesture. "Thank you, Bells," I managed to choke out. Rubbing together my trembling hands, I glanced over at Lil and Raven, who had been standing awkwardly to the side. "Bells, this is Lil and Raven. They're my family in every regard but blood."

Bells smiled at them. "It's an honor."

Lil tilted her head, as if examining Bells. Apparently, she was satisfied enough with everything she'd seen, because she pranced over to my side and said to Bells, "Your dress is cute."

"Thanks," Bells chirped. "It's from this up-and-coming designer, Monica Rose. She's amazing."

"Expensive too, I'm sure," Raven said, not having moved from his spot. "But you can afford that, what with all the money your mother inherited from her cousin, the former king. Say, do you know where Aster's portion of that money went?"

"I—no," Bells said carefully.

"My now very-dead uncle," I cut in. "Don't worry about Raven, Bells. He's moody on a good day."

Raven was still glaring at Bells, and I was pretty sure that, despite his callous words, she gave him a once-over. Hell, I didn't blame her. Most girls did the same.

Nox was eyeing Bells, his gaze flicking between her and Raven momentarily. I caught his eye and raised a brow.

He shook his head as if to say, *Nothing, love.*

I narrowed my eyes. *I don't believe you.*

His lips tilted. *Oh, really?*

"Okay, what is going on?" Bells said, looking between

Nox and me. "Can you two communicate silently or something?"

Lil snorted. "Not that I know of, but I wouldn't put it past them. Mates are so weird."

I flicked her nose and said, "You wouldn't say that if you had one, babygirl."

"First of all, *ow!*" Lil exclaimed. "And second of all, I don't think so. The whole thing is very...feral, you know? Like we have microwave meals and laptops, is it really necessary that we sniff each other to decide if we want to be with someone?"

A puff of air that I interpreted as a laugh escaped Nox. "Is that how you think it happens?"

Lil shrugged. "I mean, how the hell did *you* figure it out? Like, when did Aster go from some girl you danced with in a club to your soulmate or whatever?"

"Asteria was never just a girl in a club," Nox said quietly, and I knew exactly what he meant. He had known me in dreams—and without realizing it, I had known him too— for years before we'd met in person.

"Um, wow, intense," Bells commented as she started to walk towards the guest wing, hauling what had to be a designer suitcase behind her.

"Do you know where you're going?" I asked, following her.

She turned. "It's been a long time, but I think so."

"Great. Yeah, any of the guest rooms are yours, since you're the only family member that decided to come out of the woodwork and attend," I said.

Bells' laugh was like the tinkling of, well, bells. As we

reached the staircase, she waved her hand and the suitcase began to float next to her.

"Nice trick," Raven muttered.

Bells turned, suitcase still floating next to her and hands on her hips. "I can't tell if that was supposed to be an insult or not."

Raven's gaze lifted to hers. "It was merely a statement."

She hummed and cocked her head. "What's your deal?"

He gave her a deprecating smile. "Nothing at all."

"Are you Seelie? Or from his court?" she asked, tilting her head towards Nox.

"Neither," Raven replied. "Both. Think about it however you like, I don't care."

"You know what," I said. "Bells, you go get settled. I'm sure you're tired. We'll all reconvene for dinner."

"Sounds good," she said, her eyes still on Raven. They stared at each other for a few more tense seconds before Bells turned and sauntered up the rest of the stairs and turned the corner.

As soon as she was gone, Lil exclaimed, "Raven, what the hell is your problem?"

"She's a spoiled brat who left Aster to fend for herself as a child," Raven shot back. "Why should I have any respect for her?"

"Raven, she was fifteen when my parents died," I said. "She was just a kid too."

"Whatever," he muttered, before stalking off down the hall.

Lil rolled her eyes. "He's been moody ever since we talked to our mom about Griffin. He thinks she wasn't telling the truth."

"What did she say?" I asked carefully.

Lil bit her lip. "Well, she just didn't say much at all, no matter how much Raven pushed. She almost seemed afraid to tell us. I don't know, maybe it was me being there. I should probably let them talk alone."

"Maybe," I said quietly.

Lil sighed. "I think I'm gonna go talk to him. And Aster, take a nap or something before dinner, you look exhausted." With that, she was off, swinging her hips as she hurried after Raven.

I glanced at Nox, who said, "She's not wrong. You should rest."

"We need to look more into that symbol," I said, my voice thinning.

Nox shook his head. "Later."

"Don't you have very important kingly duties to attend to?"

"I always do. But you're much more important."

I ignored the way those words made my heart flutter and relented, saying, "Fine. I will take a *short* nap."

"Good."

I smiled, a silly tired smile, and I was surprised to see Nox's face drop. There was no doubt he was looking my way, but he looked as though he'd seen a ghost or remembered he'd forgotten to do something important.

"What's wrong?" I asked, my voice sounding oddly distant even to myself. "What is it?"

A moment passed, but before long he snapped out of his stupor. He spoke then, or at least it looked like he did; his lips moved and his face became animated with worry, but no sound reached my ears.

Weird.

Suddenly, I felt odd, both wide awake and incredibly tired; my body felt weightless, like I were completely submerged in water.

My legs began to wobble. "Nox?"

I heard nothing. All I saw was my name on his mouth.

'Asteria. Asteria.'

"Nox"—arms grabbed me as my knees buckled— "what's—"

WHEN I WOKE UP, I was lying down, staring up at the familiar canopy of my bed.

"Asteria?"

I blinked against the low light coming from the windows. Nox was sitting up against the headboard next to me, his features flooded with concern.

"What...what happened?" I rasped.

He swallowed. "You passed out."

"Oh...oops."

"Are you okay?"

Was I okay? I felt fine, truly, but admittedly it was all a bit strange. Had I needed a little nap? Yes. Was I a bottle of tequila deep and at the tail end of a three-day rager? No. Was there any other reason for me to pass out that I could think of? Absolutely not. I really wasn't the passing out type —if such a type of person existed.

"I mean, yeah," I said. "I was okay, and then I just felt like...jelly." It was then, looking at Nox's stunning face etched with worry, that the last moments came to me.

"Something happened. I remember it on your face," I said. "What was it?"

His features were sharp, his mouth set as he told me, "Right before you fainted, I think I saw something. It was odd. As if I were seeing it in my mind. I don't think it was really...there."

"What do you mean?" I furrowed my brow. "Almost like you were in a dream?"

He stared at me for a moment before murmuring, "Yes, it was."

"What did you see?" I ignored the way my limbs felt oddly sore as I sat up.

"A woman," Nox said. "Standing over you. The same one I saw on the dream bridge, with the same mark on her forehead."

"Lilith's Mark," I whispered.

He nodded. "We have a name, now we just need to know what it means. We'll go back to the Archives tomorrow."

I rubbed at my eyes, unsure if I felt any more rested. "Or we could just ask Bells," I said sarcastically.

"Why do you say that?"

"Because," I said, glancing outside at the violet-hued sky, "she was always super into historical stuff. And I mean like old, old history. I think she majored in that sort of thing too. One of my professors mentioned her once. I guess she was at the Seelie University a few years before me."

"'Super into historical stuff,'" he repeated, an eyebrow raised mockingly.

"I literally *just* passed out."

"I thought you were fine," he said, narrowing his eyes at me playfully.

"I am," I said with a wave of my hand. "I'm just saving all my eloquence for Jasper."

Nox paused, seemingly tired of my nonsense, then asked, "Can we trust her?"

"I think so," I said, tracing stars on top of the covers with my fingers. "I mean, unless she's possessed, what do we have to lose?"

"Only everything," Nox said under his breath. "But, sure, we can ask her." He looked oddly boyish in that moment, vulnerable and unsure.

I took his hand, squeezing gently as I said, "It's going to be okay."

"Perhaps," he said as a brief darkness passed over his features. "Shall we go to dinner, if you're feeling up to it? Or I can take you to my healers and make sure everything is alright."

I raised a brow. "I know which of those you'd rather do —but we're going to dinner."

"As you wish," he said, watching me carefully as I got up from the bed and stood. When I wavered for a moment, he was instantly at my side.

"Fine. I'm fine."

"I'll be here anyway."

For a moment—just a few damn seconds—I leaned against him, allowing him to take my entire weight in his arms, and whispered, "I know."

CHAPTER 16

ASTER

Dinner was quiet and a tad awkward, primarily due to the tension still simmering between Raven and Bells. He kept glaring at her from his side of the polished oak table. All the while she sat opposite him, offering polite smiles every time he looked at her. Lil was watching their entire interaction with raised brows, and Nox actually looked mildly amused by the whole thing.

"Okay." I cleared my throat. "If you two are done with the stare down, Bells, I have a question for you."

Bells' cheeks grew a shade pinker, but she smoothly said, "Of course, what do you need?"

I glanced at Nox before I asked, "Have you ever heard of Lilith's Mark?"

I figured it was best to jump in without context. If she knew what it was without involving her further, the less she knew, the better, for her own safety. We had no idea what we were dealing with here.

Bells' brow creased. "How do you know about it?"

"Unfortunate chance," I replied vaguely. "But you *do* know about it?"

Bells took a sip of wine, then said, "Lucky for you, I do. It's something that very few people are aware of. It's not even well researched. Only a handful of living historians would know about this."

"What is it?" I pushed.

"Well, it's a rune," she said, tapping her pink-painted fingernails against the tabletop. "And a very, very old one. Lost to time, I would say."

Nox sat forward in his seat, bracing his forearms on the table as he said, "It's demonic in nature, isn't it?"

"Yes, but...why are you asking?"

"Why are you hesitating?" Nox countered.

Bells sighed. "It's just kind of a taboo thing. You know, cursed or whatever."

"Great," Lil muttered. "Just what we need more of."

I placed a hand flat atop the table and said to Bells, "Look, I hate the secrecy—goddess knows there's enough of that going around at the moment—but I don't want to tell you more than I already have because I care about you. Can you just tell us what it means?"

Bells stared at her wine as she swirled it around in the glass. Eventually, she set it down and said, "Ancient historical gossip, as I like to call it, states that before Hell was ruled by mere princes, there was a high queen whose name was Lilith. The mark—made up of the four-pointed star, the waning moon, and the sword stolen from Above—is her signature. In layman's terms, it's believed this rune is how she marks what is hers." She leveled a look at all of us. "*Now* will you tell me why you're asking?"

A stunned silence followed as the information settled.

"It's a very long, very incomplete story," I said finally, pushing away the terrifying notion that I had been marked in some way for possession—that the little agency I believed I had might be even flimsier than I'd thought.

Bells held my gaze. "I have time."

"THIS IS CRAZY," Bells muttered.

"Yeah," I puffed out. "Sorry to drop it all on you out of the blue."

Bells and I sat in a small sitting area adjacent to the dining room. A low fire burned in the hearth next to us and moonlight filtered in through the uncovered windows. Bells was sunk low in a soft loveseat, and I was curled up on the couch across from her. Raven and Lil had decided to stay in guest rooms tonight instead of going home, and I knew Nox was lingering nearby, likely keeping watch. It felt totally territorial and unnecessary, and yet, with what we'd just learned, it probably wasn't.

She shook her head, the light from the flames dancing in her eyes. "No, I'd rather know than be in the dark about it all. And I'm sorry I couldn't do more to protect you from your uncle and the demon that was inside of him."

I shivered. "It's not your fault. How could you have known? None of us did. Hell, my own council still doesn't really believe me."

"Well, that's just bullshit."

"Tell me about it."

I stared at the fire, and every moment that passed, every

lick of flame, brought a new question. What did the former High Queen of Hell want with me? Maybe something to do with Abaddon? Was he her son or brother? Or maybe even a usurper of her throne? Maybe she wanted to stop me from preventing a war—but then, why mark me as hers? My head was spinning with questions, anxieties, and scenarios, so much so that I barely noticed Nox enter the room—a rarity these days.

"We should all get some sleep," he said, standing in the doorway. His wings were out and very much visible. They had been since Bells told us what the mark meant.

"He's right," Bells said, yawning. "Besides, you have your coronation in a day, Asteria. You don't want dark circles under your eyes when you stand up in front of our court."

I grimaced. I was completely, utterly, *not* excited about the coronation. Given that it was Lord Jasper's idea, it felt more like a trap than an honor, but I had already agreed to go through with it and it would look suspicious to put a stop to it now. Nox definitely didn't like the idea of it either; at its mention, his wings flared just a little wider, increasing their menacing-ness...if that was even a word.

Whatever. I was too tired to even be thinking about anything at all right now.

I stood and made for the door. When Bells didn't follow, I glanced back at her questioningly.

She smiled tightly at me. "I'll go soon," she said. "I just need to clear my thoughts a bit more before I think I can sleep."

"Fair enough," I replied, yawning. "When you do—if you do—sleep well."

Her laugh was less light than it had been hours before, but she said, "You too, Asteria. Breakfast in the same room as dinner?"

"Works for me," I said nonchalantly. Breakfast, consisting of a sugary pastry and some form of coffee, was typically consumed in my room very, *very* quickly at the earliest possible convenience. However, Bells actually grew up in a formal, high-ranking household, and I thought it might be good to maintain at least a semblance of that while she was staying here, not only for her peace of mind, but for me to keep up appearances too.

Goddess knew I could do with the practice.

Bells nodded before gazing back at the crackling fire. I turned away from her and left the room with Nox at my side. It wasn't until we were in my room with the door shut that the fear set in.

"We'll figure this out," Nox said softly, obviously sensing the shift in me.

I took a shaky breath, staring at the bed like it might bite me.

"What is it?" he asked.

"I think I'm afraid to sleep most of all. What if I see her there?"

Nox paled, and my stomach turned. He was usually fairly cool and level, and for this to bother him that much let me know it was really that bad.

He took a step closer to me, his wings curling around us as he said, "We don't know for sure who the woman on the bridge was."

I raised a brow. "I think it's pretty damn obvious. She wore Lilith's Mark. It was probably her."

He didn't say anything, his jaw clenching and unclenching as he looked at a point somewhere past my shoulder. I tried to catch his eye, but he didn't let our gazes connect until I reached out and tilted his face towards mine.

"Nox," I said softly. "Do you know something about any of this?"

He looked entirely pained as he replied, "I don't. I don't and it's killing me. I keep thinking that I must have missed something."

"Nothing," I said. "You didn't miss anything. It seems like whoever is behind all this has been hiding for a very, very long time. Even longer than your old-ass memory stretches."

He didn't smile at my words. Instead, his hands trailed down my arms and he said roughly, "If she's there, on the bridge, I'll be there too."

I swallowed, meeting his gaze. "Please don't try to do anything if you see her," I whispered. "We don't know what she's capable of. If she truly is Lilith..." I trailed off, not really knowing what exactly she could do. Nothing good, surely.

"We'll see." Nox's voice was low and dripping with primal violence. In that moment, as I looked at him in the dim light of my bedroom, the silver of his hair stark against the black clothing he wore, I thought that I could really see it now—he was like a fallen angel, forced to walk on earth, tethered to it by half of his blood, tethered by me, whatever I was.

"Let's sleep," Nox told me, his voice just a fraction softer. "Your cousin was right, you should be well-rested for tomorrow."

"Right," I muttered, rubbing my eyes.

I could feel him watching me as I slipped away from him, stripped down, and threw on one of his band t-shirts. I practically fell into the soft bed, closing my eyes. But as soon as I did, the fear set in.

The bed bowed, and Nox's arms encircled me. He brushed a kiss against my forehead and whispered, "Sleep, love."

"Promise that you'll never leave me," I said, my words barely audible as I buried my head into his chest.

"I promise," he vowed, whispering against my hair.

For some reason, the goddess' words about him echoed in my mind once again.

'*Sometimes, good wears a mask of evil so that the monsters will not find it.*'

What did a vow mean to an angel? And why did I have the strangest feeling that, despite the surety of Nox's words, he was not fully in control of deciding whether or not they remained true?

CHAPTER 17

ASTER

By mid-morning the next day, I was covered in more layers of fabric and makeup than I could count or cared for.

Lil's mom stood in front of me, her hands on her full hips as she muttered, "Hmm, maybe just a little more there—"

"Mom, I think everything is good," Lil cut in, standing to my right and already dressed in the loveliest gossamer gown. I'd insisted on paying for the floaty lavender fabric, which is as far as my personal engagement with the planning went, and then her mom and a friend had impressively formed it into the dress it was now.

She looked absolutely beautiful.

"Well, maybe just a swipe more of lip gloss or..." Evelyn trailed off, shaking her head. "What am I saying? You look beautiful, Aster."

I smiled warmly—a rarity usually reserved for her and Lil—and said, "Thank you. Really."

Evelyn's eyes grew glassy, and she chuckled. "Don't go making me cry now. Goddess, I'm just so proud of you, honey."

"I mean it." My throat felt a little tight, but I held back any tears. "I wouldn't be here if it weren't for you. Or Lil and Raven."

"There's no need to thank me," Evelyn said gently, taking my hand. "It's what family does. They take care of each other."

I pressed my lips together to keep from crying, and Lil blew out a heavy breath and said in a thick voice, "Okay, okay, we cannot all show up with smudged mascara."

Evelyn stepped away from me and sniffled before straightening and saying, "You're right. And I think it's about time. Lil, honey, we should join the others."

I glanced at the ticking hand of the clock on the wall and took a short breath. It was almost time; a good chunk of my court was waiting out there in the throne room, just waiting to see me stumble.

I wouldn't.

I was a fighter, just as Nox had once told me. Everything that had led to this moment did not define me, even if it had changed me. Now was the time to show everyone that, no matter what they thought of me.

Evelyn pecked my cheek carefully before leaving Lil and me alone for a moment. I turned to see Lil grinning at me— just grinning.

I raised a brow. "What?" I said, hardly able to hide my own smile.

She snorted. "Asteria Fairwae, you're the worst, you

know that right? But also the best, and I love you very much."

I laughed and moved to hug her, but she stopped me and scolded, "Do not ruin all the makeup my mother just slapped on your face."

"Yes, ma'am," I said dutifully, stepping back.

Her features softened, her smile warming, and she told me, "You've got this. Really, Aster, you're going to make an amazing queen. I know you don't believe that yet, and before you say anything just know I've thought this the entire time, even when everything seemed impossible. I've always believed in you."

I met her vibrant green eyes. "I know," I said softly. "And thank you."

A knock sounded at the door, and we both turned to see Raven standing in the frame. He cleared his throat and said, "It's time."

Lil smiled at me one last time and said, "See you soon."

I snorted softly. "Right."

She pranced out of the room, leaving Raven and me alone.

His mouth twitched and he said, "You look really beautiful, Aster."

"Interesting," I teased, "I thought you preferred me in ripped tights and t-shirts?"

Raven chuckled, grinning as he stepped into the room. "Once upon a time, yeah," he said then added in a softer tone, "I know I've been kind of an ass about everything, but I really am happy for you."

I nodded. "I know, Raven." Then, I hesitated a moment before asking, "Is he here yet?"

I had sent Nox away early this morning, insisting that we needed to be careful about how we presented ourselves to my court. A Seelie palace maid finding him in my bed and starting gossip on coronation day was probably not what I needed right now. Still, I hadn't been able to convince him to stay away completely. I think he was worried that with the big crowd, Abaddon might finally make a move. But I knew that no matter what we did, the Unseelie Night King showing up at my coronation—whether next to me or not—was going to create waves and start up whispers.

Raven sighed. "I assume he and Griffin will let things settle before they make their entrance."

"Right." I took a breath. "That's probably for the best."

Raven eyed me. "It is. But I'm sure it's driving Nox crazy."

"Well, he can shove his showmanship and territorial instincts up his ass," I muttered, ignoring the tightness in my chest.

Laughing, Raven replied, "There's the Aster I know."

"Well, I should probably head that way." I steeled myself, pushing my shoulders back. "And you should go find Lil and your mom."

Raven closed the gap between us further and took my hand briefly, patting it as he told me, "Alright."

He let go and turned to leave but halted as I called after him, "And please try not to kill Bells!"

He faced me one last time and said darkly, "Don't worry. No one will touch her."

My brows rose, and I was just about to tell him *that* wasn't what I'd meant at all, but he was already gone, striding out the door and down the hall.

Aside from the two guards lingering nervously outside the room, I was alone, and I took one final moment to enjoy it before stepping out.

"Let's go, then," I said, offering the guards a sideways glance.

"As you wish, Your Majesty," they said, almost in unison.

I paused, examining their nervous faces for a moment before walking past them. I heard them fall into position just behind me as I headed past the royal wing. My path to the throne room today had been planned—detailed in a letter sent to me by Lord Jasper himself. The idiot couldn't spare another hour to meet with me in person apparently. Not that I had really wanted to see him, unless it was to demand answers I knew he would likely not give.

But true to his word, Lord Jasper's route led me down a path that steered clear of curious eyes. More guards flanked me the further I went, their steps echoing behind me as the halls grew larger and grander. Finally, when I stood in the entrance hall just outside the throne room, they paused, a near-battalion behind me.

"Whenever you are ready, Your Majesty," a guard beside me murmured.

I turned to the guards and espied a strangely familiar man. His fingers were poised on his sword, ready just in case. I gave him a single, curt nod, and he motioned to someone ahead of us, holding my gaze.

That was when I recognized him. It was Julian—the guard who had accompanied me to the Trial with Ewin.

I swallowed hard. Reliving that memory was not what I needed right now.

He must've seen it on my face, because, just before the

trumpets began to sound, he said quietly, "I am sorry, my queen. For what I could not do that day. For what I should have done."

"You don't need to apologize," I told him. "We all do awful things in the name of love."

And with that, I faced the throne room.

As I took my first step forward, everyone in the room stood. I heard hundreds of whispers around me, and I walked forward slowly, the train of my dress trailing behind me. It was the dress I knew my mother had worn to her coronation, made of rich, dark-blue fabric scattered with colored jewels down the train—it looked as though sparkling light followed in my wake. Lil's mother had painted my lips red and shadowed my eyes, making me look older, more weathered—wiser.

I felt it, too, as I walked; so much had changed in such a short time.

The music rose as I stopped in front of the raised platform where the thrones sat. Two, for a king and a queen. I tried not to think too hard about what that meant for Nox and me. Even without demons and angels involved, our relationship was already near-impossible.

A guard held out a hand to help me up, and I reached out to take it, grateful for the steadiness. When our fingers brushed, my eyes flicked to his. They were an odd shade of warm brown, almost too warm, as if light shone through the cracks of his irises, trying to escape.

Quite suddenly, I knew with everything in me that this was not a guard.

And there it was, that familiar tug of the bond in my chest; its unexpectedness took my breath away, and all I could do was stare through the façade of this guard to the incredible mind within. The idiot had glamoured himself just to be here with me at this moment, and the gesture was doing things to my heart, making my chest feel tight and warm. Despite our differences and arguments these last few weeks, this was only confirmation of what I knew very well. He loved me.

And I loved him.

Suddenly, I wished I could say it, but instead of giving into the rising tidal wave of emotion, I raised my chin slightly, letting cool indifference fall over my features. This was one of the many curses of our bond. For now, I needed to be a queen. I had to set aside everything for the court I ruled over—even him.

The 'guard's' mouth tilted slightly, and it was an effort to let go of his hand as I stepped up onto the platform.

The music lulled and the entire room fell silent. In the crowd, I saw the lords of my council standing near the front, smug looks on all their faces. I ignored them, instead focusing on the ancient looking faerie approaching me. She had silvery-gray hair pulled into a severe bun, and her skin was oddly weathered for an immortal Being. I knew in my bones that she had been around for a very, very long time. Probably even longer than Nox, which was saying something.

Her eyes flicked just behind me before she said in a low voice, "Asteria Fairwae. Kneel for your court."

By the gleam in her eye, she definitely knew Nox was there. I had no idea how, since his glamour had to be pretty freaking strong for no one else to notice it, but I knew she wasn't going to blow his cover as I knelt before her.

A young faerie girl approached from behind, holding the crown of time-frozen ivy on a pillow. The older faerie gave the girl a sly smile and a dip of her head before taking the crown into her hands. Then, she turned her attention back to me and proceeded with her speech.

Nothing could have prepared me for the way time moved in those moments that followed. Nox had given me a pretty thorough walkthrough of how he'd expected the coronation would go; I knew the ceremony would be long and I'd be forced to remain vigilant and respond throughout; but what was likely ten minutes felt like ten hours. The eyes, the responsibility, the vows, the severing of my past to make way for the future, it made the minutes hurt as they passed.

Finally, just as I feared sweat was beginning to form on my brow, my final vows began.

"Do you vow to kneel for your court and your court alone?" she asked, holding my gaze.

"I do," I replied in a surprisingly steady voice.

Her chin lifted slightly. "And do you vow to shield the Beings under your jurisdiction to the best of your ability? To take to arms if needed?"

"I do."

Narrowing her eyes, she said in a voice so quiet I wasn't sure anyone else but me heard her, "Dark times are upon us."

In the corner of my vision, I swore I saw some of the lords shift uneasily. I got the feeling that this was not supposed to be a part of the coronation speech. However, the moment passed quickly, and they all seemed to relax as the woman went on.

"I trust you will fulfill your role well," she told me before placing the crown on my head.

And just like that, I was officially queen of the Seelie Court.

An unfamiliar voice bellowed, "Kneel for Her Majesty, Queen Asteria Fairwae of the Seelie Court!"

Hundreds of figures bowed before me.

After a moment of stillness, I realized they were waiting for me to give permission to stop. And for just a few seconds, I let them stay there. I let the esteemed lords and ladies, the high-ranking businessmen, and whichever other awful people I knew my council had invited kneel for just a little longer before me. After all, these were the people who had conferred and fraternized with my uncle. Some of them probably even knew what he had done to me all those years.

After a few more tense seconds, I let my lips kick up and said, "Rise."

For just a second, I flicked my gaze to where I knew Nox stood. Approval glinted in his eyes; I had just become a wolf too. Not because of the crown on my head, I knew, but because of the power I rightfully accepted and wielded like the weapon it was.

I sat on my throne then, and the chaos that I knew always followed ceremonies such as this ensued. In the bustle of ass-kissing and honey-coated words that fell before me in the next few minutes, Nox slipped away. There one moment and gone in the next.

I swallowed just as a faerie woman with too much foundation on her face cooed, "My queen, is it true?"

I turned my attention away from the spot Nox had left empty and asked shortly, "Is what true?"

She smiled at me with too-white teeth. "Rumor has it you have a mate."

My hands tightened on the throne, whitening my knuckles. I had known this was coming but hadn't exactly figured out how I was going to deal with it.

"Yes," another faerie said in a hushed voice. "And I hear he is not Seelie."

I wondered how many times in the next few hours I would be made to confirm these oh-so startling rumors, and I was already bored of it—of their amazement, of their dross perceptions of what it meant to be Unseelie.

So, in the end, I decided to go for the shock factor.

Stepping off the dais, I rolled my eyes and said flatly, "Yes, well, I do not think anyone would mistake Nox Ether for Seelie."

Eyes all around me widened and voices faded out until one said, above all the others, "No, they would not."

From the crowd emerged the faerie woman who had crowned me. She met my gaze, and I felt my eyes bulge slightly with the recognition of her esteem, of her age and power. I recovered quickly, stiffening as she moved even closer and brushed my bangs aside, her thumb brushing against my forehead.

"Hmm." She tilted her head curiously. "Interesting."

"What's interesting?" someone asked.

The woman sighed. "Nothing you would be wise nor old enough to understand," she replied blithely, her gaze fixed on me.

"And would I?" I challenged, meeting the woman's clear gray eyes.

A brow rose, and she let her hand drop. "You merely

need to open your eyes, Asteria Fairwae. The truth is standing right in front of you. It has been for many years now."

And with that, she stepped away, threading her way through the crowd until I couldn't see her anymore. I chewed on my lip, then caught myself. I shouldn't let myself look nervous. Not now, not with so many eyes on me.

To my relief, those eyes quickly averted. Mine did too, landing on a spot at the back of the enormous throne room where three figures dominated the entryway. Nox, Griffin, and another of Nox's warriors. The latter stood closely behind Griffin, and both wore snug-fitting leathers, as if they were ready to engage in battle right here in the throne room. Nox, on the other hand, wore the traditional finery of the Unseelie Court: dark pants and boots, and a shimmering midnight tunic that showed off his biceps. He wore his crown; underneath, his hair was down, the silvery strands teasing the top of his shoulders.

"Did I miss the party?" he mused, loud enough so that his voice travelled the length of the room, his gaze landing on mine.

This time, I bit my lip to keep a smile from surfacing. Presumptuous bastard, showing up at *my* coronation and making himself a spectacle. He was so maddening and endearing all at the same time.

I straightened, striding towards the back of the room, but halfway there, Lord Jasper blocked my path, a slick smile on his face.

"Do you really think that's the best idea?" he murmured, too close to me.

I stepped away from his cloying breath and snapped, "Out of my way."

"People are watching," he said in a low voice. "Watching as their queen moves to fraternize with our enemy."

"People are watching, indeed, as you audaciously step in the way of their *queen*." I narrowed my eyes and lowered my voice. "And do you really believe that? Or are you simply trying to distract me from the real enemy?"

I saw it, the moment his jaw tightened and his mouth thinned: I'd hit a nerve. Every detail, every expression, could be a clue—another piece to this puzzle—and that tick of the jaw hinted that maybe Lord Jasper was actually in league with Abaddon. The notion had definitely crossed my mind before. But somehow, I got the feeling that wasn't quite it. I just wasn't sure what *was* yet.

"Move, now," I said coldly, lifting my chin to look down my nose at him. "Your queen commands it."

People had begun to notice our little spat by now and were staring. To refuse me would now be treason. So, I watched with satisfaction as he bowed his head and stepped out of my way.

I strode forward, seeing that Nox, Griffin, and the other warrior were still standing in the entrance. Nox's eyes were smoldering, a mix of rage and desire as I approached.

"How did it go?" he asked slyly when I stopped in front of them.

My lips twitched. "I don't know. You tell me."

Nox leaned in for just a moment and breathed, "You looked terrifying and stunning all at once, love."

A rush of euphoria pulsed through me at his words and his closeness. I *was* terrifying. I had seen it clearly in the faces of my subjects. But I had also seen awe there too. For a few moments, as I stood on that dais, I was both feared and revered.

When Nox pulled back, I ignored the heavy stares on us and said to him, "Dance with me?"

His gaze roved over me, and he nodded, taking my hand as we walked to the adjacent ballroom where feasting and revelry was already underway. Fresh flowers adorned nearly every surface they could and wine was flowing freely. The air smelled like a warm, heady spring day and most everyone reveled in it. Griffin and his associate looked a little uncomfortable as we walked further into the room, but I supposed that was because this celebration was about as Seelie as it got.

I took the lead then, pulling Nox into the middle of the ballroom as a new song began. He bowed in front of me, a glint in his eye, and I knew he was thinking of the first time we had danced to faerie music in that nightclub.

The instruments swelled, and the dance truly began.

Throughout it, we hardly touched aside from the occasional brush of our hands. That was until the tempo quickened and he lifted me up in the air, his hands steady on my waist. I lifted my arms, just slightly, like a fledgling bird. I was still finding my wings; still finding my place in all of this madness.

Nox set me back down on the shining floor of the ballroom, dipping me low, his lips practically brushing the curve of my neck as he did so. I suppressed a shiver as he pulled me back up and the music faded out.

When I looked around again, every Being in the room was watching us. Many looked disgusted, but there were also curious, half-awed looks too. I ignored them all, instead leading Nox to one of the many tables of wine and food. I took a crystal glass of blood-red liquid, just for show, and Nox did the same.

"No sign of anything?" I asked him, my eyes scanning the room.

A whisper of shadow curled around his ear as he murmured, "Nothing. Not yet at least."

My gaze shot to the shadow, already fading. "I should find Lil and Bells. Make sure the wolves of the court aren't eating them up."

Nox snorted softly. "Good luck to the wolves."

I smiled but it felt tight and difficult to maintain. "Stay here with Griffin."

"Why?" he asked, his voice edged with concern now.

I sighed softly. "One, because I can do things on my own, especially at my own coronation. And two, because Lil's parents are getting awfully close to Griffin right now."

Nox's head turned quickly to see that I was right. He nodded once and murmured, "Find me later."

His lips brushed against the slope of my cheek before he was gone, striding towards Griffin. I took the moment to slip out of the ballroom, *mostly* without notice. That was going to be a little hard to do going forward, I supposed.

I entered a somewhat quieter hall, lined with shadowed alcoves that a few couples were definitely taking advantage of right now, based on the sounds drifting out from them. I walked the length of the hall and was just about to check back in the ballroom when I nearly ran into an alarmed-looking Raven.

His broad hands shot out to steady me, and I immediately asked, "What is it?"

He let go of me and replied in a low voice, "I can't find them."

I tried to ignore the chill that ran through me at his words and tried to reason, "Well, it's a big crowd."

He nodded, dragging a hand through his hair before telling me, "I know. I just—something doesn't sit right with me. It's like I can feel that something is off..." he trailed off, rubbing his chest.

I tracked the movement before raising my gaze to his. There was no way; I knew just what he was referring to. The very same tug I felt between Nox and I so often, I felt it exactly where he rubbed his chest.

"What?" he said.

But now was not really the time. So, I cleared my throat and said, "Nothing. But you're right, we should find them. Do you have any ideas?"

He ran a hand over his face. "They're probably just with everyone else."

On a hunch, I pushed, "That feeling that something is wrong. Does it have a tether, maybe? Do you feel yourself being pulled by it? Call it heavy intuition rather than anxiety."

"I don't know..." Raven's brow furrowed, then he blinked and amended, "Yeah. Yeah, I think it does—I-I am. How did you know?"

"Because I feel it too sometimes," I replied quietly.

Raven went still. "What are you trying to say, Aster?"

I straightened. "Right now, it doesn't matter. Follow the

pull if you can. See if it has a direction. Don't question it or yourself."

He let out a heavy, doubtful breath but muttered, "Right."

A few moments passed, then he began to stride forward purposefully, and I followed him until we turned the corner into a nearly empty hall, again lined with alcoves. That was when I began to hear the whispers.

Run, run, run.

He is coming.

Promised princess.

Run.

I grabbed Raven's wrist and whispered into the impossibly colder air, "Something is wrong."

"Aster?"

We both whirled at the sound of Lil's voice coming from an alcove just to our left. For a moment, Raven and I locked gazes. A thousand things were expressed in that exchange, myriad unthinkable scenarios explored and feared.

I nodded to him, telling him I was ready, and together we approached the alcove and stepped inside. I froze when I saw Lil and Bells were both lying on the floor, very much unconscious. Bells had a split lip, as if she had fought whoever had done this, and Lil looked as though she'd been in a deep sleep for hours. An immediate confusion swarmed me—Lil couldn't have been the one who spoke just now.

"Asteria Fairwae."

I jerked, spinning to find a young girl standing in front of me. Fae, but not; there was nothing remotely human or even animalistic shining in her light eyes, and I knew immediately that this was a different kind of creature, one that came from a world beyond our own.

"Raven," I said slowly, hardly moving. "Check on Lil and Bells. Make sure they're okay."

Beside me, Raven was still, staring into the alcove with an expression so full of emotion I couldn't pin it down to one thing; anger, heartbreak, adoration, it was all there on his face as he stood motionless. And, as though to punctuate the storm of emotions written across his face, on his back were a pair of magnificent midnight-blue wings, nearly dragging against the stone floor. On the tips, talons glinted in the dim torchlight of the alcove. I had seen these wings on him before, just barely, flickering in and out of existence. Now, they were brandished for everyone to see.

Finally, he turned. Raven's green eyes were wide as I met them, and I knew, deep down, the wings had nothing to do with the danger we were in and everything to do with the limp body of my cousin lying behind us.

The young girl laughed softly, pulling my attention from the wings. "Fate," she rasped. "What a funny thing."

"What do you want?" I snapped, angling myself in front of Lil.

The girl smiled. "My master wishes to see you, princess."

"It's 'queen' now."

"Hmm," the girl mused. "Perhaps."

"We're not going with you," Raven growled as he knelt at Bell's side, a hand on hers.

The girl cocked her head at him. "That," she laughed, "is where you are wrong, Son of Warriors. I will leave within the next minute. And with me, I will either take those you love, or both of you. In the end, it's your choice."

I glanced at Raven, my decision already made. I could tell by the expression he wore that he had easily made his choice too.

There was no way Abaddon was getting his hands on Lil or Bells.

Knowingly, the girl smiled and murmured, "Let us not delay then. My master waits."

In the moments before the girl grabbed us, I pulled hard on that bond Nox and I shared, trying to convey as best I could that something was very, very wrong. And right before we were pulled away into the chasm of nothingness, I swore I felt a rush of rage and panic rush down that thread that tied us together, always.

CHAPTER 18
NOX

One moment, I was talking to some simpering idiot from the Seelie Court business district, a glass of undrunk wine in my hand, and the next my chest threatened to implode, my vision flashed red, and a warning bell of panic and nausea rang throughout out my body to tell my consciousness that something was very, very wrong. The feeling lasted only a split second, but it was enough to cause my grip on the wineglass to slip. Francine, Griffin's second in command, caught it before it could shatter across the floor.

"Nox?" Griffin's voice was low but sharp, violence already building behind the single word.

I righted myself, ignoring the odd look from the businessman as I murmured to Griffin, "When was the last time you saw Asteria?"

He shook his head. "After the dance, she was talking to Raven in the hall..."

I saw it, the moment fear entered his expression and

darkened his eyes further. I knew where his thoughts had gone. The last time Asteria and Raven had gone missing, they had been in Abaddon's clutches, and I had a terrible feeling this time was not much different.

"I felt something," I said, my eyes still tracking the crowd around us. "Down the bond. It felt like a warning."

Griffin's eyes widened incrementally. "You think she was able to alert you intentionally?"

Communication through mating bonds was another thing that had become mostly lost to time, a rarity since the last Long Night. Fear was a powerful entity, though, enough to manipulate not only the occurrence of mating bonds but also the strength of them. I had always been able to send my emotions her way at will, and I often felt hers, but never because she actively wanted me to. If she had just done what I thought she had, it was big.

It was no surprise Griffin was shocked.

"It doesn't matter right now," I told him. "Something is wrong."

Francine's attention flicked between us, listening in that eternally silent way of hers. Francine was always there when you needed her, stepping out the shadows knowing exactly what was needed. I was sure I hadn't given her an order in well-over a human lifespan.

"Go," she said calmly, like this were any other day. "I'll stay and distract the vultures."

It was a fitting name for the high-ranking members of the Seelie Court, feasting on the spoils of gossip and whis-pers in the wake of Asteria's coronation. But right now, I didn't really give a fuck about them or maintaining the neutrality we'd agreed on before coming here. So, all I did was give Francine a curt nod before slipping away from the ballroom, Griffin hot at my heels.

"Check all the rooms," Griffin said gruffly, the mask of my general of war sliding over his features and hardening them. "All the alcoves. Everywhere."

I didn't even reply, shifting into the shadows that allowed me to move more freely. Ignoring the surprised squeals from the alcoves Griffin was checking, I shifted through them unseen. By the time we made our way through the entirety of the hallway, cold panic began to set in, and it only increased as I entered the first alcove of the next hallway.

The torches had been snuffed out, so I couldn't identify the bodies at first. Instinctually I knew neither of them were Asteria's, but my apprehension grew regardless. Pulling the moonstone I had on hand from my pocket, I let myself corporealize. After a few muttered words in the Old Language, the moonstone lit up, illuminating the space before me.

Lilliana and Bells were sprawled out on the floor, the latter sporting a split lip and a fading bruise on her neck. Just as I heard Griffin stop short behind me, Lilliana stirred, muttering a characteristic "*fuck*" as she tried to sit up.

Immediately, I went to her side and said as gently as I could, "Stay still, Lilliana."

She blinked blearily up at me, though her eyes widened as she saw Bells, still unconscious, next to her. "Nox," she rasped. "Where is Aster?"

I shut my eyes briefly at the fear and panic already coating her words. Lilliana loved Asteria too, in a way that even I would never fully comprehend. There was something entirely special between the two of them. A different kind of bond, and one that was admittedly just as important as ours.

I took a deep breath, supporting her with a gentle hand to her shoulder as she sat up. "I don't know."

"Someone grabbed us and flitted us here." Her green eyes bulged as her memory returned. "Fuck!"

"But you're still in the palace," I said, furrowing my brow.

She glanced up at Griffin towering above us before muttering, "They wanted her to find us."

"Bait," Griffin spat. "And she let it work. Again."

I swept my gaze over the space. "There's no sign of a struggle here. Maybe they didn't fight."

"They?" Lilliana's voice was small.

My grip on her shoulder tightened ever so slightly as I told her, "We think your brother is with her."

"Surely not," Lilliana said in disbelief. "Why would they take Raven and leave us? That doesn't make any sense."

"I don't know, but they must have wanted it that way. If they only wanted to draw Asteria here they would only have taken you as bait, Lilliana, but Bells is here. Why?"

"For Asteria?" Griffin furrowed his brow. "More leverage is more leverage. Bells is family. More reason to come running."

"More leverage than Lilliana? No." I swallowed.

"Wait." Lilliana looked to the floor by her hand. "This is Raven's." She picked up a chain, gold and plain, and dangled it through her fingers. "Maybe they did fight."

Griffin held out his hand silently to take the chain, and Lilliana obliged.

"No," Griffin said quietly as he inspected the links. "Look at the chain. It's not broken."

"He took it off?" Lilliana grimaced at a pain in her side. "I don't understand. Why would he do that?"

In that moment, I saw in Griffin something so raw and honest I could hardly watch it. In his face was pride and gratitude for the gesture his son had left us. I too had to give it to Raven, the decision was quick and the message clear. I was indebted to him for this. Information was information, and we needed all we could get.

I looked to Lilliana and said, "To tell us he went willingly. To tell us they were okay when they left." I turned to Griffin. "What Asteria did, alerting me, she had to have been focused and aware to do it. She warned me she was in danger, but it was purposeful, calculated." I ran my fingers through my hair, everything falling into place in my mind. "It was a trade. One for each of them. Lilliana was Asteria's boon. Bell, Raven's."

Griffin scoffed. "I bet they didn't even flinch at the offer."

"Bells Raven's boon?" Lilliana stared at me dumbfounded. "That doesn't seem right to me."

Letting go of her, I stood, offering a hand. "Whatever happened, we must act upon the assumption that they have been taken. We need to find them as quickly as possible."

"Agreed," Griffin said shortly. He leaned down, picking Bells up and cradling her limp body in his arms.

"She needs a healer," Lilliana said. "I can get my mom. Besides, she should know Raven's missing again."

Griffin stiffened. "Maybe it's best not to worry her."

Lilliana took my hand, rising on shaky feet as she told

him sternly, "She can decide what she can or cannot handle."

"I understand, but—"

"You lost the privilege to help her make decisions the moment you abandoned Raven."

Griffin flinched. I knew how much the words would tear through him, as sharp and painful as any blade, but we didn't have time for this, not while Asteria and Raven had already been gone for who knew how long. Nearly a half an hour by this point.

"Lilliana, please find your mother. We'll meet you in Asteria's rooms before we go."

She squared her shoulders and replied, "Fine. But I'm going with you."

"You'll be dead weight," Griffin snapped.

Lilliana looked angry, very angry at the suggestion she was useless to them, only I knew his tone had nothing to do with her coldness a few moments ago. Griffin truly cared for her as his own; fear drove his anger now, and it would be relentless.

Regardless, she glared at him and shot back, "I don't think this is up to you."

"He's right, Lilliana," I said, trying to keep my tone even as panic threatened to overwhelm me. "Stay with your mother and Bells. Now, go."

She narrowed her eyes at me. "And who are you to order me around?"

For the tiniest moment, my age and regal arrogance reared its ugly head. I was a king, after all, but I noted with a sudden and uncharacteristic humility that I wasn't *her* king.

I pushed it aside; we were wasting time here.

"We need to find them," I said, holding her gaze. "Before they are unfindable. Before it's too late. Please, Lilliana, go."

Her throat bobbed, knowing the word 'please' was not one I used often.

"I'll be there in five minutes," she said after a moment.

Once she was gone, Griffin and I hurried towards the royal wing. But just before we left the public sector of the palace, none other than Lord Jasper stepped into our path. His expression twisted as he saw Bells, still unconscious in Griffin's arms.

"Finally," he hissed. "A reason."

"We found her like this, you waste of space," Griffin growled. "Now, move."

Lord Jasper held his position, and I prowled forward until I was towering over him. My wings flared, shadowing his face, and warmth surged all over my body. Light was rising to the surface, tingling the edges of my fingertips and illuminating my eyes.

I knew, in this moment, I was more my father than anything of this world. But I would do whatever it took to get to Asteria now, even become the monster I so hated.

"Get out of my fucking way," I said, the words coated in dark promise.

To his credit, Lord Jasper hardly flinched, though I could see some of the color drain from his face.

"You have harmed and abducted a member of the royal family," he said. "That is reason enough for war."

I didn't say anything at first, flaring my wings wider. Then, I lowered my chin so that I was nearly whispering in his ear, "If I find out you have anything to do with the fact that Asteria is missing right now, your inevitable demise will come much slower and much more unpleasantly than I had initially planned."

Pulling away, I brushed past him before he could say another word, Griffin following me. Lord Jasper didn't come after us. If he alerted the guards, we would deal with it later.

Lilliana was already waiting with Evelyn when we arrived at Asteria's chambers. To her credit, Evelyn asked no questions when she saw Bells. I wasn't sure if that was because Lilliana had explained everything or because Evelyn was simply that good at hiding her true emotions. Admittedly, it was an important trait for a skilled healer, even if suppressing her true feelings had ruined the rest of her life by keeping her away from Griffin for so long.

"Set her here," she told Griffin, indicating to the bed. "Gently."

He did as she said, and Evelyn pressed her hands to Bells' forehead, Lilliana lingering behind as she worked. When I looked at Griffin, he was staring at Evelyn, his jaw tight.

"Griffin," I said. "Raven."

His attention snapped to me and he nodded, but then said, "Where?"

I swallowed, decidedly unsure of where to even begin looking. Then, I remembered the stone in my pocket. "She sometimes carries her moonstone around," I murmured. "Not often enough, but..."

"You think we can track them through yours?" Griffin asked.

I nodded. "The stone I gave her is a twin to mine. A channel runs between them, live as long as we're both in possession of them."

"Try," Griffin ordered as Evelyn began to softly chant.

Wrapping my fingers around the stone, I shut my eyes.

In the end, it was not the stone that gave me the answer, but something that was innately a part of me as much as it was a part of her. Light flared to the surface of my skin, warming me, as if it recognized the bond too. Almost as if the magic, unrightfully granted to us by those Above, was just as much a part of our connection as the tether of our own world.

I opened my eyes and Griffin tensed as he saw the Light surrounding me; a strange, otherworldly aura.

"I know where they are."

CHAPTER 19

ASTER

Raven and I sat on a velvet couch of all places. The demon-possessed faerie had taken us to what appeared to be a fancy, if a bit gaudy, house. A crystal chandelier hung above us, illuminating the space of rich maroons and golds. In front of us, on a shining coffee table, a decanter of amber liquid sat alongside empty crystal glasses.

As soon as we'd arrived, the possessed faerie had shoved us onto the couch and ordered us to wait. As if we had any other choice.

Raven glanced sidelong at me and murmured, "This is...strange."

"I know," I breathed. "Just—"

But I cut myself off as none other than Abaddon himself entered the room, wearing a similar getup to the last time I'd seen him, though without the suit jacket this time. As he surveyed us silently, he rolled up the sleeves of his dress shirt before plopping down on the armchair across from us. Both Raven and I tensed as he leaned forward.

"Ah, relax," the demon told us. "I'm simply preparing your refreshment."

Indeed, he was now pouring generous amounts of the amber liquid into glasses, and I eyed his every movement warily.

"If you think we're drinking that, *demon*," Raven snapped, "you're insane."

Abaddon clicked his tongue. "Manners, young Raven." The glasses slid our way as Abaddon leaned back in his chair. "Drink."

My spine locked suddenly, and my hand lifted.

No. I would not be made to do things I did not want to do. Not anymore. Raven was already lifting the glass to his lips though, and mine was already grasped in my hand. Abaddon was watching me closely as I fought to resist whatever strange compulsion this was.

"I...will *not* be your...plaything...again," I gritted out, my fingers spasming as I dropped the glass. It shattered into tiny shards against the glossy hardwood floor beneath us.

I expected Abaddon to be angry or shocked, but instead he simply smirked. I was so confused by it that I didn't realize Raven was already drinking from his glass. My hand shot out, knocking it from his grasp, but it was too late. As the strange compulsion faded and Raven realized what he'd done, his cheeks colored and he rasped, "What did you—"

"A test," Abaddon said simply. "And Asteria passed with flying colors."

"A test for what?" I demanded.

Abaddon chuckled. "The truth is so close, dearest. I

know you can sense it. And soon you will see the lies you have been fed for so many years."

"Why the fuck should she trust a word that comes from your mouth?" Raven growled, standing abruptly.

With a sigh, Abaddon waved a single finger, forcing Ravan to sit. "You two," he began, "are key players in this game. One by careful choice." He leveled a look at Raven. "And one by fate," he said, his gaze flicking to me.

And despite the terrible things this creature had done to me, I somehow believed what he was saying. The words rang true somehow, as though supported by a memory that I'd long forgotten.

A call.

The demon prince must have seen it on my face because he murmured, "You're learning. See, I molded you, dearest. Regrettably, it took stoking the sickest parts of your uncle's nature to awaken what needed to be awoken."

"Regrettably?" My voice wavered slightly. "It was both of you. He said it himself."

Abaddon shrugged. "Perhaps at times. But do know, I never enjoyed what he did to you. It was simply necessary."

"Hurting someone is never necessary," I replied, my voice solemn.

He cocked his head at me. "I don't know if you truly believe that. Your bastard-blooded mate surely does not."

I swallowed. If what I sent down the bond earlier had actually reached Nox, he and Griffin would likely be here soon, thanks to the moonstone in the pocket of my gown. I'd had Lil's mom sew the pockets in especially for it. And I knew that when Nox arrived, he would spare no one to get me out. I knew why, but that didn't mean I understood it.

"Details aside," Abaddon said, leaning forward, causing Raven to stiffen. "You two are here for a reason."

"Why not just tell us?" Raven dared.

Glancing at his watch, Abaddon stood abruptly, approaching my side of the couch. Raven barked my name as Abaddon snatched my wrist, raising it to his lips. But the demon must have compelled Raven not to move because he didn't come to my aid nor move even an inch as sharp teeth grazed my skin.

"This won't hurt too badly, dearest." Abaddon smiled.

I struggled to get away from him; his grip was vice-like and he was unsurprisingly strong; but I soon realized it was a futile effort. So, instead I settled for a good old, "Fuck you."

Abaddon snorted before plunging two sharp teeth into my arm. I jerked as he drank my blood, a burning sensation spreading up my arm, similar to that from the dagger in the cave. It was over as soon as it began though, the demon releasing my arm and grinning with bloody lips.

"Keeper," he breathed, as if the word itself were oxygen.

The shock of his bite winded me, and for a moment I focused my energy entirely on breathing and ignoring the pain in my arm. Finally, I looked up, pushing away the disgust at my blood dripping down the demon's chin. "I've heard that one before," I said. "Care to actually tell me what it means?"

Abaddon leaned in close, and my body locked up in fear as he whispered in my ear, "The fates have bound you to your role, sealed by the lies of your own blood."

My breath caught, and he moved away, finally releasing Raven from the invisible hold. A large arm looped protectively around my waist, and I could feel Raven shaking behind me.

Abaddon dusted off his hands and said lightly, "Ah, well, we're done here for now."

"Like hell."

My head jerked to the side just in time to see Nox and Griffin snap into existence, both of their expressions twisted into feral rage. But what stole our attention was that my mate was slightly aglow, his irises like hot coals. As I saw it, something rose in me too, urging me to meet his power with mine. And this time, I didn't know if I could stop it.

"He's using his starlight magic," Raven muttered, more to himself than to me, and pulled his arm around me tighter.

"Raven, let go of me," I hissed.

"Aster—"

"Trust me."

He hesitated a moment longer but did as I said. I stood, the familiar heat of my power burning, melting the bars of the cage I kept it in. Nox's eyes found mine as I stood, his flaring wider.

Abaddon watched us both with mild interest before he said, "You may go, Nox Ether. We are done here."

"I'm not your fucking dog," Nox growled. "And neither is she."

Abaddon took a step closer to my mate and feral protectiveness rose in me. I was at Nox's side in an instant, stepping in front of him as Light burned the tips of my fingers.

The demon smiled. "Perhaps not," Abaddon said. "But you appear to be at her beck and call." He waved his hand flippantly. "No matter. It'll all be over soon, and know that when this world burns once more, it *will* be the end of you."

A snarl worked its way up my throat at the threat, and I quite suddenly felt the many layers of my humanity peel back, revealing a creature inside that was very much animalistic in nature. Or perhaps something else entirely. Whatever it was, it was wild.

My hand wrapped around Nox's forearm, his muscles tense under my touch, but he did not move to push me aside or take my place. He knew that I could handle myself even if he liked to play the savior sometimes, and it encouraged my fight response to intensify, my confidence blossoming.

"Raven," I heard Griffin call.

Raven, who had been standing by the couch still, rushed over, and as soon as Griffin took his hand, they disappeared.

"Time to go, love," Nox said in my ear, his voice rough. He was not feeling steady right now, that was for sure.

I held Abaddon's endless, dark gaze for a moment longer before I said, "It is."

But as we flitted away from the demon prince, I felt *myself* pushing us towards our destination. I was the one dragging us through that expanse of nothingness that lay in the spaces in between.

As soon as we landed, I stumbled back, my chest heaving. I hardly recognized where we were until I saw the tiny galley kitchen and string lights in the room around us. I had somehow flitted us to my old apartment. Nox was standing a few steps away from me, his eyes tracking my every movement.

"Asteria."

I closed the distance between us, my lips crashing into

his, and he caught me, his hand splaying low on my back. I slid my hands up his hard chest, needing to feel him, to taste him. The world turning around us was completely unsure and unknown now. But we had this. I had *him.*

Nox groaned deeply as I caught his lip between my teeth. He walked us back until I was pressed against the wall next to the front door. He pulled back and met my eyes, his own wild and dark. When they flicked down to the blood on my wrist, they flared with Light.

"He hurt you," Nox said roughly. "Again."

I didn't want to talk about the demon or what he'd done right now. "I'm fine."

"I know you have your own debts to settle." Nox pulled me closer. "But if he touches you again, he's mine. Understand? I've let him get away far too many times."

"He's powerful," I said, my grip tightening on the fabric of his tunic.

Nox smiled and it was full of beautiful cruelty. "Then I'll just have to outmaneuver him."

I didn't have words after that—didn't want them. I captured his mouth with mine, my hands roughly pulling down the clasp of his pants. He understood my unspoken words; he hiked me up against the wall, pushing up the fabric of my fancy dress. I wrapped my legs around his waist as he pushed into me, his cock stretching me until I was gasping against his mouth.

"*Fuck*, you're so perfect, love," he panted, his lips skimming mine. "You feel like...everything."

"Show me," I rasped. "Show me how I make you feel."

His lip curled and he said, "As you wish, my queen."

And then, my Fae king fucked me into abandon against

the wall of my old apartment. Just like I had wanted him to months ago, when he had first been here.

Mine. He was mine. Every nerve in my body screamed it, a rhythm and a pulse as real as his touch and the feel of him inside me. What I didn't want to admit was that the insistence was fueled not only by lust but also by fear. Something was coming for us. For him.

I would be the catalyst. I already had been.

I'd known that for a while, deep down. The coming tidal wave—whatever it was—was linked directly to me. But I couldn't bring myself to disentangle myself from Nox now. It was selfish. I *knew* that, but I didn't care.

"I need you. Stay with me," I said, my words hardly more than a breath whispered against his lips. "Always."

His breath caught, and I watched his eyes as they widened, staring at me like I was the goddess herself. Like I was more than that, even.

His hands were trembling as they gently cradled my face. "You have no idea how much you mean to me, love."

I held his gaze, understanding the need in his eyes. Not just for touch, but for the truth. He and I were so similar—children lost before we could even be found, starved of the love that was supposed to be ours by right, reaching for stars on the horizon that had always seemed untouchable.

"I'll always be here, Nox," I said, my voice steadier and louder now, so that he could not mistake the words for a heated, momentary whim.

His forehead fell against mine, and his voice was hoarse as he said, "Thank you."

I touched his face too, brushing my fingers over his cheek, and said with a wobbly smile, "I'm waiting."

He let out a shaky laugh, pulling back to meet my gaze. "You know how I feel. You have me, always. Endlessly."

"Until the end?" I whispered.

Nox didn't balk at the ominousness of my words. Instead, his expression was serious as he vowed, "Until then and long after."

I kissed him in reply, no longer trying to convey words I was too afraid to speak, but because I *could*. Because I wanted to.

He was gentler now, his hips moving at a relaxed pace as he held me close. When his hand drifted between us and I neared the edge, his head fell against my neck. He let out a strangled sound as I came, following just behind me.

We were shaking as he finally let me down from the wall, and as I smoothed my dress back down, a boyish smile graced his lips.

"What?" I said, barely concealing my own grin.

He reached out, and as he smoothed down my bangs with lithe fingers, he murmured, "You did well today, at the coronation."

"About that. We should probably get back. I'm sure everyone is freaking out."

Nox sighed. "It's highly likely, yes." He stepped back, still smiling softly. "Why here, by the way?"

"Oh." My cheeks heated. "Honestly, I have no idea. I don't even know how I did it. Flitted, I mean."

He nodded. "It was the same for me, my first time. Most people learn to flit through careful teaching, since it can be quite dangerous if done incorrectly. But for the more powerful amongst us, well, I think sometimes the magic knows what it's doing more than we even fully understand."

"So, just like that? I won't need any lessons?"

Nox snorted, extending his hand to me. "No, you'll need lessons. Instinct and power can only get you so far, love, believe me."

I deflated slightly, and he chuckled. I shoved his arm and narrowed my eyes as he tugged me to him.

"Ready?" he murmured into my hair.

"I guess so."

WHEN I COULD SEE and breathe again, I found myself back in my room at the palace. Immediately, my attention went to Bells, now sitting up, awake and talking to Lil. At the end of the bed, Raven stood, his arms crossed over his large chest and his jaw ticking. I wondered, was he having to suppress those wings on his back right now? The threat to Bells—and to us all—was still very much present. In fact, we'd just been summoned by that threat. Again.

It was quite obvious that there was more to all this than we understood. Abaddon wouldn't have let us go that easily, not unless he wanted to. But he'd also made it very clear he wanted Raven and me there, claiming we both were important pieces in this game—though I was starting to feel we were more like pawns.

This was making no sense to me.

Nox glanced sidelong at me as if reading my thoughts; maybe they were playing out plainly on my face; but before any of us could speak, there was a violent rap on the door. Everyone in the room stiffened, and I had the sudden realization that no one was as protective as mates or parents, and this room was full of them.

I walked slowly towards the door, steeling myself as I opened it and found Lord Jasper waiting on the other side.

His attention landed on Bells as she stood shakily from the bed. "Well," he said. "I hate to break up this cozy little gathering but, Your Majesty, you actually have duties to attend to. With *your* court."

Someone moved behind me, and I intrinsically knew it was Nox. Holding up a hand to stop him, I replied, "Fine. Shall we?"

Lord Jasper's smile was cold as he extended an arm for me to take, and I pushed away my disgust at his touch. He was playing a carefully crafted game here, and I was already too many steps behind to back down from the challenge.

Someday, I would rip his throat out for what he had let happen to me. Alas, today could not be that day.

"Aster," Bells rasped, a warning.

I turned and looked to her—to all of them—and said, "I'll be alright. Lord Jasper isn't wrong. I should return to the party. Stay here for now. All of you."

It was a command, one of the first I had made as queen, even if not everyone in this room fell under my rule. I looked at Nox one more time, and we entered into another of our mental sparring matches.

He gave a small shake of his head. *It's not safe. Not until we know more about what's happening.*

I raised a brow. *I don't have a choice.*

There's always a choice. His hand clenched into a fist at his side, but he let me go.

As soon as Lord Jasper and I were alone in the hall, he

said, "I still expect your Unseelie mate to hold true to his word and allow for travel between our courts."

Right. I had nearly forgotten about that in the midst of everything else.

"He will," I said coolly. "When he sees fit."

Lord Jasper's nails dug into the bare skin of my arm. "No. It will happen in three days, and we will make a spectacle of it," he said smoothly.

I suppressed the urge to dredge up my power and turn him into ash, instead asking, "Why? You seemed so reluctant to ally with the Unseelie Court before."

Lord Jasper snorted. "Of course I was. The rivalry between our courts is the way of things. But you are queen, let us see what consequences your decisions land us in."

I swallowed hard. Normally, his words felt like empty threats. But I remembered what Nox had told me, about the separation of light and dark. Maybe there was actually truth to that. Maybe not. Whatever the truth of it, it was too late now to turn back, from Nox or the decisions I had made regarding our courts.

Lord Jasper and I turned the corner out of the private wing. As we passed the faeries littering the halls, I was met with sugary smiles and whispers, and I faced each pair of lingering eyes with what I hoped was regality. When we emerged into the ballroom adjacent to the throne room, the place was alive—truly as though I'd never left. Our society was long past the wild debauchery of our forefathers, but that didn't mean the Fae didn't like a party. The lords of my council were already set up there, drinking and talking around a table set up at the head of the room. In the middle of the long wooden table, laden with glasses of wine and shining dishware, there was a large, gilded seat.

My father had sat there once. A memory caught of me perched on his lap, listening to the rumble of his voice and watching my mother smile next to him. My fifth birthday celebration, if I remembered correctly.

"Your Majesty, sit," Lord Jasper snapped, adding "please" only because of our company.

And so the rest of the evening played out. Me, a specter amongst the revelry, drowning in long-lost memory as I quietly sipped a single glass of wine and watched the Fae dance, flirt, and eat.

I was biding my time here.

When the echoes of laughter finally died down and the crowd began to thin, I announced that I was going to bed. A few of the lords at the table looked my way and murmured their regards, while others were too drunk to care. And for a fleeting moment, as I left the table and slipped out of the grand ballroom, I thought that maybe this title meant nothing. Not if I didn't have the power to truly wield it. How stark a difference it made to when I stood in that room with Abaddon only hours ago, hopped up on my own confidence.

The thought flew from my mind as I approached my bedroom door, the hall around me deathly quiet. Now, it was time to face the real monsters.

Quietly, I opened the door, stepping inside to find Nox nodding at something Bells was saying. Evelyn and Griffin were gone; Raven still kept vigil at the head of the bed; and Lil was practically sprawled across the other side of the bed, half asleep. They all looked my way as I entered, shutting the door behind me.

"How was it?" Bells asked hoarsely.

I shrugged. "Loud and boring."

She laughed softly. "Parties like that often are."

I pressed my lips together. "How are you?"

She raised her chin and replied curtly, "Fine. Your mate is quite skilled at healing."

"I know," I said, still not allowing myself to look at him fully. I didn't know if I could keep it together for long if I did.

Bells sighed quietly. "Aster, I've been thinking. I might know someone who could tell us what we're missing in all this."

My brow furrowed. "Really?"

She looked pensive, and I knew I wasn't going to like the answer.

"I think it's time we go talk to my mother."

CHAPTER 20
ASTER

I said nothing when Bells suggested we see her mother. Instead, I spent ten minutes staring at the wall —calculating.

I sat on the edge of my bed, Lil sitting just behind me, cross-legged. Raven had taken up a spot on the floor, his head leaning against the wall. Bells was sitting up against the mountain of pillows on the bed, and I could practically feel her eyes on my back. Nox was lingering near the door, his eyes flicking from me to Bells.

I had few memories of Lady Marianne Waverly, my father's cousin; only fleeting images of a well-dressed faerie woman sipping tea alongside my mother. She was a woman who hardly smiled and wore her spite for the world like armor.

An ever-growing part of me was terrified of the notion that certain truths could finally be uncovered, but we needed some clarity here. We had been spinning in circles for weeks. So, if Lady Hates The World had information we needed, there was no choice at all but to go and see her. Even if it dredged up memories of the past that I didn't want to revisit. Even if a horrible, foreboding feeling had settled over me the moment Bells had suggested it.

"Okay," I said with a deep breath. "I agree. We should go."

Everyone in the room released a breath of relief, the tension having reached heights I'd been too in my own thoughts to perceive.

Twisting, I met Bells' gaze as she nodded her head once and said, "I'll call her before I go to bed."

"Do you know," I began warily, "how much of a warning she'll need before we pop in?"

Bells gave me the ghost of a smile. "I have a feeling she'll want you to come as soon as possible. You're the new queen after all."

"What is your mother like?" Lil asked, narrowing her eyes at Bells.

Bells laughed, though it was an oddly vacant sound, especially for her. "My mother tends to flock to whoever has the most power at any given time. That currently is you, Asteria. She will likely want to know what you can provide for her with that power, though she would never say that aloud."

"Every court has people like her," Nox muttered. "As the years pass, people like that always prevail. Married to nothing but self-preservation."

Bells raised a brow. "Indeed. Though I know this from reading history books, you know that from experience, I presume?"

Nox made a low noise that Lil would probably call a

'man grunt.' But his brow was furrowed as he looked at me, concern shining in his eyes. He wouldn't be coming with Bells and me, no one would, and with what had just happened tonight I was sure the idea of that made him uncomfortable. Hell, I was a big girl, but even the idea made *me* a bit uneasy.

Bells started to scoot from the bed as she said, "I'll go and call her now."

Before she could make it very far off the bed, Raven was instantly up and moving to her side. "I'll walk you to your room," he said gruffly.

Bells snorted softly. "I'm quite capable, but thanks."

"You were hurt," Raven said flatly. "And unconsciousness. Just let me walk you to your damn room."

She paused, and puzzlement entered her expression as she looked at Raven. "Fine, then," she relented, finally. "Goodnight. And Asteria, I'll text you with her answer after I'm done talking to her."

I nodded and muttered, "Thanks."

Bells left, Raven keeping a close eye on her as they walked out into the hall together. When only Lil, Nox, and I remained, Lil said heavily, "Well, I think I need to sleep."

She did look exhausted, her eyes red-rimmed and lips pale and dry. I patted her hand and said, half-sarcastically, "Do you need me to walk you to a guest room too?"

She managed a dry laugh. "No thanks, Daddy. I think I'll be able to manage on my own."

I smiled, just barely, as she stood shakily and headed for the door too.

"Let me know what Bells says about her mom, okay?"

she said just before she left, "I'll probably be sleeping, but text me anyway."

"I will," I assured her.

She took a deep breath and left the room, the door clicking softly behind her. Nox stayed where he was by the door, and I fought the urge to call him over. Would I tell him I needed him or tell him I was fine? When it came down to it, I absolutely wasn't fine, but I had never been great at asking for help.

"Are you just going to stand there by the door all night?" I said in the end, hating myself a little for being so bad at this.

He crossed his arms over his chest. "Are you ever going to fully let your guard down around me, love? I can see it in your eyes, you know."

I bit my cheek and looked away from his unflinching stare. Soft, practiced footsteps sounded on the carpet as he walked over to the bed—assassin's footfalls —but despite how dangerous Nox could be, I had come to trust him. Truthfully, just trusting him was the least scary part. What was truly terrifying was *telling* him how much I trusted him.

And telling him just how much I cared.

What we had said hours ago in my old apartment was sacred and important in its own right. Still, I knew I'd yet to give him everything.

The mattress bowed slightly as he sat down next to me. "Planning on ignoring me and looking at the wall until Bells contacts you?"

"Very funny," I muttered.

He took a breath as if he were going to say something, but the room remained silent.

Finally, I looked at him and asked, "What is it?"

His answering smile was pained. "I'm just sorry."

"For what?"

"That you are coming to truly understand the burden of ruling. I wish…" he trailed off. "I wish so badly you did not have to know it."

"I can handle it," I said, bunching the fabric of my dress in my hands.

He lifted a hand, lightly stroking his fingers down the slope of my cheekbone as he replied, "I know. Despite how much I loathe the burden you're coming to know, I was proud of you today, Asteria. You carried yourself with a grace that many leaders fail to ever find."

Heat blossomed in my cheeks for some reason. I wasn't bashful about the way I had acted, and yet it was still new for me. Being complimented by someone like Nox, someone who had ruled successfully, summoned an odd burst of pride.

"You are allowed to feel it," he said softly, his hand now cupping my face gently. "The sense of achievement."

"That feeling has destroyed people," I said softly. "Especially rulers."

He chuckled. "Only the cold-hearted ones. And before you say anything, that could never be you. You burn, Asteria. You always have, and I dare say you always will. It's part of why I love you so much."

I stared at him. And those words I had been fighting for so long almost found their way onto my tongue. But then, my phone buzzed, and both our attention was drawn to the message Bells had just sent me.

My mother would like to speak to you as soon as possible. She claims it is a matter of urgency.

I swallowed hard before replying:

If you're feeling up to it, I say we go tomorrow.

"It'll be fine," I said, my voice uncharacteristically soft. I reached out, tangling my fingers in his hair and bowing our foreheads together.

Nox brushed his nose against mine and murmured, "I just have an odd feeling about all of this."

Bells was to flit us to her mother's estate, which was west of here. Apparently, Lady Marriane had given no indication of how long this visit would be. A part of me hoped that it wouldn't take long. The more time we spent there, the more serious the information likely would be.

"I do too," I admitted, "but I don't have much of a choice. If Bells' mother has any sort of information about—"

"I know," he said. A shadow passed over his face, a wisp of darkness curling around his ear. I couldn't hear what it said, but a general feeling of unease was communicated to me.

"Don't be afraid," I whispered. "We'll figure this all out together, alright?"

He smiled through an otherwise sad expression. "I should probably be the one comforting you right now."

Lil, Bells, and Raven wandered over from breakfast and lingered in the entryway. The look on Nox's face must have said it all: he wanted time with his mate.

"Tell me if anything seems amiss," Nox said, gently tilting my chin up towards him. "Alright?"

I sighed. "I'll be fine, Nox. Seriously."

He searched my face. "I know, love. Just...try not to take any unnecessary risks."

I smirked and winked as I muttered under my breath, "But I love taking unnecessary risks."

Nox groaned, his expression grave. "Gods, if I weren't so concerned I'd be completely turned on right now."

"My mother's estate is far from risky," Bells said airily, stepping into the room, telling us our time was up. "Don't worry. It's mostly just dull, and that includes her company."

Nox attempted a smile, the corners of his mouth twitching awkwardly, but he only communicated his agitation further.

I touched his cheek and said, "Relax. I'll see you later."

"I'm serious about the risks." His throat bobbed, but he relented, nodding, and finally stepped back. I gave Lil and Raven quick hugs before following Bells to the courtyard outside.

She glanced sidelong at me as she took my hand. "Ready?" she asked, her eyes bright in the morning sunlight.

"Why not?" I replied.

She laughed, but the sound was lost to space and time as she flitted us away from the Seelie palace. When I could breathe again, we were standing in front of an enormous house. A porch wrapped around the front and the siding was an odd, muted shade of lilac.

Beyond the house, the grounds included a small pond, a garden of stone statues, and several stone structures that extended beyond the house itself. One appeared to be a cottage of sorts, leading me to wonder if a groundskeeper lived there. The two others were small and dilapidated, a contrast to the prim, pristine beauty of the rest of the grounds.

A heron flew above us, landing in the pond, the clear, blue water rippling as it gracefully touched down. But beyond the bird and the low hum of insects, the estate was oddly still. Quiet and almost devoid of life. Suddenly, the reason for Bells' hesitance to come here made sense to me. This place was beautiful but empty.

"Home," Bells said, though there was little warmth in her tone.

I glanced at her. "It's nice."

She snorted. "Yes, well, my mother does like to keep up appearances."

And with that, she led me to the front door. Before she even knocked, it opened, revealing a faerie woman wearing a gray dress. Everything about her was faded, from the silver blonde hair to the storm cloud color of her eyes.

She avoided our gazes as she said softly, "Welcome home, Lady Bells." She curtsied low. "And it is an honor, my queen."

I grimaced. "It's nice to meet you."

She stayed in the low bow until I realized she was waiting for me, and I added, "You can stand—rise, I mean."

She did and then said, "Follow me. Lady Marrianne is waiting in the drawing room."

"Phenomenal," Bells muttered.

It was only then I noticed Bells was wearing a far less modern dress than she had upon her arrival at the Seelie Palace. This one fell past her knees and was made of thick, green fabric. Her makeup was also sparser, revealing the pallor of her cheeks and the purple tinge underneath her eyes. On the other hand, I had worn one of my nicer blouses, but still just dark jeans and lace-up boots. For a moment, I felt self-conscious—that knee-jerk response I once felt when my lack of status meant things like wardrobe and manners mattered to get what I needed—before remembering I was quite literally a queen. I could wear whatever the hell I wanted, despite who I was meeting.

The girl—a servant, I presumed—faded away into the hall as we entered a large, airy room. Fragrant tea and a plate of delicate cookies were already set up on a low table between two blue satin couches. And sitting, facing us, was Bells' mother.

She was how I remembered her: pristine. She sat with flawless posture in a high-necked azure dress, her makeup flawless and hair pulled away in a severe bun. Her thin, pale fingers were folded atop her lap, and she lifted her head from the book she had been reading as we entered.

"Asteria," she murmured.

"*Mother*," Bells said in warning, a tone of genuine surprise lacing the word. "This is our queen."

Lady Marianne ignored her daughter, instead ushering both of us over and saying, "Sit, please. And I apologize, we will have to serve ourselves today. The conversation will be too sensitive to allow others in."

As she spoke, I felt something heavy settling around the room, a metallic taste coating the back of my throat.

"You feel it, Asteria?" she asked me as she picked up a teacup. "The ward?"

I met her stern gaze, unease turning my stomach. "Does it prevent us from leaving?"

She shook her head. "No. Just others from entering and listening. You could cast one too if shown how. In fact, I'm surprised you haven't been shown already. Does your mate not want you to have the ability to protect yourself?"

"Mother—" Bells began, but Lady Marianne held up a hand.

I took a steadying breath, balling one hand into a fist. I needed to be patient here. This entire visit was a calculated move to put us ahead, and I could not risk losing the information she might provide because my temper ran too hot.

"I'm not here to talk about Nox," I said carefully. "Bells thought you might have some insight into my past."

Lady Marianne's eyes fluttered shut momentarily. I noticed that, as she set her teacup down, her hand was trembling. When she looked at us again, she directed her gaze to Bells and asked softly, "Is it worth the price?"

I glanced at Bells. She furrowed her brow and said, "I don't...Mother, I don't know what you're talking about."

Lady Marianne settled back on the couch and said solemnly, "It must be. Time is coming to a close, and I presume you are running out of options. Someone must bear the responsibility."

Unease stirred in my stomach as I waited for her to go on.

"Let us begin, then," Lady Marianne said, her gaze falling to me. "And I will tell you the tale of the daughter that Theodore and Dianna Fairwae both loved and cursed."

CHAPTER 21

NOX

"You need to relax."

I whirled, seeing Griffin approach. I was pacing in my study in the Unseelie Palace—had been for the last hour since Asteria and Bells left.

"Easy for you to say," I muttered. "We have no idea who this woman is. She could do anything."

"Asteria can handle herself," Griffin said, and I swore I heard a hint of pride in his voice. "You must be aware of that by now."

"Yes, but if it came down to herself or her cousin, you know very well who she would choose to protect first."

Griffin didn't reply, his silence answer enough. Asteria was self-sacrificing to a fault, even if her selflessness was something I loved about her.

And there it was again. That one word.

Love.

I'd let it slip again last night, and for a split second I'd thought she might finally say it back. I could be patient for as long as it took, forever if need be—if we actually had that long.

"Is Asteria being gone today the only thing bothering you right now?" Griffin asked.

Damn bastard knew me too well.

I glanced at him. I wasn't going to talk to him about my longing, my desire to hear her say those words to me. It was personal and irrelevant to the political nightmare we were currently facing. So, I summoned a different anxiety: "She's not the biggest fan of Wista," I said stiffly. "I ended up telling her why I allow her to remain in the palace."

Griffin's eyes widened. "And did you tell Asteria about the prophecy Wista made too?"

I ran a hand over my face. "No."

"Shouldn't you?"

"I don't know, Griffin." I huffed out a breath. "She's already had so much loss."

"And you want her to be blindsided when she encounters more? If the prophecy even remains true."

I leveled a look at him. "Prophecies seldom change."

He shrugged. "People like you are seldom born. We don't know how that could affect things."

I shook my head. "Don't get your hopes up."

"So, you've just accepted it, then?" he asked, holding my gaze.

I tilted my head. "Given how things are shaping up, the likelihood of my death is becoming more and more realistic as the days pass."

"That could be said for any of us," Griffin insisted.

With a heavy sigh, I brushed past him. "I'm going to the library. I need to find out more about that mark."

Griffin said nothing as I left. I knew I had upset him, though he wouldn't be quick to admit it. Neither of us were like that, especially with each other, but I simply couldn't dwell too much on it now. There just wasn't time.

In the day.

In my life.

As I entered the stacks, I reached out, brushing my fingers against the spines of worn books. I pulled a few out and brought them to one of the desks in the study arena, scouring the texts for anything about the mark I'd seen on the dream bridge, but there was nothing— nothing about a demon named Lilith, and nothing at all about any queen of hell at all. There had only ever been princes.

But there had to be more.

I returned to the stacks, wandering further towards the back where the sunlight grew sparser and the scent of paper and leather was heavy in the air. I crouched down, reaching for what appeared merely to be paper bound together with thick twine—old texts, before the leather binding of books was common—but just as my fingers skimmed the paper, a breeze touched my neck. It smelled of crackling fire and spices that I could not name. Ancient scents, lost to the centuries as they passed.

I remembered them, though.

My heart pounded, the beats resounding wildly in my ears as a low hum of energy filled the air. Slowly, I turned to see the specter of a young man before me. He appeared to stand on the ground of the library, but upon closer inspection, he hovered above it. He was dressed in a simple white shirt and dark pants, his silver hair a halo around his head.

Where his eyes should have been, there was nothing but blinding, white light.

My jaw set as I waited for him to speak.

His lips twitched, and when he finally spoke, it was both a tenor rumbling through the air and a whisper in my head. "You've become quite stoic over the years, Nox."

I swallowed, my throat paper dry. "What do you want?'

Sameul's half-smile fell, his features sharpening. "Are you not happy to see me? Much time has passed in this world since I last appeared to you."

I eyed him skeptically. "Do you not understand why I wouldn't be happy to see you? Or is that emotion too subtle for your kind?"

He raised a single brow. "Do not forget, blood of my blood, that you are of my kind too."

I scoffed like a naughty child. "How could I?"

He drifted a step closer. "It pains you, the pull between worlds, does it not?"

"My pull to this world is much stronger," I replied, refusing to back away as he stopped directly in front of me.

"Ah," he said, the word like a breath. "Yes, your mate. She is the reason I have come today."

I stiffened. "Keep her out of your meddling."

Sameul looked almost pitying for a moment. Then he said heavily, "I must go soon. But I came to give you a warning."

My pulse pounded, but I managed to reply, "How thoughtful."

He didn't react beyond narrowing his gaze ever so slightly. "The consequences of centuries of actions are finally coming to a peak. The bridge was never meant to be broken. The key never meant to be kept. There is too much imbalance, and I fear this realm will not survive it. I…"

He trailed off, and I narrowed my eyes. Nephilim were not typically the kind of creature to hesitate or shy away from the truth.

"I admit to having been a part of it all," Sameul finished. He was beginning to fade away now, becoming even less corporeal than before. "My only regret is your mother. You are right to think we do not feel emotions the way those in your world do, but I feel as close to sorrowful as you could understand it when I think of her."

And with that, he was gone, leaving only a trail of glimmering powder in his wake.

CHAPTER 22
ASTER

"Nearly three years before you were born, Asteria, your mother was told by a healer she could never have children."

I stared at Marianne as she paused, processing the words. Truthfully, I had zero idea of where this was going, and it was making me uneasy. Shifting on the stiff material of the couch, I said, "Go on."

She pressed her lips together, and I swore I saw her jaw tremble.

"Your mother was devastated, for more than one reason. She herself desperately wanted a child. But most importantly it was part of her duty as queen to continue the royal bloodline. Your father, as always, masked his true disappointment so as not to upset her, but he was greatly troubled by the news. Time passed, and he searched for a solution. None showed itself. Not until the visit."

"That makes it sound so ominous," Bells muttered.

Her mother raised a brow. "I am not being dramatic.

Dianna Fairwae claimed she was visited by an angel shrouded in light, bearing wonderful news. There was a way she could have a child. Her mistake was not asking what the price was." Lady Marianne sighed. "Still, less than a year later, you were born, Asteria. The kingdom rejoiced and so did your parents. It wasn't until I first visited you that your father told me about the dreams."

Outside, rain began to pound on the windowpanes. Fitting, I supposed, for what was starting to feel like a ghost story.

"Your father confided in me that Dianna had strange dreams while she was pregnant, ones that often left her in distress. And in the dreams, she saw the same mark—over and over again."

My stomach turned.

"Has it been presented to you?"

I swallowed. "You haven't said what the mark was yet," I replied a little defensively.

"I have not, but your face told me this means something to you, vague as it is." Lady Marianne grimaced. "They didn't know at first what it meant. When they searched old records, nothing appeared, at least nothing concrete. It wasn't until your father confided in his brother that they had a name for it. Lilith's Mark."

A shiver ran down my spine. How had Uncle Calum known of the mark? Had he already been meddling with demons at that time?

"After you were born, your mother's dreams stopped for a time. But not a year later, she began to have them again, and they became more disturbing. She saw a world burning, a figure shrouded in heavenly light from Above, an avenging angel with massive, dark wings. And that was just what your father told me. I am sure there was more. It all came to a peak a week before they died.

"Your father called me to the palace early one morning in a panic. He had begun to trust me explicitly by that point. He had no sisters and had stopped putting his faith in Calum. Besides Dianna, I was all he had of family.

"When I arrived, Dianna was half-conscious and muttering nonsense, curled up on the bed. Theodore was in a panic, claiming she had been in this state for most of the night after she had awoken screaming. I approached her, and when I was close enough, she grabbed my hand and... well, when she spoke, it was not Dianna. She made me swear on my life not to speak a word of what she was about to tell me. I did, thinking the oath empty, but the Beings of light and darkness do not play games."

Thunder boomed outside, a dramatic interlude to the confession. Beside me, Bells had gone still, staring at her mother with wide eyes. It took me a moment to realize why she looked so afraid.

Lady Marianne had sworn not to tell this story on her life.

I almost stopped her then and there, but she raised a hand before continuing.

"Dianna told me she had been deceived. It had not been an angel that had visited her that night all those years ago, but the goddess—The Maiden—and she had tricked Dianna. For once upon a time, the Maiden, Amely, had lost her entire family to that first Long Night, despite her victory as the Evening Star. But she could not rest and could not be at peace with them, as she had been cursed with an existence of duty. When she begged the Beings of Light to let her do so, they refused, claiming it was her eternal destiny to remain as she was, a servant to her realm. Ultimately, she sought her wish elsewhere, with other powerful Beings. You can imagine what I am saying."

"Demons," I whispered.

Lady Marianne nodded. "In a vision, Dianna saw the past—saw the Maiden summon a demon. Amely's mother, Lily, appeared to her, but her form was merely a disguise for a Being much more powerful. Amely's mother was, in truth, the fallen queen of Hell, wiped purposely from history and forced to live an eternal sentence on the earth plane."

Marianne settled back, the teacup still resting in her hands. "You are descended from the Maiden, Asteria. I am sure you know this by now. And what your mother realized too late was that your birth was a calculated move on Lilith's part. That mark you are dreaming of is hers. It is her way of claiming you. You are the key she created through centuries of careful maneuvering. A bridge between light and dark...between worlds. You are Lilith's revenge."

Nothing settled over me. No shock or fear. No real response to the gravity of the information I'd received. My mind was completely blank.

Bells, however, seemed completely engaged and serious as she asked sharply, "Then why on earth did the Beings of Light choose Amely or Asteria to be their warriors?"

Lady Marianne shut her eyes and said softly, "Amely was chosen by a Light warrior named Sameul to further punish Lilith. The fallen queen was cursed not to tell anyone who she truly was. He thought it would pain her to see her human daughter used as a tool for the Nephilim. I doubt he ever even dreamed the consequences of his actions."

A tool.

Amely...

Me.

We were just tools for Beings who assumed they were greater than us. Why hadn't the goddess told me all this when I died under that tree? And *should* I have died? Should I have decided not to go back? Because by doing so, I had doomed the world and everyone I loved in it.

"Mother?"

Bells' sharp voice pulled me back to reality. I looked up just in time to see the teacup slip from Lady Marianne's hand and shatter on the floor.

"Do," Lady Marianne slurred, looking only at me, "with this information what you will. But know...this Long Night will put the others to shame."

And with that, she slumped against the couch. I felt the ward around the room fall, along with something else—I felt something break. It was like that day by the dying winter flower bed with Nox. I could feel the threads of life tugging and pulling.

Lady Marianne's had just snapped.

"Bells," I whispered, glancing at her.

"She's gone, isn't she?" She was staring at her mother, stone-faced. "That's what she said, right? That this information was tied to her life?"

I shook my head slowly. "Bells, I..."

"You didn't know, Asteria," Bells said, her chest rising and falling quickly. "Neither of us could have." Her voice wobbled, but only for a moment; it was the only crack in her composure as she made a believable play of rushing out of the room and crying for help.

∾

NOT AN HOUR LATER, Lady Marianne's body was moved from the room, leaving it empty.

"You should go, Aster," Bells told me, her voice thin. "I'll need to stay here to take care of further affairs."

"Bells—"

"The information is safe with me. I vow it," she cut in, facing me.

I wrung my hands together. "Bells, I wasn't doubting that. Are you...this is just a lot. Are you alright?"

I wasn't exactly the queen of talking about emotions, but someone needed to check in with her.

Bells shifted on her feet. "This will make me sound heartless," she said in a flat voice, "but mostly I'm worried about what will be expected of me as the head of my household going forward. My father died before I was born, and now there will be roles I am going to need to fill. Different pressures. I'll probably be expected to marry promptly to ensure our bloodline continues, as I'm the only child."

"Do you want to marry?" I asked, and for a split second my mind landed on Raven.

She sighed. "No. Not now. Perhaps not ever. But I won't have much choice."

"We'll see about that," I said quietly.

She swallowed. "Aster, don't worry about me. Focus on figuring out how to save the world. Then we can worry about my upcoming nuptials."

Her words felt a bit like a slap to the face. She made the issues of the demons, Nephilim, and inevitable war sound more like a fairytale than a very real, very quickly approaching reality. But I suppose, with her mother's body growing cold in the other room and the press of her new responsibilities, maybe she just didn't have the capacity to think about those things right now.

I took a step back, keeping my emotions in check, and said, "Alright, Bells. I'll keep you informed."

"Do," she said softly. Then, after a beat, she added, "I'm sorry, Aster."

It took me a moment to realize what she was apologizing for—the truth her mother had revealed after so many years of hiding it.

I only shook my head and lied, "I'll be fine."

She nodded, accepting the falseness of my words. "Will you call Nox or Griffin to have them flit you back to one of the palaces?"

"Of course," I replied.

She sighed heavily, then pulled me into a gentle hug before letting me go. I turned and left her in the mess I had unknowingly created for her. I suppose that's what I did to people—walked into their lives and created chaos.

After that, I didn't call anyone. Instead, I walked the grounds of the estate in the rain for what felt like hours. I always seemed to end up like this, alone and in the rain when reality became too much. But I couldn't go back, not yet. I couldn't see the hope on their faces fade as they realized I was the catalyst and the reaper in all of this. That I *was* the answer to the riddle we had been searching for—and I needed to be eradicated in order for the world to survive.

I didn't see any other way.

I had been a pawn before I had even come into existence. Nothing but a chess piece in this game of gods, angels, and demons.

The rain picked up, and I shivered. My phone buzzed in my pocket, and I ignored it. I knew I should get back, but I wasn't going to call anyone.

I would do this myself. And if it accidentally killed me, well, problem solved.

I closed my eyes and breathed deeply, feeling the rain on my skin and imagining home. It wasn't exactly a physical place that I saw in my mind. It was Lil laughing and Raven grumbling. Even Griffin, yelling at me to do another lap. And Nox.

Always Nox.

A rip in time opened, and I stepped inside, feeling the air cut off from my lungs. For a moment, I flailed, forgetting where I was or where I was supposed to be going. My lungs seized, but at the last moment before my vision began to fade, I grasped onto a line—a string connecting me and someone else. A moment later, I was flung from the darkness, landing on the floor, sputtering.

"I did it," I muttered to myself between heaving breaths. "Again."

Strong arms encircled me without warning, and I leaned into them. I didn't even need to look to make sure it was him. But when I felt him trembling, I glanced up to see his eyes ablaze, quite literally.

"Nox," I said, touching the sharp planes of his face. "Chill."

"Chill? You do realize how entirely reckless that was?

You've flitted once before this—once—and you were with me. If something had gone wrong this time, nothing could have been done."

"I was fine," I said flatly.

His brow creased, the light in his eyes dimming. "What happened? Where is your cousin?"

I looked around, realizing I was in his bedroom in the Unseelie palace. Then, I took a shuddering breath and said, "She stayed back to deal with the affairs."

He cocked his head. "Affairs?"

"Lady Marianne is—dead," I choked out the last word. "There was a binding spell of sorts tied to the information she told us. She must have decided it was worth it; it became obvious she was aware of it."

Nox held my gaze. "What did she tell you?"

I looked away for a moment. Would he hate me after hearing who and what I truly was? The descendant of a demon, with the soul of her half-blooded daughter. And not just any demon, the lost queen of Hell. I was Lilith's revenge on the world. The key she would use to rip the seams of our realm apart and send our world into chaos like never before. Perhaps she even wanted to use me to reach the Beings who dwelled Above. Maybe my purpose was far more terrible and greater than I could even imagine.

But I knew deep down Nox wouldn't care. We were both too entwined at this point to even see logic. Logic was love's bitch.

And so, I looked my mate in the eye and relayed what Lady Marianne had told us, starting with my mother and the 'angel' that had appeared to her. Nox didn't move from the floor as I spoke, and I didn't try to either. When I told him about Sameul's involvement in all of it, his hands tightened on my arms where he was holding me. But otherwise, his expression did little to betray what he thought of all of it.

By the time I finished, I was shaking and my stomach was churning. Nox ran his fingers absentmindedly down my arm, his expression still blank.

When I couldn't take the silence anymore, I prodded, "Nox?"

His eyes flicked to mine, but he said nothing.

"What are you thinking?"

His jaw tightened. "I am thinking," he began, "I'm thinking how afraid I am that you are going to do something reckless and self-sacrificing now."

I stiffened. He wasn't exactly *wrong*. I had been thinking that this could all be solved with me out of the equation.

"I thought so," he murmured, his eyes roving over me.

Lowering my chin I said sharply, "It's not as if it isn't the obvious solution. Don't act as if it didn't cross your mind too."

He went still, his muscles taut under my touch, and when he looked at me again, there were sparks of starlight in his eyes once more. "It didn't," he growled. "Because it isn't an option. You are not dispensable, and it would not make you a hero—"

"I'm not looking to be a hero!" I exclaimed, pulling away from him. "I just want the people I love to be alive! To be happy and safe, for once."

His eyes flickered, and I wondered if I knew why. If it was because he questioned whether that one little word included him.

But as always, he didn't push, instead saying quietly,

"Your death would not make anyone happy, Asteria. It didn't before, and it won't now. And besides, I have every intention of leaving this world when you do."

Shock coursed through me at his words, said so starkly and plainly. I stared at him, wide-eyed, and whispered, "Don't say that."

He shook his head. "I've lived a long time, love—"

"And you can live a long time more," I cut in. "You can't bind yourself to me like that. It isn't fair."

"You talk of your death as if you're already planning it," he said, his brow creasing.

I looked away. "Whether I choose it or not, the likelihood that I'll survive this war isn't high."

"You could say that about either of us."

I said nothing in reply. We were both still sitting on the floor, but he stood and moved towards me. Wordlessly, he scooped me up into his arms. I didn't fight it. I didn't want to. I wanted comfort now, even if I didn't deserve it.

"Where is everyone else?" I muttered against his chest. "We need to tell them what happened."

"At your palace," Nox said, his voice rumbling against me. "But they can wait a moment longer."

He sat down on the bed, still holding me. I peered up at him and whispered, "I don't know what to do."

"We'll just stick to the plan," he said. "Finding a way to help the possessed faeries. Readying for the demon's attack. Joining our courts, as your advisors requested."

I shut my eyes. I had forgotten about my stupid council and the fact that we were going to have to appear as a spectacle before them in just two days.

"Do you really want to do it?" I asked, not looking at him. "Open travel between our courts?"

Nox's chest rose and fell in a sigh. "Honestly, love, it's the least of my concerns at the moment. If it keeps the vultures at bay for a little longer, I'm fine with it."

"Right," I muttered. "We should get back. Raven, he'll be worried about Bells."

Nox was silent for a moment, before he asked, "Do you sense it, between them?"

I sighed. "I didn't tell you this in the aftermath of everything, but I saw Raven's wings when he saw Bells unconscious."

"Does she know?" Nox asked, his voice quiet.

"No. But she should."

He shifted so that I was forced to look at him as he said, "Should she? Sometimes I wonder if you would rather have not known we are mated."

The words stung like a cold slap. "Why?" I whispered.

His hands were gentle as they cupped my face. "I don't regret a second of it," he said. "But I cannot help sometimes feeling as though I brought all this upon you the moment I showed you my wings."

I rolled my eyes. "Don't give yourself that much credit, Nox. I've been in a mess my entire life. You showing up only opened doors that I would have been shoved into at some point anyways."

His thumb brushed across my mouth, and I stiffened.

His brow creased. "What is it?"

"I thought there would be at least some part of you that would be a little disgusted at what I am."

He stilled, his expression momentarily blank. Then, he

traced my lips once more, his gaze growing heavy as he said in an oddly restrained voice, "Never."

"I'm descended from the lost queen of Hell."

"Yes."

"A demon."

"I know."

I pressed a hand to his chest. "Nox. It seriously doesn't bother you?"

His heartbeat was a drumroll against my fingertips as he leaned in and breathed, "I don't know if you quite understand, love. You have me completely. You could ask me to burn the world to ashes and I would do it."

My breath caught, and I whispered, "I wouldn't want that. If something happened and I became corrupt or even possessed, I would want you to just end it before I—"

He cut me off with a searing, desperate kiss. The press of his mouth was almost angry, but he never hurt me.

Between kisses, he whispered, "Never. You—I could never."

Despite the day and despite all my fear, a low curl of heat bloomed in my belly. I didn't just need to feel grounded —I needed *him*. Too often these moments between us felt stolen, and I was sick of it. I wanted to *take* a moment. To stop time and carve a fucking hole in the wall of all these Beings' plans for us.

I pushed him back so he was leaning against the headboard as I straddled him. His fingers traced the curve of my hips as I began to move them, already feeling his cock rock-hard beneath me. As I ground against him, he lifted his hips to meet mine, his mouth moving to my neck, sucking and licking. I rolled my hips again, and he groaned, one hand diving clean under the hem of my shirt. His hand moved to a hard nipple, and a gasp escaped me as he brushed calloused fingers against it.

"Nox."

"What, love?"

I practically ripped my shirt off and ordered, "Stop teasing. Not now."

His eyes blazed, and he flipped me over so I was lying flat against the mattress. His lips brushed across the dips and curves of my torso as he murmured, "As you wish."

"You're still—"

There was no time to respond as he shoved down my pants and parted me with his fingers. He groaned as he discovered how wet I already was and tugged my pants and underwear completely off, spreading my legs.

"I'm not going to take this slow," he murmured against the soft skin of my thigh as he glanced up at me.

"Don't," I replied.

His answering smile was all devious faerie king. I knew that being half-Unseelie meant his very being craved moments like this, whispered oaths against skin in the dark and hot seduction. It was in his nature, and I was beginning to feel like it was in mine too.

He dipped two fingers inside of me, curling them the moment he sucked on my clit. I cried out, my back arching and my hands grasping the quilt. He pulled back a moment as he began to pump his fingers in and out. Then, as my mouth opened to plead for more, his finger circled just the right spot.

It was all I needed.

I shattered. The world shattered. My vision fractured into beams of starlight, and my body soared.

He hardly gave me time to come back down to earth before he leaned over me and rasped in my ear, "Are you ready, love?"

I hardly had the wherewithal to nod before he pushed into me, slowly filling me. I lifted my hips up, desperate for more, but he rasped, "Patience, my star."

My lips brushing his, I said, "We don't have much time."

He tilted my head back, trailing his mouth across the curve of my neck as he murmured, "Perhaps not. But right now, we'll make time."

I felt the prick of his sharp canines brush my skin, the same moment he snapped his hips against mine. Digging my fingers into his back, any words I might have said were lost to me. Soon, we were both lost in the abandon of it, the world and its worries fading away. My vision was reduced to him and the only sensations that mattered were the feeling of him inside of me and of his hands on me.

His body stiffened and he gasped, "Asteria."

I only kissed him and moved my hips in encouragement. Wings flared from his back, and his body shook as he came, a mix of groans and nonsense that was mostly my name escaping his mouth.

When he finally stilled, we were both wrapped in the cocoon of those wings. I reached up, and he didn't stop me as I gently dragged my fingers across one. A shudder ran through his body, and I took a deep breath.

"What is it?" he asked.

I forced myself to look at him, even as my heartbeat kicked up. "Nox?" I whispered.

His gaze was steady. "Yes, love?"

I paused. I knew what I wanted to say. But I was so damn *afraid*. It was my life; it was the way the people I loved tended to leave; it was the mess we were in, and the fact that anyone could be torn away from me now.

It was me—my mounting fear of who and what I was.

But we could be running out of time. And I needed to say this. I was sure of that.

So, I looked him in the eye, my heartbeat speeding up as I said softly, "I love you."

A faint smile played at Nox's lips. And for a moment, that was all I got. Then, the smile broke into a full grin, and his eyes shone with unshed tears. He reached out, cradling my face. I didn't even realize I was shaking until he touched me. And for the breath of a moment, my lungs ached with anxiety. What if, despite his sharing of the words, my admission was too much? Too soon or too late?

"Thank you," he breathed, his own hand trembling as he swept a stray tear falling down my cheek.

I felt my eyes widen of their own accord, hardly in control of my own movements or even feelings. Too many emotions were barreling through me, mixing and twisting in my stomach. Hope and love, and just the slightest hint of fear because so few had wanted to stay in my life. Deep down, I knew there was nothing to be afraid of. But I had to make sure.

"Does that mean you..." I took a deep breath, my breath uneven. "It's just, typically, in these types of situations, the other person responds with—"

He chuckled softly, cutting me off.

I adjusted so I was looking at him, demanding, "What could possibly be funny right now?"

He smiled widely and my heart ached a little at the sight of it.

"I love you too, Asteria," he said, twisting a strand of my hair in his fingers.

I raised a brow, taking a shaking breath as I said, "Now, that's more like it."

His smile softened, then he shifted, standing as he said, "Wait here just a moment."

"Nox, we need to go soon."

He turned. "I know. This won't take long."

I sighed, pulling the sheets up over my chest. To his word, he returned shortly, pants slung low on his narrow hips. He sat back down on the bed, and I pushed up onto my elbows.

"Well?" I prodded.

He chuckled. "So impatient."

Then, he opened his palm. My breath caught as I saw what was in his hand.

It was a ring set with a delicate amethyst stone.

"Nox..." I began. "We can't—"

"I'm not asking you to marry me," he said, smiling. "Well, not exactly, at least. I just want you to carry it with you until you're ready. It was always meant to be yours anyway."

I raised my gaze, meeting his eyes. "This was your mother's, wasn't it?"

He swallowed, then nodded once. "She wore it on her right hand. Her wedding band was on the left, of course, but I think this was the ring she meant for my father. Anyways, she always told me when I found my mate, it would be theirs."

"*When*," I whispered. "She expected it?"

Nox's answering smile was sad. "As I've told you, mates were much more common at that time. And I suppose the shadows may have whispered to her too."

"Did they whisper to you about me?"

He nodded. "All the time."

"Still?"

"Still."

I wanted to ask what they said, but we really did need to go. So, instead, I said, "Do you have a chain? So, I can wear the ring around my neck."

Nox nodded and slipped off the bed. He returned with a delicate silver chain, looping it through the ring. "Turn around," he murmured.

I did so, sweeping my hair over my shoulder. He clasped the chain around my neck, and I felt the weight of the ring on my chest. When I faced Nox again, he seemed to hesitate before saying, "There is something else too."

My stomach dipped. "What do you mean?"

My phone began to buzz on the floor where I'd left it. I met Nox's eyes, and he said, "You should probably take it."

I pressed my lips together, frustrated at the interruption, but picked up the call.

"Hey Lil—"

"Where are you and Bells? And where is Nox?"

I took a breath, then told her, "I'm with Nox. We'll head back to the palace in a sec. And Bells is still at the estate."

"Why?"

"I'll explain when we get there."

She sighed into the phone. "Good. Raven is freaking out for goddess-knows what reason, so please hurry."

"We will. I'll see you soon."

I cut the call and glanced back at Nox. "We should go. Can what you wanted to tell me wait?"

He looked a little pained as he said, "It can wait."

I held his gaze for a moment. "Alright."

A feeling of foreboding settled over me as I looked at him. And I wasn't sure if it was because of the looming threats on the horizon or whatever it was he'd yet to explain to me. Ultimately, I let it go for now; even if I wasn't thrilled about the prospect of more secrets between us, there were more important things going on.

We would take this one secret at a time.

CHAPTER 23

ASTER

We flitted back to the Seelie palace just as the sun set. Avoiding the lords of my council and the courtiers, Nox and I walked straight to my room, where Raven and Lil were waiting.

"Where is she?" Raven immediately asked, twisting to face us as I opened the door.

Lil put a hand on his arm, but he shook her off, staring at me with wild eyes.

"She's safe, Raven," I said quietly. "But I don't know when she's coming back."

His brow furrowed. "What happened?"

Deciding not to ease into things, I simply said, "Bells' mother is dead. It was the cost of the information she shared with us today."

Lil's green eyes were wide as she whispered, "What the fuck?"

"Indeed," Nox muttered behind me.

"Is no one going to make sure she's alright?" Raven asked, his body still tense as he stood a few feet from me.

"She wanted—had to stay back at her family's estate," I told him, adding a tad more softly, "It was her choice, Raven."

"But—"

"Raven," Lil snapped. "Bells will be fine. Let Aster tell us what Lady Marianne told them."

Raven peered at Nox, his expression almost pleading, but Nox shook his head slightly as if to say, *Not yet.*

Nox knew all about waiting and holding back, and while he understood the primal instinct of a bond, its intrusive potency, it was sometimes best ignored—now was not the time to go to Bells.

Raven would have to learn to resist that urge many, *many* times.

Lil glanced at me, and I mouthed, *'I'll explain. Later.'*

Raven relented, relaxing his posture and folding his arms as he leant against the wall. "Okay, so, what happened?"

"What Marianne told us…" My voice drifted off, and I suddenly realized I was shaking. "You might despise me," I whispered.

Lil raised a brow. "I assume you told Nox already, and he's still here? Are you really thinking our reactions would be any different?"

I wanted to say no, but Nox understood it in a way neither Lil nor Raven could. Maybe even in a way no one in this realm could. We were half-children of other worlds, blessed—or rather, cursed—by Beings that were much more powerful than anyone here. I had worried his reaction would be negative, but I didn't expect him to be afraid in the same way Lil and Raven might be. Still, they deserved to know the truth, to be given the chance to stick around like they had all these years for me.

I sat down on the floor and told them everything, looking at my hands the entire time I spoke. When I finished, silence fell over the bedroom. I could feel Nox lingering behind me, but I dared not look; by the way the shadows were falling, I thought his wings might be out.

Finally, Lil snorted and said, "That's it? You thought we would be what...scared?"

I looked up. "I guess."

She laughed. "Aster, I love you, but please don't be stupid. I've seen you do some scary shit, the most terrifying involving *way* too many shots and Professor Hendricks from second year—"

"Um, okay." I cut her off quickly. "We do not need to relive *that*."

She grinned. "See? You might have super-scary magic power, but it will never top the wild university years."

Relief softened me a little, and it gave me the courage to lift my chin, to stop averting my gaze.

I looked to Raven to find him smiling. "Man, I knew lots of things, but I did not know about that story."

I rolled my burning eyes. "It isn't important now," I muttered.

Raven sighed and knelt down in front of me, holding out a broad hand. I took it as he said, "We're not saying this doesn't change things or that it isn't important. But to us, you'll always just be Aster. Stupidly reckless, wild, amazing, Aster. Okay?"

I couldn't help the tears that rolled down my cheeks as I nodded. Raven brushed them away before moving away and standing tall again.

A sharp rap sounded on the door.

I was immediately on my feet, wiping away the last of the tears from my face and striding to the door.

Nox's wings flared, and he said sharply, "Asteria, wait."

I paused, looking back at him just as I heard none other than Lord Jasper speak from the other side of the door. "Your presence is required."

Nox brushed past me, and before I could stop him, he opened the door. In the blink of an eye, he had Lord Jasper gasping and pinned against the wall.

"Give me one good reason not to rip your throat out right now," Nox ground out.

Lord Jasper's cold gaze found mine and he rasped, "I just heard that Lady Marianne Waverly has passed. How tragic."

Nox's wings swept out wide, nearly blocking my view of the lord.

"You knew," he snarled, "and you chose to remain silent at the cost of another."

"Why...why should I have sacrificed myself for the information *you* so desperately desired," he said, struggling for air, "when there was someone else so willing to die for it? She knew what she was doing. We all took the vow."

"All?" Raven echoed.

"Nox." My voice was clear as it rang out. "Step away from him."

Nox looked back at me, still pinning Lord Jasper to the wall. "You're sure?"

I nodded. "Release him. For now."

Nox let him go, and Lord Jasper took a heavy, gasping breath. His face was still all harsh cruelty as he panted, "Good. You're learning."

I took a step towards him. Then, I said flatly, "We'll endure the spectacle you and the other lords demand. We'll 'unite' the courts. And then, you'll be removed from your place on my council, along with most of the others."

Lord Jasper sneered. "And who will you replace us with? Your inexperienced, unsavory band of friends?"

I shrugged. "I don't know yet. But at least I won't have to deal with griping old men constantly trying to stab me in the back."

Then, I witnessed a delightful rarity: a true flash of anger on Lord Jasper's face.

Nox angled himself in front of me as the lord took a step forward. "If you even attempt to touch her," Nox said, "you're dead."

Lord Jasper stiffened. We all knew Nox meant what he said and was very capable of carrying it out.

"You'll regret this," Lord Jasper finally said, backing away.

I rolled my eyes. "I have bigger problems than you. Go run off and scheme while you still can." I smiled cruelly. "Thanks to the courage of Lady Marianne, you are officially useless to me."

He gave me one last glare before turning and swiftly striding down the hall.

When he was gone, Lil let out a breath and muttered, "Jeez."

Nox ignored her comment and turned to me, saying, "There are things I need to do, to prepare for opening a channel of travel between our courts. I'll need to return to my palace to do so."

I took a deep breath and replied, "Then go. I should stay here, for now."

His brow creased. "You're sure?"

"I'll be fine."

He didn't look convinced. Still, he sighed heavily and said to all of us, "Stick together. I'll be back tomorrow evening."

Raven gave him a curt nod, and Lil put both her thumbs up. I turned away, but not before Nox caught my hand. I let him pull me closer as he said quietly, "I don't like this. Leaving right now."

"I can handle myself. Besides, it's just one night."

His jaw tensed. "I know."

"Go," I whispered, placing a hand on his cheek. "Seriously, we're good here."

He sighed again, his chest expanding. Then, for the briefest of moments, he pressed his lips to mine before flitting away, right out of my arms.

When he was gone, Lil shook her head and said, "He's always gotta be so damn dramatic, doesn't he?"

"I understand it now," Raven said quietly.

Lil shot a look at him. "What on earth is going on with you?"

He glanced at me as he said, "Do you want to tell her?"

"Tell me what?" Lil demanded.

I strode over to the bed, flopping down, truly exhausted. Into the pillows, I mumbled, "It's your deal, Raven. Your turn to be dramatic."

He grunted, a manly, discontented noise I heard from

him so often these days, before he said, "Aster's cousin, Bells—"

"Yeah, dummy, I know who she is," Lil cut in. "You didn't need to preface it...she was just here."

"Just, shut up for a second," Raven grumbled.

"Why, yes, of course," Lil cooed.

"Lil," I mumbled, already half-asleep. "You should let him say this."

She sighed. "Fine. Go ahead."

There was a pause before Raven blurted out, "She's my mate."

Lil didn't say anything at first. Then, she let out a sound somewhere between a cackle and a shriek before shouting, "You have *got* to be kidding me!"

I REACHED my hand out across the dream bridge. Shadows swirled into a form, and Nox appeared a moment later.

"Are we alone?" I asked, my voice echoing through the space between us.

His shadows surrounded and caressed me, almost affectionately. "I think so," they whispered.

I took a step closer, pure light bleeding into the swirling darkness that made him up. It was so odd, the way we appeared here. He was the son of a Light warrior, yet he appeared in the shadows. And me, a child of darkness, wreathed in starlight. We were day and night bleeding together in those few stolen moments that dawn provided. Maybe the converse nature of our beings was both what linked us together and what would ultimately try to tear us apart.

"The shadows say you're worried," Nox said.

I watched as one twirled around my finger. "Can you feel it?" I replied before I knew what I was saying. "There's something on the horizon."

The shadows quickened around me, whispering.

"Yes."

"Yes."

"She sees it."

"She knows."

"You hear them?"

I looked up. "I do."

The ring around my neck floated in front of me, the stone slightly aglow. Light flared, and an unfamiliar, deep voice spoke my name.

I DIDN'T HEAR from Nox for most of the next day. I tried not to worry, but with the distant memory of that odd voice from the dream, unease stirred low in my gut. By four in the afternoon, I was pacing in my room. Lil and Raven had tried to come in earlier, but I'd told them I needed time to think. Mostly, I just didn't want to worry them any more than they likely already were.

At six, I finally texted Nox. And not five minutes later, there was a knock at my door. Quickly, I strode over and opened it. To my surprise, I found Griffin standing there.

"You shouldn't be so trusting. I could have been anyone."

I took a short breath. "Where is he?"

Griffin grimaced. "He sent me here to tell you things are taking more time than anticipated. But that he'll be here before dawn."

I tried to hide the disappointment. Apparently not well enough, because Griffin added, "Sorry."

"It's fine," I muttered. "You can go."

When he didn't move, I raised a brow.

"He asked me to stay with you."

"Um, why?"

He shrugged awkwardly. "I don't know."

I narrowed my eyes. "You're not a very good liar, Griffin."

Stepping into the room and shutting the door behind him, he sighed heavily and said, "He mentioned something about your dream bridge. Someone else was there."

My attention piqued. "Do you know who it was? Did he say?"

Griffin looked uncomfortable, shifting on his feet as he said, "He alluded."

"And?"

Griffin stared at me, then said, "If I tell you, will you promise to stay put for now? I'd rather not chase you across court lines at the moment."

"No promises," I said slowly.

"I'm serious." He looked away and sighed as if already regretting his decision. "The Light warrior gave Nox a visit the day you went to see your father's cousin."

"You mean he saw his father?" I asked, feeling my own eyes widen.

Griffin nodded, meeting my gaze. "He seemed to think that's the voice you both heard last night."

I nodded once, then slowly made my way to the bed, sitting down.

"Asteria?" Griffin said as he approached me, his brow furrowed.

I glanced up at him. "It's just a lot. I understand why he didn't tell me right away—I had my own shit to share."

"Right," Griffin said. "Do you need...anything that I can offer?"

I smiled, but it felt forced. "I think I just want to sleep. Raven and Lil are in the room just across the hall if you want to hang out with them."

Griffin shook his head. "Only if you want me to. Otherwise, if you're comfortable with it, I'll watch over you while you sleep."

"Careful, you'll make yourself sound creepy," I said in a half-assed attempt at a joke. Goddess, I was so, so tired.

Griffin saw past my charade though and replied, "Just think of me as a guard. I'll sit over there and read until he gets here."

"Overprotective faeries," I muttered, even as I closed my eyes and collapsed against the pillows.

When I awoke again, Griffin was gone and Nox was curled around me, his breathing even. Even in sleep, his wings were visible.

"Nox?" I whispered.

His arms tightened. "What is it?" he breathed into my hair.

"I'm afraid."

The words were so simple, whispered into the dark of the bedroom, but we both knew it was monumental for me to admit them.

"I am too," he finally said, after a few seconds had passed.

"I think something is going to happen tomorrow."

His answering silence told me all I needed to know. He felt it too.

But for the rest of the night, we didn't say anything else. Neither of us slept; I was too afraid of what dreams would bring. Instead, he held me tightly, and I counted his heartbeats as if they were my own.

CHAPTER 24

NOX

Early in the morning, when the sun was still barely up, a knock sounded on the bedroom door. From the moment my eyes opened, my senses were on high alert, my body rigid with anticipation.

"It's fine. I think it's just Lil," Asteria murmured at my side, her hand softly cupping my stiff shoulder. "She said she would give me a warning before they all come in."

"Who?"

She glanced at me. Her eyes were dim and tired with sleeplessness. I couldn't help but think that I had done that. But truly, I hadn't been able to return until late in the night. I had been putting off rearranging magic channels in the Veil to allow for monitored travel, and if the spectacle was to occur today, it had to be done.

"Just the maids," she said, yawning softly. "To help make me look pretty or whatever."

I paused. It wasn't that I didn't trust Seelie Fae at all, it was only that any of those maids could be possessed by a demon. Then again, I could say the same about anyone in my court. My mind wandered to the possessed faeries still locked away beneath my palace, and my chest tightened. Though we had no choice but to keep them there, it still pained me. I knew some of them personally.

"If anything happens, I can handle it," she said with a confidence that almost made me feel better, the hesitation within me clearly obvious to her. "Besides, don't you need to get ready too?"

"I suppose," I muttered, slipping off the bed.

She caught my wrist. "This is for the best, for now. Besides, maybe it'll actually be a good thing?"

If this had been completely her decision, I wouldn't have second-guessed it, but I was certain the lords of her council still had ulterior motives. And despite what she had said to Lord Jasper about taking him and others off the council, this move would make that more difficult. It would make people in the Seelie Court trust the lords more fully and strengthen connections to business partners, both savory and unsavory. If she pulled away from them now, things could become even more dangerous for her.

But she didn't need me putting doubts in her mind right at this moment; everything was already in motion; so, I nodded and said softly, "Perhaps, love."

Her brow creased, and she looked as though she wished to respond, but the knocking grew louder. She sighed and walked over, opening the door to reveal Lilliana.

"Sorry, but they're going to be here any second," Lilliana said brightly. "Good morning!"

"You are seriously messed up for being like this in the mornings."

"In the morning, anything is possible!" She turned to me with a forced smile and said, "Shoo. I'll see you in a few hours."

I didn't want to leave. That foreboding feeling was strengthening by the second, and my feet had planted themselves so firmly it was as though my shadows conspired to root them to the ground for good.

"Nox," she said, her voice a shade quieter.

Taking a deep breath, I strode over to where she stood by the door. Instinct had me pressing my lips to hers, my hand tangling in her hair.

She clung to me for a moment before pushing me away and muttering, "It's fine. Go."

But as I let her go, she stumbled. "What's wrong?" I demanded, gently grabbing her arm to keep her from falling. Alarm bells went off at her sudden unsteadiness. This would not be the first time she'd fainted under circumstances beyond their control.

"Woah," Lil said, her brow furrowing.

"I'm fine," Asteria muttered, her voice thin.

"You can call it off if you're not feeling well," Lil said, her voice sharper than usual. "Seriously, Aster, you don't look—"

"I have to." Asteria gave a half-attempt at rolling her eyes, but I could see the barely concealed pain in her eyes. "Stop it, both of you. It's probably just nerves."

Without looking away from her, I said, "Lilliana, please give us a moment."

She cleared her throat and said tentatively, "I'll be just outside."

Once she was gone, I turned back to Asteria. "What are you feeling?"

Asteria's eyes fluttered shut. "It's probably nothing."

"It's not."

"And you're so sure?"

"Yes."

She opened her eyes again. "You feel it too, then?"

Her hand was ice-cold as I took it in mine again and said, "I feel something. Something I've felt before."

"Which is?"

Something was amiss, a low hum vibrating through the air, one that I'd come to recognize as signaling a presence that was *other*. It was the sort of energy that sounded alarms in the mind of anything close to human. "I believe a demon is near. Or coming soon."

She stiffened. "Well, there are probably possessed faeries around somewhere."

"I believe this is more than that. And I think you know that, or at least sense it?"

Looking away, she muttered, "On today of all fucking days."

"Lilliana is right. We can call this off."

When Asteria looked back at me, her expression had shifted; a hardened, albeit begrudging, queen stared back at me, a ruler willing to do whatever it took.

"No," she said. "It has to be today."

She slipped her hand from mine, swaying again as she did so. And again, I caught her.

"Asteria," I rasped, every instinct in me screaming to take her to safety. Away from whatever was coming.

"Don't. Just stay by my side today, alright?"

"Always," I said immediately.

A FEW HOURS LATER, dressed in traditional ceremonial wear, I stood outside Asteria's door again, alone. I had sent Griffin ahead of me, about an hour ago. Though I didn't want to leave her side at all, I'd thought Asteria might appreciate the space; I knew she often lashed out when she was nervous or stressed, and somehow I didn't think my nagging presence would help her as she prepared to face her court. Still, I didn't exactly trust Lilliana to protect her, not that I would ever tell either of them that. I'd likely be met with protests and annoyance that I didn't trust them to fend for themselves when danger was near.

Because I did feel it, the danger. The constant resonance in the air that unsettled me so.

I knocked on the door, the sound echoing in the strangely quiet hallway. That was when I realized there were no servants rushing around, no guards lingering nearby. No guards meant no Asteria; they would have followed her until she reached the balcony overlooking the courtyard, every Seelie guardian protecting her, adding themselves to the hoard as she passed through the halls; but I pushed open the door just in case.

"Asteria!" I called.

When no one replied, I opened the door to find her bedroom empty, and the only sign that she or Lilliana had been there recently was the small pile of candy wrappers atop one of the couch cushions. I smiled slightly, but even alone, the movement felt forced.

The hum I'd been tuned into all day changed, increased in intensity, and I resolved not to linger in its presence, to meet Asteria as quickly as I could. I turned on my heel, striding out of the bedroom and back into the tomblike silence of the hallway. As I swept through the palace, I expected to come across someone, anyone stationed to guard doors above all else, but just like the wing of the royal chamber, each new corner I turned was vacant and still.

I sighed sharply through my nose. I would just have to meet her and the others at the balcony for the announcement. But as I turned to begin making my way there, I stopped short.

"Nox."

Someone was whispering my name. Over and over, so quietly I could hardly tell if it was in my mind or aloud. I swallowed hard, fear surfacing and threatening to corporealize the wings on my back. The feeling only multiplied tenfold the moment another name snuck in amongst the whispers.

"Asteria."

There was nothing that piqued my attention like my mate's name, and my body instantly heated; a rising anger and creeping fear had my vision darkening around the edges, and with every moment that passed, there was another utterance.

"Promised one."

"Evening Star, fallen from Above."

"Princess of the Abyss."

I whirled, but the hushed, hurried words didn't stop.

"Nox."

"Bastard of Light."

"Promised princess."

A door to my left slowly opened, and I unsheathed the single dagger I had on my belt. But as I raised the weapon to meet whoever was responsible for the whispers, I saw no one. Instead, I stood alone, staring at the open door that revealed a stone passage, leading down.

I knew where those steps led, the dungeons, but I didn't think the Seelie lords kept any possessed faeries within the palace? Perhaps I was wrong. Perhaps this was another piece of the puzzle Jasper had been hiding.

My better judgement screamed at me to turn away, to go find my mate and leave the whispers behind. But a louder, stronger force within me insisted that I *needed* to follow the sounds. That I could not turn my back on whatever taunted me so. I had to know who was calling to me. Who was calling her name.

With one step and then another, I followed the continued, maddening whispers into the passage. As soon as I passed over the threshold, the heavy wooden door clicked shut behind me. Still, I did not turn back; I followed the worn stone steps down, deep under the palace.

The staircase eventually led to another door, this one with a small, barred window. I paused in front of it, my mind a mess of the unending slew of whispered phrases.

"A reckoning."

The words resounded in my mind until, for a moment, the voices abruptly stopped. With barely a nudge, the barred door swung open, and I took one final step into the Seelie palace dungeons.

"Who's there?" I spoke into the silence, almost wishing the voices would come back to give me some sense of reality, an idea of what was going on, and where they—whoever they were—had gone.

Just as I began to think I'd heard it all inside my mind, that my sleepless nights had amounted finally to paranoia and hallucination, clarity rushed through me, cutting through the clouded haze I'd found myself in over the last few minutes. With it, I realized suddenly that there were no guards here either—this time an unexplainable fact—as in almost every cell that lined the hall beyond, faeries stared at me through the bars, eerily silent.

"Was it you, demon?" I said, stepping toward the closest faerie, "talking just now?"

Still, the faerie stood in silence, seemingly possessed more by tranquility than evil.

I turned to leave, certain that whatever the situation was here I no longer wanted any part of it, but the barred door slammed shut as soon as I neared it. Then, someone cackled; that was my only warning.

Between one moment and the next, the faeries in the cells began to shriek and scream, their words vicious repeats of the whispered phrases I had heard moments ago. Soon, they began to scream another name, a strange name that alarmed me for reasons I was unaware of.

"Azazel!"

Soon, they were all shrieking the name. Some shrieked in unison, like one mind with many mouths, others seemed taken by their own chaotic energy, dancing, almost, with flailing limbs. They didn't sound afraid or angry. Instead, they sounded as if they were rejoicing, chanting in cele-bration.

A shiver raked itself down my spine, and I turned, trying

the door. It was locked, and I swore quietly. I prayed there were no wards on this place preventing me from flitting out, but the hope was futile; this was a prison, one that had surely held Unseelie faeries before, and as the seconds passed and my magic refused to cooperate, I found I was no exception to the rule.

I turned away from the door, scanning the area for any other possible exits as the possessed faeries continued to screech that odd, terrible name. That was when the guards finally emerged from the end of the hall. But as soon as I saw them, I knew they were no friends of mine. These guards were possessed too, and they were heading for the locked cell doors, keys in their hands.

This had been a trap from the beginning, a danger I had surely acknowledged at least on some level, but one I had idiotically failed to estimate.

I unsheathed the dagger again and readied my shadows to fight. But as soon as the first cell door opened, the torches lining the walls abruptly extinguished, plunging the entire cellblock into darkness. For a few moments, the sound of heavy breathing was the only thing I could hear. Then, a click resounded through the darkness, then another, and another. Still, no one came at me.

I took a deep breath, widening my stance. I had no doubt they were simply readying to attack, building their numbers in order to overwhelm once they finally did. And overwhelm me they would. I was gravely outnumbered here, especially given the fact that I could see nothing. I had a hunch too that the demons could see much better in the dark than I could, which left me at an even greater disadvantage.

The last click ringing through the stale air was my final

warning before an uncountable number of footsteps rushed my way. With a sharp inhale, I swung into action the best I could in the dark, but no sooner did hands claw at me, sharp nails tearing at my clothes and skin. The faeries snarled and shrieked in my face as they grasped to pull me down; the sounds only did more to disorientate me, but the true fear set in as I felt the sharp bite of a sword slice across my back.

There were armed guards here. *Possessed* armed guards. And I, with my short dagger, the unnatural darkness, and the others already overwhelming me, was in no state to fight them off, at least for long.

Another blade caught my bicep, the cut deep enough that I couldn't help the cry of pain that escaped me. There were bodies crawling all over me, scratching and clawing at my skin as I tried to sidestep the next blow, and I heard the sharp whistle of another blade just before it hit me. I was barely able to move because of the swarm at my feet, the sword slamming bluntly into my side. I barked out again in pain as the wielder pushed the blade further in. I reached for my starlight then, cursing myself for not trying it sooner, but when I tried to drag it up, there was suddenly nothing but embers.

For a few seconds of cold clarity, the world slowed.

I might actually die today, I thought. After everything that had happened, this could very well be how I met my end, alone and in the dark of a Seelie dungeon, while crowds gathered above. Crowds which Asteria would soon be addressing without me. I had *promised* to be there. Promised I would never leave her side, promised I would always show up for her. And almost as if in response, I felt a violent tug on that bond that lived between us, a rush of panic akin to what I'd felt the day of her coronation.

Something was wrong. She needed me; I had to get to her, if it was the very last thing I did.

With a roar, I reared back, the sword ripping away from my body. I ignored the blinding pain and the rush of slick blood. Instead, through the chorus of shrieks and shouts, I inserted whispers of my own. Shadows, who bowed to me and me alone, working to disorient the demons just as their whispers had done to me. Some of the possessed faeries momentarily moved away from me, confused by the whispers from down the hall that spoke with my voice. The slight reprieve gave me just enough time to hear the steps of a guard rushing towards me. I sidestepped, and based on sound alone, swung my dagger into what felt like his gut. He grunted and by some small mercy relinquished his sword. I grabbed the blade as he dropped it, ignoring the pain as it sliced open my hand.

Just as I got ahold of the grip, banging resounded on the barred door behind me.

"Nox!" a familiar voice roared.

A weak sliver of light filtered into the dungeons as Griffin held a glowing moonstone up to the small window. Moments later, a heard a lock snapping in two.

"They're all possessed!" I gritted, my hand gripping the blood-soaked wound at my side.

Griffin didn't even deign to answer me, instead springing into action the moment he flung the door open. The light from his moonstone was just enough for us both to see the demons as they rushed at us. And one by one, we cut them down. After all, this was what we were both trained to do; successfully win a fight with impossible odds.

What felt like hours but was likely just minutes later, the last demon-possessed faerie fell to the blood-soaked floor.

I stared at Griffin, my breath heaving. "Where is she?" I finally gasped.

"She had just finished when I left. They…" He took a deep breath. "The crowd didn't take it well. They were beginning to protest when I left to go look for you."

"We need to go," I said, my hands still gripping my side.

Griffin's gaze fell to the wound. "Nox, you need to—"

"Something is wrong," I snarled. "I felt it. I need to get to her *now*."

My friend stared at me then. Not my general, who would have insisted I get to safety and find a healer, but the man who had been with me through the very worst and seen me come out on the other side. This was the man who knew just how much Asteria meant to me, the friend who understood that I needed to get to her side right now more than I needed to be safe.

"Let's go then," he said shortly. "Come on."

He offered an arm to help support me as we walked out of range of the ward preventing us from flitting.

"Ready?" he asked.

He knew as well as I did that flitting with a wound like this was going to hurt like hell. But I gritted my teeth and said, "Now."

I tamped down my scream as he flitted us to the balcony, my side feeling as though it was being ripped into all over again, but my focus was soon drawn from the pain as I heard the screams.

Below us, in the courtyard below the balcony, all hell had broken loose. Faeries openly attacked each other, and children cried out for their mothers as they were snatched from their arms. Blood already stained the cobblestone, and the metallic tang hung heavy in the air.

Beside me, Griffin's eyes widened as he took in the carnage. "This...They were not doing this when I left," he said, his voice rough.

Even through the horror of the violence, I focused on one thing and one thing alone. "Asteria," I said. "We need to find her."

Griffin tore his dark eyes from the senseless fighting below, letting me go as I moved as quickly as I could past the balcony and into the room just beyond. But as I took in the scene before me, I froze. The entire line of Seelie lords had fallen, all of them crumpled and unconscious on the ground. Raven was the only person still awake, his eyes wide as he knelt on the ground, holding an unconscious Lilliana. I met his terrified gaze for a moment before I shifted my attention.

In the middle of the room stood a man. Except, I knew in my bones this was no mere man, not even faerie nor shifter. He had long, dark hair tied into a single braid down his back. Bone-white antlers jutted out from his head, and he wore a tailored suit. His eyes were fathomless pools of shadow, meeting mine as he smiled at me, revealing sharp fangs that snagged on his lip.

"Where—is—she?" I snarled, each word bleeding with every desperate emotion rushing through me.

He chuckled, shifting his stance. The air shimmered to reveal Asteria, held in his arms, her eyes shut. On her forehead, a mark was glowing.

Lilith's mark.

My heartbeat pounded in my ears. I had to move carefully.

"Who are you?" I demanded, one hand slightly outstretched. I tried tugging at the mating bond. It was there, still flickering with life between us. But despite my efforts, Asteria did not wake.

The man cocked his head, still smiling as he said, "I think you know who I am, Son of Sameul."

"*Azazel.*" The name fell from my lips before it even came to my mind. The demons in the dungeon knew he was here, and I was going to kill this one just the same as I'd killed them.

He chuckled softly, and an unbidden snarl escaped me as he stroked a finger lazily down Asteria's arm. My chest tightened as I saw the wound there had reopened, a bloody twin to the glowing symbol on her forehead.

"Give my regards to Abaddon. My dear brother will need it after his failure here. Though, perhaps I should send him a thank you card. He carried out most of the difficult parts for me."

For a brief moment, Azazel's gaze landed on Raven, and his smile grew. Then, he flicked his gaze to me as he took the smallest of steps back.

I didn't dare look away from Asteria for more than a second, still trying to reach her, but instinct had me shifting forward, my wings flaring wide.

In a split second, a rip opened in the air behind him.

A portal.

Though I had felt the strength of my starlight power return the moment we had left the dungeon behind, I couldn't risk using it on the demon, not when Asteria was so close to him. I would have to get to her by sheer speed and strength alone.

My anger and panic swelled to a nearly unbearable point, and I lunged forward. Griffin shouted my name, but I ignored him, ignored the way my weakened body protested as I collided with what seemed to be a solid wall of air. Azazel laughed again as my wings flared wide, catching me before I could completely slam into the barrier.

"Too late," Azazel taunted as he stepped backwards into the portal.

I pounded on the invisible barrier, practically screaming down the mating bond. And just before they disappeared through the portal completely, I got my wish as Asteria finally opened her eyes. The barrier fell away, and I lunged forward, my hand outstretched. Her eyes were aglow, blue irises nearly blotted out with Light as her hand reached towards me. Her lips formed my name and our fingertips brushed...

But it didn't matter.

Azazel stepped through the portal completely, and they blinked out of existence, the rip closing swiftly behind them. The force of it knocked me backwards, slamming me into the far wall.

"Nox." Raven's voice caught as he said my name. He was still holding his sister as she stirred in his arms.

I looked at him blankly, but there was a storm brewing within me, threatening to overtake everything. There was another noise, someone pounding on the door, yelling, but it all felt a world away.

"Nox." That was Griffin's voice now. A moment later,

Unseelie warriors flooded the room. I sank to my knees as Griffin approached me, his blade raised.

I raised my gaze to him and said in a strangled voice I didn't quite recognize, "He took her."

Just outside, a fresh uproar of cries pierced the walls of the palace. I couldn't bring myself to care.

"The citizens!" one of our warriors called from the entrance to the balcony. "They're attacking each other!"

I knew. I knew and had seen that the demonic attack we'd been bracing for all these weeks was here. But the fact hardly registered in my mind.

"Seal the exits and entrances," Griffin was saying to the others in a deathly calm voice. "Quickly."

I moved to stand.

To end.

To kill.

To take, because *she* had been taken.

But just before the burning rage overtook my senses, I felt a pull, a slight tug in my chest—a rope across that bridge of light and shadow that I had come to know so well.

Asteria.

Asteria.

"Asteria," I whispered.

CHAPTER 25
ASTER

I was at a bridge, shimmering with starlight. I twisted sparkling plumes around my fingers, watching as they slithered between my digits.

At the other end of the bridge, a shadow caught my attention. It grew, becoming a great cloud of swirling darkness. I took a step back, even as an invisible string tried to pull me forward.

"Who's there?" I called, my voice echoing.

A figure formed in the shadows, and then a man, hardly corporeal, stepped towards me. Tendrils of shadow made up his features, making it difficult to read his expression. Still, I sensed he was on edge.

"It's me, love," he said, his voice a caress. "I am so sorry. I failed you. I fought to be with you, I swear."

I opened my mouth, then shut it, unsure of how to respond.

"Don't you know who I am?" he asked.

Did I? His presence felt oddly familiar, but I could not pull his face from my memory.

Finally, I took a breath and replied, "I don't think so."

He took a step closer, those shadows trailing him like a cape. Lifting a hand, he ghosted cool darkness across my cheekbone. "Then it is a pleasure to introduce myself to you, love," he murmured.

My breath caught but I managed to ask, "What's your name?"

A shadow mouth tilted in a wry smile. "My name is Nox."

"Nox," I breathed. "And we've met before?"

Howling silence filled the space between us for a moment, before Nox spoke again. "We have met many times before."

Even in this place of things both there and not, I could feel my pulse pounding. "In what way?" I dared.

Shadows shifted as he leaned in and murmured, "In the way that night meets the dawn."

"How sad," I whispered. "We didn't have much time, then?"

He took a step back. The bridge was fading, and I reached out a hand made of starlight towards him. Even as the cloud of darkness began to consume him, I saw his smooth expression flicker.

And in farewell, just before the bridge fell out from beneath me, he said, "Perhaps, love. But I will fight to gain back those few moments, even if it is all we get."

And with that, Nox was gone.

In the sudden moment of awakening that followed, where consciousness stirred and dreams faded, an image flashed in my mind's eye: I saw amber eyes, hair like starlight, and a smile, just for me. Then, as I caught the smell of citrus-scented night as the sun rose in the distance of my vision, there was a word, a name, uttered in a soft voice I knew wasn't my own. A man's voice.

"Asteria."

~

I OPENED my eyes to see a strange man with antlers leaning above me. His eyes were fathomless pools of night, sparkling with a hint of stardust.

"Sleep well?" the man asked.

I looked around carefully, slowly, furrowing my brow. We were in the center of a spacious sitting room. A fire roared in the hearth, the flames a strange, blazing white. The excessive furniture and decor was borderline gauzy, all velvet and dark wood.

I felt utterly lost.

"Where am I?" I asked, forcing my gaze back to the stranger in front of me.

"Asteria."

There it was again, that name in my mind. My chest tightened, and I lifted my hand, pressing it against my sternum. The man followed the movement with curious eyes but said nothing.

Panic surged in my throat, tightening my lungs. "Who are you?"

His lips curved as he sat back and flipped his long braid over his shoulder carelessly. "My name is Azazel, cherub," he said, his voice charming and wicked. "And this is my home."

Acknowledgments

We made it to the end of the second installment in this series! 'We' because this book has been just as much of a journey for me! But before I dive into that, I want to thank everyone who made this book possible.

To my parents, Brian and Sara. I will always credit a portion of my creative works to you. You began my love for imagination and creativity, whether it be through reading at bedtime or piano lessons, and you have always supported the pursuit of making my dreams a reality.

To MK Ahearn and Ky Venn at Azala Press. I have been able to take my books to places I could not have imagined mere months ago because of your support. The publishing industry can be a lonely place, especially when you're doing it all by yourself, but you both have provided not only logistical support, but also encouragement at a time when I had begun to doubt my ability to really 'do' this thing. I am forever grateful that you are always open to answer my endless questions and hype up my stories. I can't wait to see what else we can do together!

To Amy Davies, the editor of this book. It was an amazing and humbling experience working with you. I can truly say this is one of the best finished projects I've done because of the work you did on the manuscript. You not only did an incredible job staying true to my vision and voice, but you also gave me tools to better all of my writing projects going forward.

To Kayla Hill, my bookish bestie. I am so glad we took that English class together and that you decided to email me after I wrote that paper on ACOTAR. You are my favorite person to send book memes to and are one of the few people in my life who truly understands my obsession with winged men. Without you, this book series would have never taken flight. And I cannot wait to read more of your amazing writing. We got this, girl!!

I thought writing this book would be easy because the first book was the kind of project that just kind of wrote itself. But it turns out it's true what they say; writing book two in a series is an immense vortex of pressure, self-doubt, and what-ifs. What if this one falls short? What if I lose the momentum? And my favorite... "Now, *that* was a negative review" (Writers, please never look at your Goodreads page unless you have to, like I used to make the mistake of doing). All that being said, I think the struggle made this book what it is. It forced me to take more time than I had planned with the manuscript, which in turn gave me longer to reflect on Aster's struggles as a character, and also to craft our favorite POV chapters... *wink, wink*

At the end of the day, I can truly credit my ability to finish this book to you, my readers. You all are quite persistent, especially following a cliffhanger! Which I love—it gives me motivation to get you the next installation in the story. I hope you enjoyed this book, and again, I apologize for the cliffhanger. Though, I'll wager to guess you'll be even more upset with me after this one. Guess I'll just need to get to work on book three!

Until then, happy reading and again, thank you.